Tales of Spiral Castle

Also by Patricia Kennealy-Morrison

The Books of The Keltiad
(in chronological order)

The Deer's Cry
Blackmantle
The Hawk's Gray Feather
The Oak Above the Kings
The Hedge of Mist
Tales of Spiral Castle: Stories of The Keltiad
The Copper Crown
The Throne of Scone
The Silver Branch

Strange Days: My Life With and Without Jim Morrison

ROCK CHICK: A Girl And Her Music
The Jazz & Pop *Writings, 1968-1971*

Son of the Northern Star

The Rock & Roll Murders: The Rennie Stride Mysteries

Ungrateful Dead: Murder at the Fillmore
California Screamin': Murder at Monterey Pop
Love Him Madly: Murder at the Whisky A Go-Go
A Hard Slay's Night: Murder at the Royal Albert Hall
Go Ask Malice: Murder at Woodstock
Scareway to Heaven: Murder at the Fillmore East
Daydream Bereaver: Murder on the Good Ship Rocknroll (forthcoming)

TALES *of* SPIRAL CASTLE

STORIES OF THE KELTIAD

PATRICIA KENNEALY-MORRISON

Tales of Spiral Castle: Stories of the Keltiad

On the Web:
www.facebook.com/patriciakmorrison
pkmorrison.livejournal.com
mojohotel.blogspot.com
myspace.com/hermajestythelizardqueen

"The Last Voyage" originally appeared in *Crusade of Fire: Mystical Tales of the Knights Templar,* edited by Katherine Kurtz and published in 2002.

Produced by Lorrieann Russell and Jesse V. Coffey
Jacket artwork by Lorrieann Russell
Interior book design by the author
Author photograph by L.D. Bright

ISBN-13: 978-0692236100 Lizard Queen Press
ISBN-10: 0692239103 Lizard Queen Press

AUTHOR'S NOTE

As some of my readers may have noticed, I was
not born to write short stories. I was meant to be a
marathoner: epic novels are as shopping lists to me,
I toss them off like epigrams, like crackers into soup.
Well, okay, it's a bit more work than that, and certainly
nothing to brag about. But basically, yeah, complex
400-pagers with a cast of thousands, all of whom
have weird and unpronounceable names, come easily
to me. It's only the typing that's bothersome…

So, being thusly predisposed to hefty sagas, I
had a very hard time indeed with these four stories.
In fact, writing them was probably the hardest
writing work I have ever done in my life, and I'm
just not used to that kind of slog. Blood, tears, sweat,
screams…not always my characters', either.

In any case, I wrote them because I'm not yet ready to
go back to my science-fantasy series, THE KELTIAD, in any
kind of big way. At the moment, I have two more books
planned out, one to fill in between the two trilogies, the
other to conclude the series in a blaze of glory. Things
will happen. People will die. More people will die. I'm
going to make you weep. I'm going to make *me* weep. And
I'm not ready to face telling those two stories just yet.

But readers wanted a taste of Keltia, and they wanted it now. Heck, even *I* wanted a taste of Keltia. No matter that I'm still working on other projects that consume all my time: I wanted to see Aeron and Gwydion again. And so I wrote us some little visits.

The first of these takes place long ago, in a time of great religious struggle on Earth, and is a hitherto untold part of Keltic history and Earth history alike, incidentally detailing how the great Clann Douglas, as well as the fabled Knights Templar, arrived in Keltia. Other than that, it's not really connected to the other three stories.

Which take place congruent to our Keltic present, more or less: we see Aeron as a child of nine, discovering her magic in a formal test; Gwydion as a youth from fourteen to eighteen, learning to use his own magic and being tested himself; and the Terran lieutenant Sarah O'Reilly, just after her arrival in Keltia with Captain Haruko and the rest of the crew of the Sword, learning that magic is real, and being set up for a test of her own. And finally we meet Gwyn ap Neith, king of the Sidhe of Keltia, as more than merely a very appealing deus ex machina; though he does still serve that function, a little, he's become more of a person and more of a player now—I'm very fond of him, and he has long since elevated himself into the ranks of my Keltic Top Ten favorite characters.

While these stories can be read as little vignettes that fill in backstory, expanding history with and of familiar characters, they are also meant to serve, eventually, as connectors back to *The Beltane Queen* (when I get around to writing it) and lead-ins forward to the final book of the series, *The Cloak of Gold* (likewise). And they are to be taken as canon, so don't forget about them when you read the extant, or indeed future, books.

All of which I will gradually be publishing on Kindle/ Amazon, and perhaps tinkering a bit with them as I do so. Just some harmless retconning, to bring the existing work into line with the new stuff, and to get me out of the inevitable corners into which I have painted myself. And there are more of those than I quite like to see, so it will be nice to have a chance to fix them. Or some of them, anyway.

Thanks to my most excellent betas, the Usual Suspects: Donna L. Brown, Jesse V. Coffey, James Allen Davis, Susan Harwood Kaczmarczik, Carole McNall and Lorrieann Russell. You are all fabulous.

For Dr. James Sullivan of North Babylon High School and
Dr. Russell J. Jandoli of St. Bonaventure University,
who taught me well, long ago,
and from whom I hope I have learned well enough
so as not to shame their teaching

KELTICHRONICON

In the Earth year 453 by the Common Reckoning, a small fleet of ships left Ireland, carrying emigrants seeking a new home in a new land. But the ships were not the leather-hulled boats of later legend, and though the great exodus was indeed led by a man called Brendan, he was not the Christian navigator monk who later chronicles would claim had discovered a new world across the western ocean.

These ships were starships, their passengers the Danaans, descendants of — and heirs to the secrets of — Atlantis, that they themselves called Atland. The new world they sought was a distant double-ringed planet, itself unknown and more than half a legend, and he who led them in that seeking would come to be known not as Saint Brendan the Navigator but Saint Brendan the Astrogator.

Fleeing persecution and a world that was no longer home to their ancient magics, the Danaans, who long ages since had come to Earth in flight from a dying sun's agonies, now went back to those far stars, and after two years' desperate wandering they found their promised haven. They named their new homeland Keltia, and Brendan, though he refused to call himself its king, ruled there long and well.

In all the centuries that followed, Keltia grew and prospered. The kings and queens who were Brendan's heirs, whatever else they did, kept unbroken his great command: that until the time was right, Keltia should not for peril of its very existence reveal itself to the Earth that its folk had fled. They were joined in this by the folk who had journeyed with them to the stars: the Sidhefolk, those beings of magic, of Light and Dark alike, with kings and queens and powers of their own.

It is when Kelts and Sidhefolk come together for a high purpose that the greatest things are accomplished, and the greatest tales are told…

THE LAST VOYAGE

October, 1307

A CHILL DARK NIGHT in autumn, a whipping wind from off the
land, out of the heart of sleeping France, an outflooding
tide obedient to the reins of an unrisen moon. In the Atlantic
port of La Rochelle, chancy starlight made a ghost parade
of the eighteen ships, too ill-assorted to be called a fleet,
leaving the harbor, strung out stern to prow, silent under
sail and tow and muffled oar.

On the deck of the first and largest, a war galley which
bore upon her side the name Great Mary and an icon of
the Holy Mother at her bows, a young man leaned on the
taffrail, staring out at the foaming water. Strongly built, tall
and broad of frame, he was much, much younger than first
glance made him appear—just turned twenty-one—and
for that, the somberness of the handsome features and the
tanned skin were all to blame. He had dark hair and a well-
trimmed beard, and his alertness of bearing and posture
proclaimed him warrior no less than the sword that hung
at his side.

His name was James, Lord Douglas, of the House and
Name of Douglas, and he was a knight of Scotland—*Sir*
James, a title to carry proudly; more proudly still, he was

close friend to the new-crowned King Robert, first of that name, called the Bruce. This night he was leaving France for Scotland, going home for the second time in two years, having completed the mission on which his king had sent him—a mission that, though successful, had not been accomplished entirely according to plan. He was muffled warmly above his mail in a thick dark wool cloak, collared with the fur of a wolf; as the Mary slid past the harbor mole and seawall and the east wind began to cut clean and cold from the distant Alps, he huddled the cloak closer, brushing his fingers over the rough weave as over a woman's hair, touching not wool but memories—sight of heathered hills, scent of bonfire leaves.

"Good Scots web," he said, no hint of apology in his tone for the wistful gesture. "Shield as well as shelter."

A snort of companionable agreement from his left. "And us still in need of both, I am thinking."

James nodded, knowing that the other—his even younger cousin Walter Stewart—understood both sentiment and situation.

And a good thing too, he thought, bracing himself as the galley set to the first big Atlantic rollers like a hunter to a fence. *For all our present peril, this is but one strand in a far greater weave strung upon a far greater loom. Before the weavers are done, the web spun here will come to cloak the world, and that we knew or ever we sailed from home...back in this year's summer, when I came to France for only the second time in my life, and that on royal business...*

Glancing over his shoulder at the little carrack that had brought him from Scotland and had just decanted him on France, James Douglas took a deep breath of the butter-warm July air off the Bay of Biscay, and approvingly scanned the bustling quays of La Rochelle, chief Atlantic port of the Knights Templar. As his retainers made arrangements for suitable horses and a proper armed escort to take them the last stage of the long journey from their home — to Paris itself — James's thought ran back to the event, or not-yet event, that had sent them.

Earlier in that tumultuous summer, Robert Bruce, who now held the Scottish crown in both gauntleted hands — as he had seized it the year before in despite of English Edward, known as Longshanks, and also, though even less in compliment, as the Hammer of the Scots — had been troubled by rumors blowing across Europe like wicked winds, rumors concerning the Knights Templar. Rumors that Philip, the corrupt and avaricious king of France, and Clement his equally corrupt puppet pope were plotting the Order's doom — a doom that was very much not to Robert's purposes nor likings. When those rumors began to buzz too loudly to ignore, even in the midst of his own woes Bruce had thought to send James — without whose loyalty and sword-arm Robert would have still been merely the Earl of Carrick and not the King of Scots — to the Templar preceptory in Paris, where James had been received a few years before as a lay knight, to seek out his brethren and, in Bruce's name and Scotland's, to both ask a favor and offer one.

Which favor was the greater, the proffered or the sought,

none could say, at least not yet. But James had left Scotland at once, a royal commission sewn into the lining of his cloak and his cousin and four men-at-arms as all his tail. They had landed at La Rochelle, and now the tiny company was hastening to Paris, up beside the quiet blue line of the Loire. His ostensible errand, or at least so it was given out in public, was to petition the warrior monks for military guidance—for swords upon the field too, if it came to that, and did it seem possible. But the true purpose of the embassy was vastly more important, and it would come to be more strangely accomplished than could ever have been thought.

Yet however urgent they might seem, or even are, such high matters are never swiftly decided, and James found himself enjoying quiet days in Paris as the official envoy of the King of Scotland. A very different state from his first visit to that city, and he was not unaware of the irony. As he walked by the Seine one sunswept afternoon with Walter, he recounted the tale of how, four years before, when he was scarce sixteen, he had lived here adrift, too proud and too powerless to go home. In truth, there had been little or nothing to return to: the English had executed his father, Sir William Douglas—known as "the Bold", and with good reason—in their Tower at London, on Edward's express order. Further, they had seized the substantial Douglas patrimony of castles and land, bestowing it upon one of their own; and there seemed vanishingly small chance of James ever being in circumstances to win it back. When he went to Court to petition for its restoral to him, sponsored by a family friend, King Edward, on the mere hearing of the Douglas name, had gone black as thunder and ordered James out of his presence and his kingdom alike.

With nowhere else to go, he had fled to France, to try to work things out, and, as he had written to his cousin with touching faith, "to see what help God may send me." But divine aid — working as usual to a more than mortal timeframe — was not swift to show itself. Angry, sad, often drunk in low company, more often hungry and houseless, James had wandered Paris, accepting the kindness of hospitality where he felt he might do so honorably, or at least with as little dishonor as possible, knowing and resenting that he would not soon be in a position to repay.

Then one day he had come upon the Templar preceptory, a forbidding fortress on the Seine's right bank, in a marshy district near the royal palace, and his heart went out to it on sight. With his name and title for entrée, he had ventured the acquaintance of some Templar officers, who saw in the tall Scots youth if not exactly monk material then surely warrior metal, while he for his part had been glad and grateful of the martial training and spiritual comfort they bestowed.

Perhaps God had shown His hand at last, or maybe it was merely fate's usual trick of favoring the favored, but once safe lapped in the protection of the Templar mantle, James's luck had changed dramatically. His fellow countryman Bishop Lamberton, aghast to learn of the youth's miserable straits, took him in at once as ward, so that between bishop and knights James had been both well cared for and well educated, in lore and war alike; and with the inborn loyalty that would mark his name forever, he had vowed never to forget.

But just as he was settling into a far from comfortless exile's life in Paris, as many had done before him and would again after, the year 1306 had called him home. William Wallace had been executed in London—the Lion of the North butchered like a steer, by jackals—and all Scotland was aflame. Robert Bruce had been first excommunicated by the pope for a murder in sanctuary—admittedly a grave sin, though no reasonable person thought it deserved quite so strict a punishment—and then defiantly crowned in the pope's despite by his own Scots, in the wild, deep, ancient way at Scone; Clement, furious, had responded by promptly placing the entire disobedient country under papal interdict. Which, however it worked on the people, meant at a higher level no damned papal interference in Scottish affairs, which many besides Robert considered no bad thing: so James had returned home like an arrow to the gold, to be present at that king-making, and his Templar training and his unceasing hatred for those who had brought him low and his willingness to be used as a sword against the English made him more than welcome.

Indeed, he had gone straight into the inner circle and close confidence of the new king—and also into the speculative notice of every marriageable lass in the land, and many more who, if not weddable, were certainly eagerly beddable. But such romancing was best left to the ballad-makers. For those who stood with Robert of Carrick, there remained a kingdom to be secured, and for his part James had found in Bruce not only a monarch's cause but a lifetime's friend.

As such, he rode by Bruce's side, and despite his youth

was entrusted with the strategy and captaincy of many a raid; he did not fail at the test. Not just in battle did he serve: when Bruce and a handful of dispirited followers were hiding in a dank, sand-floored cave in the western isles, he it was who noticed a spider desperately trying to anchor its web; and though the tiny creature had failed twelve times running, yet on the thirteenth it succeeded. Thinking to cheer his king, James had made a parable of the incident— and Robert took the homely little tale so passionately to heart that, come spring, he had roared out of the isles and back to the mainland, newly revitalized for the fight.

And from that tiny web, victory had blossomed like the spring itself and perched upon their banners like a wingwide eagle, with James retaking his father's castle in a raid that would become a byword for savage ferocity, and Bruce going steadily, doggedly on, with the cunning of a wolf and the spider's own persistence, and Edward of England fallen dead at Whitsun, the Hammer of the Scots hammered in his turn upon God's own anvil, none but a weakling son left behind him to rule in the South. And scarce had they all turned round and drawn one deep quiet breath than the Templar rumors began—the rumors that, reaching a royal ear, had sparked this present errand.

In good time was that spark set. No sooner had James arrived in Paris in July than the smolder of rumor became certainty's flame, and Bruce's fey Scots foreboding proved a true one. Though the knowledge was as yet shared by only a few, the Templars were indeed doomed; very soon now, in all lands that bowed to the pope's rule, as the pope himself bowed to the rule of the French king, all knights of the Temple were to be arrested and bound over for trial as heretics, their wealth and properties stripped and seized. And there was for heretics in that time only one fate...

As summer drew inexorably toward harvest, James considered all this as he and Walter walked again upon the riverbank. *I have not told Walter the whole tale, not yet, but he is fitting things together – well, in the two minutes at a time he can spare from sighing for douce bonny Marjory Bruce...*

As if he had heard his cousin's thought, now the younger man frowned, and with a deep breath turned to James. "I have been thinking... Templar spycraft is the finest in the world — surely the Order has known what is coming?"

"Oh aye," said James, staring upriver at the glorious towers of the cathedral of Nôtre Dame de Paris. "They have not been sleeping, they know fine what will come to pass — and they have been taking steps. I could not tell you before, but that is why Rob has sent us here. Since even the smallest bairn in Christendom knows how charges of heresy must end, for weeks now, even months, Templars have been fleeing their commanderies by night, clad not as knights but rough as any peasant. They have been driving wains or riding packhorse convoys or sailing riverboats down the Rhone and the Seine and the Loire, all of them heading to La Rochelle, hiding up in the town, or in the countryside roundabout."

Walter stopped dead upon the cobblestones, fixed his cousin with an almost accusing gaze.

"They are planning flight," he said, in the arrested undertone that is the polite concealment for a gasp, though none was near enough to overhear them. "From Philip and Clement— To keep the Templar treasuries, and themselves, out of their hands, the knights are bringing it all to La Rochelle. To escape with it to Scotland, at Rob's behest."

"Nothing has yet been decided," replied James with a warning look. "Well, if it has, it has not been revealed to overmany, and certainly not to me. But aye, Scotland— Rob has promised them refuge, since he and Clement are hardly on terms just now, and the chance is too good to miss. Sanctuary for the knights, as Clement's writ, thanks to the excommunication and interdict he himself imposed, need not be obeyed by our king or any Scot else; a matchless fighting force for Rob to wield against Edward; and a vast treasure to fend the knights and pay due tax to the Crown. A win all round, at least for us and the Temple, and foul scorn upon France and Rome."

"You have spoken to the Temple masters?"

"After a fashion. I have offered Rob's terms privily to the senior preceptors, who have so far said neither aye nor nay, and I have yet to address the brothers in public conclave. Though we can all see how this must go... But the treasure is being safely stowed; and every seaworthy Templar craft now moored at La Rochelle, or that can get there timely, has rutters and charts for Scottish waters in its sea-chests, and navigators and seamen versed in Scottish seas are already aboard. There will not be many. But it is to be hoped there will be enough."

"Because of us, and the word we bring—but Jamie, surely they must say aye, how not! Yet Clement and Philip swear themselves blue-arsed that none of this is about money, only possible heresy."

His cousin snorted. "Oh, it is never about money with those two, to hear them piously tell it. Yet money is all that they have ever been about, or ever will be. That is the only reason they unleash these blasphemies, make no mistake. But the treasuries of the Templars will be denied them."

And that is the nub of it, the real reason hell is going to be loosed upon the Templars — money and power as always, at the root of things, with this lying midden of trumped-up charges, sorcery and heresy and blasphemy and buggery to cloak it in before the world, as pathetic excuse...

Well — not saying that that last, at least, might not have sometimes chanced. But what if it had? As a soldier and a young man, James knew well enough that those who most profess to scorn the flesh are often the first to secretly indulge it — leave it to such whited sepulchres to make it more a sin than it was, and by Christ's sweet mercy, there were many sins in the calendar far worse than that. But for the rest of it, no; one had only to look at Templar history these past two hundred years — and to scan the account books of pope and king, noting particularly the huge debts owed by both to the Templars — to see the true reason made plain. No, there was no sorcery or heresy or blasphemy afoot, though those sins were to be used as excuse. The sins, and crimes, lay instead, truly, on that royal French popinjay and his venal lackey of a pope...

But though escape was planned, destination had been uncertain. Since every Christian man, woman, child and nation were expressly forbidden to aid heretics, on pain of death themselves, where on this earth might fleeing

Templars go to find safe haven? Many had wondered that very thing. Then Jamie Douglas had arrived in Paris with the answer…or at least *an* answer.

So it went for some weeks, with James becoming more fretted by the day, the hour even, at how short time was running for his brother knights. He knew well, few better, how much there was to set in order; he also knew they were not wasting an instant of the pitifully short time they had. But as the summer days ran past and began to turn to cool gold autumn, and still no word came, he resolved that if he did not hear soon from the masters of the Temple, he would go himself to the preceptory and make himself heard, and let things chance as they would.

As it fell out, he did not have to. One midnight, at a secret, well-attended conclave in the preceptory chapterhouse, to which he had been unexpectedly summoned but no reason given for his commanded presence — though he had a fair idea — James caught the eye of the Grand Master of the Temple, great Jacques de Molay himself. No more than a glinting glance, a tiny nod — and both recognized the moment for which the one had been sent and the other had received him; the moment, and the purpose, for which, perhaps, they had both been born.

Rising up from his wall-seat in the lovely stone-arched chamber, its carved stone ribs and decorated vault glowing above him in the candlelight, where he sat as a lay knight of the Order as well as the royal envoy of Scotland, James made his offer, Robert's offer, for all to hear, speaking with the authority of his king and the warmth of his own heart the plan that he had been empowered to speak.

"Brothers, time has come to choose. Doom walks in France, and treachery in England, but in Scotland there lies sanctuary. Philip's greed cannot reach there, and Clement's writ does not run there, and the King of Scots takes no heed of either. I bring his offer before you all of a secret refuge and a new life—look where he has set his royal word and seal upon it."

He drew from his tunic breast the precious commission he had carried—a single piece of vellum with Bruce's seal affixed as king, which could have been his death warrant had he been caught with it by Philip's men—and held it out. But no one made a move to take it, and after a moment he put it down behind him on his chair, and remained standing.

"And what payment does Robert Bruce seek of the Templars, for so great a service done us?" asked the Paris preceptor, after a fraught little silence and a swift side-glance at de Molay, who had made no sign that anyone there could read.

"My lord the King of Scotland," said James, a bit more sharply than he had intended, "asks only that the Temple support him in his reign, as and if he should have need, and if it may be done without violence to vows. Anyone's vows. Beyond that, he asks no more than that Templars should survive, in Scotland if nowhere else. Surely that is a wish we all share full measure," he added, with a little sting of exasperation plain in his voice.

What in all hells is their difficulty with this? True, it is a dreadful thing, that they must flee, and most likely set aside at least certain vows if they wish to thrive and survive. Surely God will understand; has He not sent them this calamity in the first place? They will die in the flame after unspeakable tortures if they do not go...

"As excommunicates, only," muttered a blond Burgundian from a seat over against the farther wall. "Like your king himself."

"But safe," said James evenly, "and with a fine chance to stay so and be one day restored. For the interdict will not last forever, and neither will Clement and Philip."

A good point. Silence hung heavy as incense in the chamber. No eye turned to James as he stood there, and no gaze dared even flicker to the great central throne, where Jacques de Molay sat sunk in thought.

At last the Master of all the Temple stirred in his seat, and when he spoke more than a few heads snapped round at the strange new note they thought they heard in his voice. But the lined old face that he turned to James Douglas was gentle, suffused almost with light, though it could not be said that he smiled.

"No... No—my dear son—you have the right of it. They will not last—forever."

Not long thereafter, at the fine tall house near the Sorbonne where he and Walter were Temple guests, James was shaken ungently and urgently awake one night before dawn to hear a grim message. Dressing swiftly, hearts hammering, the cousins roused their few retainers and gathered up their gear, and rode like the Wild Hunt itself to the preceptory across the river, for the message was as terrible as it was certain, and men had died to discover it: on Friday the thirteenth day of October 1307—mere days hence—Philip's officers throughout France would open sealed orders, and when they did, the Temple would be cast in chains.

Yet, however passionately James besought them now, when he and Walter came hastening into their presence, Jacques de Molay and other high officers steadfastly refused to flee, knowing that their absence from Paris would alert Philip and deny escape to their brothers; and they were resolved to bide the issue, and to die for the Temple if such should be their fate.

As surely it shall be, thought James, anguished. His best arguments lay in ruins and his native Scots prescience was chilling his soul: what could be done had been done, and now it only remained to face what might be done. Yet at least something lastingly Templar might be salvaged from the wreck.

But time was now, and no more. He and Walter knelt humbly to receive the Master's blessing, felt the strong old hands rest upon their bowed heads in benediction and valediction ("until the end of our lives or the end of our Order, whenever it shall please God that that should be"), all three of them knowing that the thing would play out as it must, and that whatever way it ran, God's purpose would be truly served.

Them the party—not just James and his men but such Templars as the Master ordered to accompany them, and there was sorrow at that parting also—mounted and rode off in twos and threes through the narrow choking back lanes, not to the great main gates of Paris but to lesser portals, where guards — persuaded, bribed, slain where necessary — let them pass in secret from the city; they would join up again outside the walls, taking not the main roads but rough hidden tracks through deep forests. Not a few times the guards stood silently aside for them, porting arms in proud salute as they passed, honoring them for what they were, and had been — a valediction in itself, for come the dawn no servants of the Temple save Jacques de Molay and his brave companions would be left in the city.

And so it was that the last of the Templars — brothers and sergeants, men-at-arms and knights — rode out of Paris, and heard as they rode the gates of history clang shut behind them.

To their surprise, there was no pursuit on the roads to La Rochelle; then, as word and suspicion spread behind them, much pursuit; arrows too, three of which were balked of their destination in James's back only by the weight of Scots wool and the tempered mail beneath it. The general alarm for escaping Templars had not yet been raised, but Philip's officers were alert all the same; it was they who followed the riders with arrows, and they also who died for their efforts.

Galloping on unchallenged, the fugitives passed empty Templar outposts as they went — a glad sight, meaning safety for others — and picked up fresh mounts as and where they could.

They were long days and nights on their way, riding swift and light, keeping to lesser roads as much as possible for safety's sake, but in the end they could not have cut it much finer. Pounding into La Rochelle mere hours before

Philip's officers unsealed their orders and were set to strike, they found the ships of the Templar fleet tugging at their anchors and cables like hawks in jess.

But the Templar captains, calm and far-eyed as sea eagles, dared wait for the outbound night-tide and any last-minute stragglers, knowing that these ships were the last way out of France for their brothers, and their gamble well repaid. As Great Mary left harbor, she and her seventeen sisters were carrying near a thousand men and over two hundred horses, and all the gear and supplies necessary for both; and the fabled Templar treasure, as much of it as they had been able to gather in haste, was crammed aboard as well, like gleaming ballast.

Now, safe in sea-darkness under filled sails, James sighed and stretched within his cloak and looked away to the northwest, and beside him Walter smiled, knowing how his cousin fretted not entirely for their distant homeland but for action in this most righteous cause. Passing the nearby Ile de Ré, the ships caught up still more refugees from secret assembling places on empty rockbound coasts, hove to briefly near Finisterre, where they took on the last of the exiles, and now were headed west, straight out to sea. France had vanished; by dawn the Templar fleet, carrying the wealth of the Order in both men and gold, would have vanished also, into mystery and legend—ultimately, at least some of it, into the secret service of Scotland's king. Still, battle before journey's end was not so much likelihood as certainty, James reflected with some hopefulness, so the adventures were far from over.

They were lucky, or blessed, or both, to have gotten away

with as many strong ships as they had: the main fleet was far distant, at sea in the Mediterranean, plying the waters of the regular pilgrimage routes between Palestine and the southlands of Europe, as Templar vessels had done for two hundred years, ignorant of the doom that stood waiting for them on the quays of Europe when they should come again to land.

Swift messengers had been sent to every port, certainly, hoping to catch and warn the ships as they docked en route, but many of the couriers would not arrive in time to deliver their warnings. Those ships and the mariners aboard them faced a grim fate: seizure and imprisonment, ultimately execution. Jacques de Molay had wept for them, and prayed for them, and then he had turned mind and hand to saving those he could. Indeed, until James had come with Robert's offer, the Master had had little alternative but to send as many knights as he could to Portugal and the Teuton lands, there to disband and disappear into other knightly orders, to save themselves. The unexpected offer of a Scottish sanctuary where they could remain Templars, or as near as might be, was truly a gift from God, and James had been much honored for bringing it. The acceptance of the offer was a gift from on high also; and surely Robert Bruce would see it so—trained knights, war-horses, weapons, ships, treasure to support them. A gift that gave to both sides was the best gift of all…

All these thoughts cheered James now, and he twisted round to look at the line of sail strung out behind the Mary: sleek hounds of the sea, coursing steadily under the great autumn constellations that slowly heaved themselves over the horizon. If he strained his nightsight, he could just discern the sure quick movements of the mariner knights, barefoot or hide-shod, in rough breeks and short tunics, quietly seeing to their arcane tasks; the others had all tucked themselves prudently out of the way, asleep below or huddled here on the maindeck. Some on each ship were down in the holds looking after the horses stabled on the orlop deck, keeping them calm and fed; destriers, trained war chargers, were far too valuable to waste—either to be killed or left behind for the French officers to seize—and the ships had taken on as many as could be safely boarded.

Suddenly James felt a fierce exaltation out of nowhere, a soul-surge and lift of spirit that caught him squarely in his middle, almost doubling him over, and which owed nothing to the rise and fall of the billow beneath the Mary's hull. *This is the Templar fleet!* he thought exultantly, *such as remains of it, any road, and I am bringing it home to Scotland and to my king. Perhaps not as any of us had planned it, but even so…*

He saw in his mind's eye the ships' lovely names writ proud along their sides, gilt-lettered in Latin and English and French, saintly images gracing the prows, Templar crosses painted on the sails—which might not have been over-prudent, but was something the knights had insisted upon, and he approved. Of the eighteen sail, Great Mary, Michael Archangel, Idumaea, Holy Wisdom, Magdalene, Arimathea and three others were headed to Scotland; three more were bound to sympathetic Baltic ports, where folk cared only for merchantry and let religion shift as it pleased, and where the fleeing knights would be beyond

Clement's power. The remaining six had just turned south for Portugal, and every soul on every ship had been on deck to lift sword in what was almost certain to be final farewell this side of heaven's own shores.

Of the several hundred vessels that had comprised the mighty war and merchant navies of the Temple, these eighteen alone were free, at least that they knew of for certain. Twelve were war galleys; the others were graceful nefs, coaster cogges, river carracks that had seldom tasted salt. But all were strong and sturdy craft built for their purpose, the shipbuilders knowing that even the humbler vessels might be needed for war-work one day. And knights manned them: the ships would all make it safely to journey's end, and would not sink with their cargo. Well, they would if permitted peaceful passage, at least, and that was by no means a certainty. Perhaps even some of the other ships might yet escape the traps set for them in the Mediterranean, and sailing to freedom through the Pillars of Hercules, come to join them in Scotland; it was a thing to be prayed for.

Though the need for flight had put their pride in pocket— Templars were forbidden by their rule to turn their backs on their enemies, and only the direct orders of Jacques de Molay himself had forced them aboard the ships in the end — one thing the knights had been as iron upon: each ship's mast streamed the Beauséant upon the wind, the black-and-white Templar war flag that had flown proudly above many a victory and even more proudly above a defeat. *And this will be a victory*, James vowed now, but a leaching sadness took him in his bones as his exaltation died.

Very like this is the last voyage of the Templar fleet; the last time the Beauséant will ever fly so, a Templar flag over Templar ships of a Templar navy... And to fly it now was, if not sheer madness, then imprudence at best, on a level with that of displaying the great cross-painted sails; but faith and honesty and something that could perhaps be called defiance – though it was not really like defiance at all – had constrained them. If it be indeed the last voyage, then at least it will not be sailed under false colors beneath the eye of God...

But it needed no vexillum or crimson-crossed sails to tell even the most casual observer that these were ships of the Temple: if anyone were to glimpse them, even the merest fisherman out at sea off the coasts of England as they drew near, the hunt would be up. So, driven by a strong clear-weather easterly gale that set the sheets creaking like trodden-upon snow, the ships went in a great sweeping curve out of the Bay of Biscay and far out to sea. For several days they were out of sight of land, going past Cornwall and the Sullia Isles, then briefly raising the southern Irish coast, rounding to the west and on to the north. In all those anxious days and nights they met no other ship, had not even a glimpse of distant sail.

Still, all knew that such luck, or grace, could hardly hold. Before they left Paris, they had had word of an English fleet stationed off Ayr, in Galloway, to bar the Irish Sea and that part of southwest Scotland against just such an escape; and even more than that, against aid landed on that coast coming to King Robert. Likewise they had been warned of a few ships of the MacDougals of Lorne, blocking the waters farther north. But neither the English nor their bought dogs of Lorne could have dreamed what course their Templar quarry was soon to take…

Luck held longer than they dared hope, or perhaps it was that heaven dared not let so many warriors' prayers go unanswered. After the first few days at sea, the mist and fogs of those western waters veiled them from pursuit— often from one another also, but there was no help for that. Still, even prayer cannot balk fate when God has planned things otherwise. With the Templar ships on a long beat to the northeast, from northern Ireland across toward the Mull of Kintyre, where they had thought to seek shelter, with Scotland a low blue line against a daffodil dawn, the mists drew aside on a changing wind, and strung across the channel like a shieldwall in the sea was the English fleet.

Because of what came after, in later days James recalled but little of that fight. The strategy was to avoid engagement if at all possible: the tiny fleet's cargo was far too precious for that—they must do whatever they could to land it safe ashore. To that end, a pair of ships were already tacking to make a noble rearguard sacrifice stand, and he could see others diving back into the safety of the fog banks. But the Holy Wisdom, the Michael Archangel and the Great Mary had been cut off by part of the English line, as neatly as wether lambs are cut from the flock by a working sheepdog, and James prepared himself for battle as the enemy ships plowed nearer.

I had never thought to die on aught but Scottish earth, unless it was English earth and I getting my vengeance…still, Scottish waters are no doubt next best...and I daresay a sword cuts the same on sea as on land...

He drew his sword, the blade glittering as it had always done; he held it up to heaven like a cross, Templar fashion, kissing the hilt and breathing a brief prayer before battle commenced, as he always did. But then came something he had never seen before, and would never again forget, as long as he lived, and after ...

One moment all was as it was, desperate, fierce, final; after that, nothing was ever the same again. A sudden gigantic shadow fell upon sky and sea and ships, dimming the morning like some great dark wing. Then, parting the mist and cloud like the hand of God Himself and blazing like the sun come down to earth, something silver and tremendous, something stronger than a thousand London Towers and a hundred times vaster than Edinburgh's mighty castle-rock, came settling in silent majesty through the clouds. The waves churned and flattened in white spray, under a wind from all quarters at once; the three trapped Templar ships bobbed and jinked like seal pups caught in shore break.

Then, with a sound of ten thousand drums, the wild waters were drawn up like a road into the sky, summoned home, a billion raindrops suddenly returning to the clouds where they were born. Before James or anyone else could draw breath to shout or even pray, the galleys were drawn upward also, sailing up that broad glittering path, straight into the dark yawning belly of a ship from the stars.

Within — *well, within* whatever *it is, in God's holy Name, that we* are *in, where are we, what has happened to the English ships, what has happened to us?* – James pulled himself upright from where his buckled knees had brought him. Clutching the gunwale for support, he looked wildly around, first for his sword, then for Walter and the others, who were clinging, equally dazed, to the rail nearby.

Then all of them stared drop-jawed at their surroundings, all thought of swords forgotten. *No sword ever forged – not Durendal, not Tizona, not Caliburn itself – would be any use against this...*

They were in an enormous, well-lit, vast-vaulted chamber, roofed and walled and floored all of metal. The soft rosy light seemed to come from everywhere and nowhere, and though it was a far brighter and steadier light than any they had ever known, it did not hurt their eyes. The seawater was gone, and the English ships were nowhere to be seen. But the three Templar galleys hung – and this they could not, literally could not, understand – suspended and motionless in the air, fifteen feet above the floor.

Although his heart was racing as never it had done in battle, James was neither afraid nor ashamed; this was something so far out of his sphere that there was no point in either shame or terror. He would give in to neither until he knew for sure that he must, and then he would overcome it – as he had done before.

Only fools are never frighted: I will save my fear for when I know there is something real to be afraid of... Surely there is a natural explanation, though what that might be I cannot think! But this ship of the air is a made thing. It is not magic, it is merely some natural enginery and philosophy we do not know. Men created it, therefore men can understand it...even if I do not, or at least not yet…well, if they are *men, and not angels, or folk from lands beyond the sky….*

That last was a shrewder guess than he knew — though not than he would come to know. Then, putting paid to his wondering by opening up a whole new slate of questions, doors hissed and smoothly slid apart at one end of the chamber, and a knot of entirely human-looking men — and women! — came in. One who seemed in command spoke briefly, and several turned aside to do mysterious things at a glowing panel near the door. Whatever it was they did, James and the officers of the three ships — the crews were somehow singled out and left aboard — found themselves no longer on their vessels but standing upon dry decking made of some unknown material sure to the foot. He mastered himself with an almost physical effort, and turned a level gaze on the newcomers.

They returned his look with friendly, interested curiosity, and no hostility that he could detect. *We are not prisoners, then – at least not yet…* To his eye they had a familiar aspect: tall men with warriors' builds, many well-mustached like Scots or Irishers, some full-bearded as any Templar. But, however unchivalrous it might be, and it was, James could not stop staring at the women. Long-haired as proper ladies should be, they were not merely unwimpled but clad as no proper lady had ever been in all the life of the world, garbed like the men in tight-fitting trews and doublets of dark green cloth, with badges and other marks of rank upon breast and collar and sleeves. They moved not like decorous court madams but with a straight-backed stride and forthright stance, and they spoke to their male counterparts as equals, with easy laughter and comradeliness, even with command. For their part, they returned James's uncivil stare with serene expressions and a warmly appraising smile or two, attending to their work with the same swift assurance as the men.

"My sorrow to put such fear and confusion on you," came a calm voice then, "but we saw that quick action was needed, and we knew a little of your plight, as your thoughtspeech gave it us."

Though the words were meant to soothe, the fact that they were in resonant Latin every bit as good as a churchman's own, and Irish-accented Latin to boot, only unsettled the new arrivals even more. The voice's owner saw this too, and stepped forward smiling.

"We are folk of many different tongues, so Latin will serve us easiest and best—you do speak Latin?" Seeing nods all round: "So then! I am Connla mac Nessa vhic Dhau, captain of this ship. This is the Cabarfeidh. And as you have doubtless worked out by now, we are not from around here."

James found his voice. "Nay—aye—may I ask where—who—how?"

Connla mac Nessa—tall, brown-haired, blue-eyed—chuckled. "You may well ask indeed! I would be surprised did you not have goleor of questions...which will all be answered in good time. For a beginning, know that we are Kelts, folk of a very distant realm called Keltia, here on a—yes, you may call it a visit."

Keltia... "We—I—have never heard of such a land."

"Nay, you would not have. This will take some time, sirs,

give me a little sword-room here... Well. Keltia. It is not a land, just so, but a world; not one world but many, under not one sun like this above us but seven different suns. Under the guidance of Saint Brendan the Astrogator, we left Erith—Earth, this planet now beneath us—in the year 453 by your reckoning, fleeing the intolerances of Pátraic the slave, Patricius the Roman priestling. After sailing the stars for two long years, we came to our new home, and called it Keltia.

"Now Keltia is as far from this world as it would take light to travel in a thousand years; Brendan, whom later we named as saint, taught us the principles by which we can voyage in such craft as this, and greater ones still, making the journey in a matter of weeks, or even days."

Connla saw the utter incomprehension on the faces turned to him like blank wondering sheep, saw too that some of them had begun to tremble with the sheer strangeness and terror of it all. *As well they might,* he thought with sympathy, *and these are no cowards by any means, but brave fighters... Slow and easy! Do not expect them to understand all in one telling; they have no smallest idea of how light moves, barely of astronomy itself. Indeed, they still believe the Earth is flat, poor devils – do not affright them any more than you must!*

So Connla spoke to himself, in his own mind; and he spoke aloud more gently still, not as to children, but as a teacher might speak to a pupil, or a healer to one who has had a great and terrible shock.

"I know how strange and fearsome this must be, even to warriors. For now, may I know to whom I speak? To put a name to a thing, or to a person, makes it less frightening...

We know already what you are, and why you are in such straits; it is why we have removed you from your peril just this moment, and now we must discuss what you wish to do next."

Easier would that *be,* James thought wildly, *if I did not feel as ignorant as a pig and stupid as a noonday owl...*

He glanced quickly at the Templar officers beside him, hesitant to usurp a privilege of honor, but the three ship's captains quickly backed away and indicated as one that they were more than willing, indeed quite happy, to let him, as ranking noble, royal envoy and presumed man of the world—whatever world that might be!—return the foreign captain's civilities. His mouth pulled down at one corner and his heart had not ceased to pound almost out of his chest, but he bowed to the outworld commander as he would have bowed to his king, and his courtesy was returned.

"I am Sir James Douglas, lord of the House of Douglas, knight, captain of war to King Robert of Scotland, first of that name..." He introduced Walter Stewart and the senior Templars; more bows—it seemed that all of them were clutching at the traditional forms of greeting, simply to cope with the moment. *Truly, though, these Kelts have not lost the courtesy of our people by going to the stars...*

"A fellow countryman," said Connla, smiling. "My mother's kin hail from beside the Gala Water, not far from Douglas lands, though my father's people are from Valentia, in the Irish west. Not they themselves, of course; both kindreds left Erith long ago, with the first immrama. But we will talk of that presently. Come now...your folk will be cared for, and your ships also."

He drew James aside with him; Walter, not without a desperate backward glance as of a drowning man, went off with the Templar officers, each of them escorted by a Keltic counterpart, while other crewmen approached the ships to attend to the rank and file who had remained aboard, paralyzed with shivering bafflement as they watched things play out—even Templars could not be expected to accept something of this magnitude with perfect equanimity.

Are these then our guides? Or are they rather our guards? James dismissed the thought even as it formed. *Nay, these are folk of honor...surely we can trust in that for our safety. Thank God for Templar training, that no one panicked and loosed an arrow in sheer terror! Though I have a feeling any chance ill-thought attack would somehow not have found a target...*

After walking down what seemed leagues of cool smooth-walled corridors, Connla mac Nessa turned aside into a small chamber, gesturing James to precede him, as a host to an honored guest, and for all his resolve to keep a stern demeanor James could not suppress a gasp. The entire opposite wall was sparkling window, a single huge clear crystal pane framing a view such as never man of Earth had seen. He found himself at the glass, if glass it was, with no memory of crossing the room, one hand raised as if to caress what he saw.

Scotland lay at his feet, the Highlands a bright white comb, so near it seemed he could reach down and touch their snows, while England and Wales were swathes of misty green silk and Ireland a burnished shield upon the waters. He could see the Mull of Kintyre and the little islands below, even the ships of the English fleet from which they had been saved, tiny as a child's toy boats; raising his eyes, he saw the Borders, the hills of Eildon, Edinburgh's great Castle Rock off in the distance like a carved pebble, even his own Douglas lands...all laid out before him like a giant and perfect map.

Surely this is what the lands must look like to the eye of God...

As he watched rapt, though he felt no motion, the huge craft rose higher still; to one hand, he beheld France where it lay across the choppy waters of the narrow Sleeve, while to the other the coast of Europe was plain to his sight, all the way up to where the Danemark vanished into mist and cloud.

These folk can cross in an effortless instant what distance takes us long painful weeks and months – and such farther distances as we cannot even reck of...

James sensed the silent presence of Connla behind him, standing away, patient, giving him time to take it in; but for all his best efforts, his voice shook as he spoke – though only a little.

"Sir and captain, perhaps you would now of your great kindness speak of what I must know."

Mac Nessa felt a surge of great relief. *Good! This is a brave man – he has mastered his first shock and is beginning to accept this new reality; and once he does, so too will all the other newcomers, which will make everyone's life all that much easier. Especially mine...*

"As you will have it, my lord of Douglas," he said aloud, smiling, "and gladly will I tell." He motioned to a wide padded couch below the great window, and James gratefully sank down into it, as much out of sheer exhaustion and bewilderment as to hide the fact that his legs were beginning to tremble.

Pouring a mether of ale from the keeve that stood on a low table, Connla offered it to his guest with the proper formula, and then the good bread and cheese and meat in the dishes beside, that he had earlier ordered to be left there awaiting their arrival. For a moment, James stared uncomprehendingly—he had not broken his fast that morning, knowing it was to be a day of battle—then accepted the small platter as mannerly as he might manage, trying not to gobble like a hog, but by God and all angels, he was *hungry*...

Connla nodded approvingly. "You will feel more yourself once you get on the outside of some good food... Well, now. We know of the Templar Knights from our return voyages—oh aye, we have had some dealings and encounters with your order, of varied natures and outcomes—and as I said, we know also a little of your current straits. But the whole tale will serve us both best."

It took a long while, and much repetition and long involved side-explainings and backtrackings, for Connla to make all clear about Keltia, and for James to make things clear in return. But at last James sat back and shook his head—he was feeling much better now, and clearer in his mind, though still hopelessly staggered, and still he could not tear his gaze from the view below. *Sailing among the stars, and round planets, and magic of the*

Sidhefolk, and light as motiving agent, and demonstrations of incredible power…

"Your tale is more amazing than anything I have ever heard, lord; it stands above the stories of Fionn and Roland and Arthur himself. Yet I cannot deny the evidence of my own eyes—this is beyond not belief but beyond disbelief, for that I see it before me, all around me. But that you dared leave Earth at all—"

"We thought we could do no other," said Connla quietly. "Pátraic was too close behind us, and we saw that the forbearance we had given him and his faith was not going to be given us and ours in return." He fell silent a moment, then spread his hands and shrugged, a gesture more eloquent than speech.

"So we left. Great Brendan and Nia his mother, who was a princess of the Sidhe, the faerie folk, built us ships to sail the overheavens, and found for us the road through the stars, what way those of Atland, the great island nation that was whelmed in the waves, had left it for us. Found too our promised home among those stars. We have dwelled there ever since." Looking straight at James: "And I make this offer to you now, lord knight. You and your fellows, who I perceive are as direly threatened in your time as we were in ours, and for the same reasons, or as near as makes no matter, are welcome to join us there, to live in peace and freedom as you choose."

James had not been expecting that, and to buy himself time for thought, he reached again for the keeve of ale—which had already been replaced twice, unsummoned, by a silent kern who came and went without a word—and poured himself another mether.

Nine hundred years they have been out there, out among the stars...nine hundred years! And on the world they left behind, no one knew; or if they did, they did not say — save perhaps the bards, in those wild poet's tales that none ever took for truth...all those legends about craft that could sail over land or sea, and flaming swords that could cut through any thickness, and magic armor, and crystal ships that knew their owner's mind...who could have known it for plain, not so simple truth? Or knowing, who could have spoken to be believed?

"We kept it that way a-purpose," said Connla, seeing James's expression and knowing his thought—the incredulous half-laughing, half-angry disbelief. *Ah well, poor soul, it is no easy thing to be hit with all this in one go. Not exactly easy for us either; though we at least have seen it before, and thank all gods we have been trained to deal with it...*

"Not that we had any real fear that others would follow—the secret of the shipmaking was ours alone, and we have kept it well—but we preferred not to leave to Erithfolk a bitter legacy, the gnawing resenting knowledge of something that they could not have for many centuries to come, if even then; it would have been too cruel. Also we did not wish to be pursued; we were escaping, not exploring, and we did not want our conflicts following us to our new home. For who knows what the haters would have done with the knowledge of Atland? Spreading their poison to the stars would have been the least of it."

James frowned slightly. "But you said you have encountered folk in your return voyages; surely this must have posed a problem?"

"Oh aye, for a certain value of 'problem' only. Those who discover the secret and the truth, we bring away to Keltia, though of course never against their will, so no problem there; the rest must bide — at least for now — and should they be ill-advised enough to prattle about us they are thought mad by their hearers, so again there is no problem. Your own plight confirms how unready they still are to know our truth: your folk still persecute one another for that most utterly stupid of reasons — difference of faith. They have not yet managed to learn that all spirit comes from the same place, that differing faiths are merely differing cloaks for the same mighty and loving truth. The Light wears many faces, and many are the roads that lead to it."

Connla paused, stared out the window a few moments, sighed. "For their own souls' sake, they must learn to honor different beliefs, as the Highest did give them to different folk; to dwell side by side and in peace with those who believe differently, and to respect all gods as they respect their own. And this fault of not doing so seems for some reason to lie more with the Christers than with others. Though such prejudice could be said to be with all People of the Book against those not of their kind — Christling and Saracen and Jew alike. All they ever do is destroy: temples of other faiths, even fellows of their own faith, if they deem them out of line. Perhaps it is your Book itself that is at fault. There are many good words in it, to be sure, but also many others that are not so good, and some are even evil."

James acknowledged the truth of the charge with a tightened mouth and a curt nod. "When my brothers of the Paris Temple served in Palestinia, they were not always at the sword's point with their so-called enemy. Many spoke with wise men, aye, and wiser women!, of the Saracen folk — their commanded foe who often became their friend — and they told me that those learned ones said the same as you have said just now, to the confoundment, or worse, of their own priests, their mullahs. So hateful ignorance is by no means limited to infidels, nor words of light to Christians. But that is a truth that most have yet to master."

He shifted on the leather seat, looked mac Nessa in the face. "My Church did terrible slaughter in France a hundred years ago, against blameless good folk called Cathari — men, women and children all horribly tortured and slain. And those Cathari were true Christians, sons and daughters even as we are of the faith that vaunts itself the only true one; they had committed no sin except to think for themselves and not lie down before Rome like ignorant slaves to be trodden upon. And so they died for it. I flatter myself that I am a good son of Mother Church, my lord, but when I see how readily that same Church visits pain and blood and death, when such suits her purpose, on her own folk and on harmless others — the Jews, the Cathars, now the Templars — aye, and doubtless more still in time to come, I would gladly bring her roof down upon her own head if only I could. Mother Church can be a very harsh parent indeed. Ploys of worldly power and control, made in the name of Christ Jesus — dare I blaspheme to say it, but I do not think that such is what He had in mind. But you are not Christians at all."

"Indeed we are not!" came the amused answer. "We follow the draoícht way: Eolas, the Knowing, Shan-vallachta, the Old Road of gods and goddesses—as our foremothers and forefathers did, before the White Druid of the Tree was brought by Pátraic to conquer our lands. Thanks be to God and Goddess alike that we got out just in time... So we too have felt the hand of Rome against us—I daresay we are not so unlike, the Templars and ourselves."

"But—"

Connla waved a dismissive hand, but he was smiling. "Your Christ was a mighty teacher sent by the One, the Great Creator of Being. Your Church says that he took man's form but he also bore god's nature. Well, you are more right than you know, and he is not the only such one, god or man, who has ever done so, or ever will. Avatars, such beings are called in eastern lands, easter far than your Templar Outremer—Ch'in and Persia, Nihon and Hind. Nay, we have no quarrel with him, only with what was made of him once he was gone and could not prevent it.

"Others of your faith are in Keltia, you know," he added, seeing James's trouble—and his sudden start of surprise. "There are not many, but they are there, and glad to be so; fine Kelts they are, too. If you come with us, you will not be alone, and you may follow your faith as you will—as it was meant to be followed and never yet has been. The Celi Dé, we call them, the Servants of God—they joined us and the Sidhefolk on the Great Immram, the First Voyage, when Pátraic drove the Old Ways out of Ireland and brought in new ways that even these sheep of his own flock could not, and would not, thole. After, Pátraic called us serpents and snakes that the power of his new god had driven from the land."

"To a realm beyond the pope's reach—"

"Far beyond the reach of Rome, right enough. But—as my Celi Dé friends are always telling me—never beyond the reach of God."

"Well, far beyond the reach of Clement and Philip—that is more than far enough for me! But how can God have made one truth—and so different a truth—for you, and another for ourselves? And other truths still for other folk?"

But Connla smiled, and declined the gambit. "Who dares put limits on the One? Or limits on the power of Goddess or God—aye, there is a Goddess, I promise you, maybe even you shall come to know Her… That is the only real blasphemy: to believe there can be boundaries to the Highest's creation or manifest Self. And the only real sin is to act as if there are."

James rallied one time more to protest, though he wanted to believe and accept this impressive and immensely likeable stranger more than he could say; indeed, already felt in him a friend. "Yet churchmen have ever said that any other way than Rome's is a lie."

Connla grinned, and James flushed, feeling suddenly unsophisticated and even naïve. "Every man banks the embers to his own loaf, when he can get away with it… That is only what churchmen *say*. What *is*, is a very different matter. And once even Rome herself held otherwise. I ask you: what you have seen here today, what I have spoken to you—does it feel like a lie?"

"A lie?" James flung back his head. "No, by the splendor of Heaven! It feels like truth and freedom. And yet my way too feels like truth."

Connla's smile widened and warmed. "And we do not say that it is not! Nor would we. But—and this we do say—it is not true in the way you now think that it is true. And that is a thing you may and must yet learn, if you come to dwell among us; or even if you do not."

"Still"—he added, rising from the window seat, and James rose with him, startled to see that the sun which had been climbing during the sea-fight was now nearly set even at this height, they had talked for hours—"you will have ample time to consider. We remain here at least a sevennight, though at such a height and behind such a cloak that folk beneath cannot see us."

Reasonably, seeing James's dismay: "You and your companions need time to rest and recover yourselves before they can wisely choose their fate; you know that this is so. We will repair your vessels as well as your wounded; also we require time to complete our own duties—we are tasked with responsibilities of our own, you know, we did not come here merely to rescue you timely from your foes! But you are free of this ship." The implication being, though Connla was far too courteous to say it aloud, that the Templars were no peril because they were much too ignorant to understand what they saw, and much too incapable of harm against the Kelts to pose even a physical threat; and, James admitted privately, the captain was far from wrong to think so.

"You may go wherever you will and speak with whomever you please; I am at your service at any time for any need or reason. You have been through many shocks this day; all of you need to heal. I must leave you now, my duties call me; but I will join you again for the nightmeal,

and any of my folk will gladly converse with any of you."
Connla added with a smile, "You are as great a mystery and
new thing to us as we are to you, I promise!"

James looked up, all his longing and confusion and
wariness and hope battling it out in his eyes and upon his
face, and he did not care greatly if the other saw; also, to his
chagrin and shame, he realized that all day long, while he
and Connla had spoken, he had not given a single thought
to his companions, not even to his cousin Walter.

"Truly?"

Connla mac Nessa vhic Dhau laughed outright, but it
was not a mocking laugh or a cruel one. "Truly! There is
very much to learn and explain, on both sides and to both
our benefits. Do not worry for your folk; they have been well
cared for and explained to, as our guests; as you yourself
have been. Brehon law still holds among us: hospitality to
the stranger does not change simply because it has gone out
to the stars."

On the morning of the sixth day, in the chamber with the
huge window-wall where he had spent his first hours
aboard the Cabarfeidh, James Douglas restlessly waited
for Connla mac Nessa. Presently he must give the Kelts an
answer to their offer of sanctuary, by comparison to which
his own offer of sanctuary to the fugitive Templars was as
a rushdip to the sun. Over the past days—and wondrous
days they had been—he had talked to any Kelt who would
have speech with him, and he had learned much, so much
that sometimes his head had spun with it. Then he had
put the choices to the knights, and to all the folk down

to the least squire and smith and horse-handler who had accompanied them from France. He had set it out for them squarely, honest enough to let them see his own feelings on the matter — though he also took care not to influence their decision. The choice must be their own.

Indeed, all Templars who had made the sailing to Scotland had now been given the choice that Connla mac Nessa had given James Douglas: not just the crews of the Mary and the Michael and the Holy Wisdom, but those on all the surviving ships below that had made their way to the safety of a secret inlet in Kintyre. Three only, sadly: one, the smallest, had been captured by the English, and two had been destroyed in the rearguard defense — the three vessels destined for the Baltic, which had accompanied them thus far, had by orders not engaged in the fight, and were by now, it was to be hoped, sailing far past the northern isles and safely on their way.

James had charged Connla and his officers, diffidently but firmly, with the unfairness of it: how it was hardly justice that only some of the refugees should have this amazing chance of sanctuary in a new world; and the Kelts had agreed at once. So James and Connla had gone down to each vessel, spoken privately to each captain; then the captains and crews had all been brought up to the Keltic ship, to speak to Connla and his crew, to see the wonders the others had seen before them, and to make their choice along with them.

Some Templars had been resolved from the first to have none of it. For them it must be Scotland or nothing; others held the whole thing to be a strange waking nightmare or evil magic illusion, in any case the undoubted work of Satan, and the Kelts must be devils or fallen angels, or at best the duped mortal minions of the princes of hell—at which James only shook his head and sighed for his brethren's rigid minds.

Yet many were afire to ride out, or sail out, on this new adventure, even though it was made very clear to them that they could never return to Earth, and that anything like crusading or missionary work among the Kelts, or any other race (for there are other races, James recalled with wonder, many of them, and they not human at all!), would not be tolerated. "Though tolerance is truly our way," Connla had said, "you will be the ones to whom that gift is extended, and we expect you to return the same back to us. If you feel you cannot, speak now: for that will be the price of your freedom. If your pouch is not deep enough to pay, do not think to be buying in any market of ours, and better for all of us do you remain here and face your natural fate. My sorrow if that sounds harsh; but we are a nation of realists, have had to be so from the start, and we have learned to speak our minds, tide what may betide."

There had been many solemn conversations between Kelt and Templar, and also between knight and knight amongst themselves, discussing the countless ramifications of this— staying or going, Scotland or Keltia. But also there had been many merry meals and meetings, and bonds of friendship had already formed between such different folk who were in truth not so very different at all. James, reflecting, found that he could not predict who would stay and who would go; but he knew already what road he himself would take ...

Strangely, it was a childhood recollection that had decided him: in a brief period of peace, he had been out riding with Walter and Marjorie Bruce, and they had come to one of the carved wyrdstones that were so common in Fife and the neighboring lands. They had dismounted to examine it more closely, seeing the usual odd-looking beasts, the crescents and V-rods, the double discs and Z-rods, the combs and mirrors and lines of horsemen. But this stone had borne upon its weathered sides a new and strange thing: the carving in question appeared to be a line of rowers sitting in a longship of old. But around its stern was what seemed to be a flurry of flames, and the prow of the craft was pointed straight upward toward the heavens…

Could it be? Was that stone not merely a carver's fancy but a true depiction? Once, then…

Now mac Nessa entered, a new air of command wrapped about him like a cloak. Greeting James warmly, he ushered him into a bigger chamber adjoining. At a long, polished stone table, the officers of the Cabarfeidh were seated, and all down the table's other side sat Walter Stewart and the captains and chief officers of the Templar galleys — who to a man looked intensely relieved at James's entrance.

There was a palpable feeling in the room, James noticed as soon as he took the seat facing Connla's own across the middle of the table, the memory of the chapterhouse meeting in Paris coming to the fore. Not fear or tenseness — more like the feeling on the night before a battle, when you know you are committed to the fight but cannot yet see what shape that fight may take…

"Well now," said Connla mac Nessa easily, though the

air of solemnity remained. "We have met, and we have spoken, and now it is time to decide." Swiftly he outlined the offer and its alternatives once again, so that all might be perfectly clear on the matter. "There it is, then: sanctuary in Keltia for all who wish to go, peace and freedom within our laws to live and worship as you choose; or to be safely set down again in Scotland, beyond the reach of the English fleet, though that will be all the help that may be given.

"We may have overstepped ourselves in offering even this choice to you, and I am quite sure our High Queen will wish to discuss it with me when we get home," he added, though he did not seem much alarmed at the prospect of possible queenly displeasure; no doubt he had encountered it before. "But here, now, we give you the choosing, and ask only that, whether you remain or come with us, all of you take oath to your god to keep our secret. The King of Scotland may know, and we will deem his royal oath as spoken; but none else."

He ceased, and his eyes sought James Douglas across the table's width. For his part, James glanced at Walter, then he squared his shoulders and lifted his head to meet Connla's gaze.

Now I know how Jacques de Molay did feel, that night we rode from Paris…

"We have considered among ourselves, lord and captain," said James then, formally, "and taken advice of your folk as well as our own counsel, and we accept." Smiles, and great relief, and murmurs of approval. "Not all of us will come, but many will. We know an adventure when we see one, and we thank you, either way, for what you give us. We hope to furnish good and loyal service in your land, for that is our knightly purpose. Nor are we strangers to oathfast secrets: we will swear upon our swords—no oath is more sacred to us than that."

"But for yourself, lord?" asked a tall, vivid, russet-haired girl with the eyes of a mermaid and the carriage of a young stag, whom he had noticed on that first day in the landing bay—as he now knew to call it—and whom for some daft reason he had fought shy of approaching until a whole day more had been lost to his idiocy. After that, they had talked for hours, for days, with that shining, bubbling eagerness that comes when a young couple first meet, when they know each is drawn to the other and that more than talk will come of it; and he had learned, to his chagrined but proud surprise, that she was second in command to mac Nessa himself.

I think I would beggar my soul to buy such freedom, such a life, for my folk and for myself— -and beggar it still more to have her in it—but...

"Scotland is my home, lady," he said at last, looking straight at her, letting her see his agony of choice, his divided heart. "But this"—he raised both arms in an oddly ceremonious gesture, looking round at the shining ship, the star maps on the walls, the jeweled orrery depicting Keltia and its worlds that hung in the air in the middle of the room—"this too is mine. Only I did not know it until now."

"Will you come, then?" said Connla with soft urgency. "You and Keltia would go strong together, and we are friends already, you and I."

James was silent a long time, and they respected his

silence. "I will not, then," he said at last, and they could hear what it cost him to say it. "Not now. Not yet. I must return to my king, and help him in his work. I pray you understand, though I am not sure I understand it myself... But when that work is done, I will come, if I may, to call you all my friends in Keltia as I call you so here and now. Or perhaps I will send my son to you, if ever I have one—a scion to graft a Douglas slip on this distant rootstock. Failing all else, the Low Road, by which we Scots believe a soul in death does come to its true home, will take me there in the end."

He met the warm sympathy in Connla's eyes, and though he dared not turn his head to look, he felt the keen sorrowing disappointment in the girl's, and knew both feelings in himself.

"We understand very well," said Connla mac Nessa, and though he did not smile, it felt as though he had. "A hero's choice, either way, and we honor it and you together. Know that the Name of Douglas will be a thousand times welcome among us whenever and however it comes. And I for one have no doubt whatever but that it shall."

On a stony beach on the ocean coast of the isle of Skye, ankle-deep in cold kelpy surfwash that swirled around his boots, James Douglas stood with lifted head, shading his eyes against the sea-glitter off the hull of the Cabarfeidh, as it hung a hundred feet above the waves.

Cabarfeidh, the Antlered One—a title of their god, so my bonny lady said; the ship being named for him as Templar ships are named for our own holy ones. But only look! Not beholding this, who could possibly believe it? Even seeing as I see and have seen, knowing what I know, still I am dumbfounded.....

He took an involuntary step back as, in total silence, the gigantic craft began to rise, laughing at himself for so doing — no step's distance could have saved him if the craft had crashed, or chose to aim a light-volley at him where he stood. Then he took three steps forward in uncontrollable longing, feeling his heart rise with the ship, laughed again as a thought struck him.

However will those English mariners even begin *to explain what they will claim to have beheld? I would not be in their boots for any money...*

As the Cabarfeidh mounted higher in the heavens, James drew his sword and lifted it in salute, and the others who stood with him on the strand instantly followed his example. Standing off from shore, reunited with the remnant of their fleet, all their crews now much depleted — and their treasure likewise, James and the Templar captains having insisted on a fair share of the gold accompanying the voyagers, to fend them in Keltia — the Mary and the Michael and the Holy Wisdom and their three sister ships paid their respects to another sister: on each mast the Beauséant dipped in homage to the great starcraft above.

Surely they can see us, as we can see them, and I wish to bid them proper farewell. Such things my brothers shall see and know! Things that might have been mine too: a life and a love — but duty is pre-eminent, and maybe yet one of my clan shall carry the Name of Douglas to the stars...

He saw the ship unfurl her star-sails, and tears stung his eyes as the vast silver sheets inclined and rippled in return salute. As he watched, the Cabarfeidh pulled in her sails again, then, accelerating from a standing start, vanished at the zenith on a trail of white fire; and when even that was gone, still he watched. Then he sighed, and turned about, and went with the knights who had watched with him, all of them as subdued and as awed as he, to land the warriors and horses from the ships.

The Kelts, true to their word, had magically, or perhaps not magically, though so it certainly seemed, transported all six remaining ships north to Skye, beyond the reach of the enemy fleet, a service and a kindness much appreciated; they would be safe hid in the deep-watered narrow sea-lochs between the mountains' arms, and could sail out at their leisure wherever they might be needed. Now all that remained for James was to find a mount and companions to ride with him to where he could speak to King Robert.

And just as importantly, with my friend Rob...

"If it were anyone but you, Jamie, to tell me such a tale..."

"I know. But it is I. And it was so."

In the hall of Inverlochy Castle, deep in the Highlands at the entrance to the Great Glen, which stronghold he had just recently taken, Robert Bruce leaned back in the carved wooden chair. His reddish hair was tousled as ever and his keen glance was fixed on the eager glowing face of his young friend and captain—the friend who had just told him the most fantastical story he could ever have thought to hear.

"A realm of the stars—a ship to sail the heavens—" Bruce drank from the mether that had stood untouched at his elbow for the past two hours as he had listened entranced;

now he shook his head, marveling anew. "How I would have liked to be there, to see it for myself...."

"It would have amazed you."

"God's feet, as it does!" The king was silent; but the man's eyes sparkled at the thoughts racing through his mind. "New worlds, new suns — and all of them ruled by our blood! Who could have prophesied such a weird? But once safe settled in their new home, in this Keltia" — he pronounced the unfamiliar name with care and wonder — "did they never think, or wish, to return?"

"Oh aye, they have done so many times by all accounts. Though only to keep an eye on the home lands, and to take away those who longed to go and knew how to make contact. When first they left Earth, they pledged themselves never to interfere more with Earth's problems; that pledge has not been broken, though I was told that it has a few times been bent, or tested sore... We have sworn on our swords, as Templars and as knights of Scotland, to keep their secret."

Bruce, no stranger to nuance, immediately saw what was being so delicately asked. "As will I," he said at once, and solemnly touched the hilt of his own blade in token. "It will not be the first secret we have kept, you and I, nor yet will it be the last."

James relaxed, knowing he had kept his word to Connla mac Nessa. "Still, Rob, the errand was not bootless: many knights left, right enough, but many more remained, ships and treasure with them, all of them vowed to our need and your service."

"May heaven reward them for it," murmured Robert

Bruce, "and avenge them upon their betrayers."

"And likewise protect our brothers wherever they now may be," said James presently. "And those among whom they now dwell."

And the king joined him in "Amen."

So the wars went on, to break the English hold on Scotland; and if Edward Longshanks, Hammer of the Scots—who had died that very year of the Temple's fall and James Douglas's encounter with the Kelts—had pounded those Scots hard, those same Scots now pounded his England even harder. Edward had left to succeed him a weakling son, a second Edward, said to prefer his luxurious favorite, Piers Gaveston, to the tasks of governing and the crusade to conquer Scotland, and so had withdrawn his forces, at least at first, though now, under the goading of his barons, Edward was again making inroads on Scottish soil.

Thanks to the balladeers, James had already gone into legend as the Black Douglas, as much for his methodical ferocity in war as for his dark handsomeness: he had learned early on that fear could do as much for a commander as a schiltron of troops, and his actions were devised to sow terror among the English, through raid and rout. As for Robert the Bruce, he had settled the crown of Scotland more firmly upon his head than ever. With James's help and battle genius, he was slowly and successfully clawing back the lands that Longshanks had ripped away, defending his gains against Edward by means of "secret war"—a tactic of lightning-quick strikes followed by a melting-away into the mists and moors where the English forces could not follow.

The secret war was greatly successful: by the year 1314, there remained in English hands only the border town of Berwick—and the great strategic prize of Stirling Castle, rising on a mighty rock above a stream called the Bannockburn.

Seven years after the Templars came to Scotland, three months after Jacques de Molay, dying in flames at a Paris stake after long imprisonment and torture, had summoned Clement the pope and Philip the king to join him ere the year was out before the throne of God's judgment—as, eerily, they would indeed come to do, dying within weeks of one another—on the morning of the twenty-fourth of June 1314, a clear warm Midsummer Day, Robert Bruce and James Douglas, and Walter Stewart newly betrothed to the king's vibrant daughter Marjory, who had been held hostage all that time, and the assembled force of the Scots with them, met the English armies below Stirling Castle rock for the second day of battle, on the flat plain hard by the Bannockburn.

It was a desperate day for the outnumbered Scots; for all their valor, several times the battle, and Scotland with it, seemed lost. Beneath his tressured-lion standard, Robert Bruce was silent, as if he waited for something and dared not say for what; James Douglas, away commanding the right flank, said no more than his king.

Then, as suddenly as if they had ridden out of the air, a force of mounted knights came over the ridge and reined in, looking down at the battlefield. They were cloaked in pure white, the famous crimson cross was gone now from

the left breast of those mantles; but the warhorses they sat
were full-boned Flemish destriers, the bared swords in their
hands bore the plain Templar hilt, and their standard-bearer
gripped a lance-staff from which flew the Beauséant itself.

They were not many, they had not come in their full
numbers; but they were enough. One after another, the
English soldiers looked up to see them motionless against
the skyline; an ominous silence began to settle over the field,
like the breath-caught stillness before the thunder cracks in
the heights of heaven, and a whisper ran swift as lightning
along the lines.

Templars, the hissing fearing word went up as English
sword-arms faltered. *The Knights Templar are come to fight for
Robert Bruce!*

And so they had, and so they did; so great was their
skill in battle, so feared the Templar name, that the day was
turned and carried for Scotland and its king.

And at last there came a time when the horrors were done.
The mighty Temple had been broken and was now no
more, and both France and papacy were stained with blood
that would never be washed entirely clean. Many knights
had perished under torture, great and lesser alike; many
more had survived, finding sanctuary in other orders and
other lands, though no knights in Templedom had found
sanctuary stronger, or stranger, than had those who sailed
from France with Jamie Douglas.

But in Scotland, a different tale was told. Early in the
reign of King Robert, in the far west of Argyll, a small village
had taken root in remote Kintyre. It was called Kilmichael,

Saint Michael's Church—those newly settled there had wished to sanctify their new home ground, by placing it in the protection of the prince of angels and the captain of heaven's forces. From many lands had they come, these once-Templars: they were Scots, English, Welsh, Irishers, French, Burgundians. Knights still, by the pope's decree they were monks no longer, though some continued to comport themselves as such and keep to their old vows, as a matter of honor. But for the rest, to ensure their survival past the present generation they had set aside their vows of chastity to wed with the flower of Scots noblewomen—suitable matches having been carefully arranged by Elizabeth de Burgh, Bruce's formidable queen.

Now they were raising herds and tending crops and keeping their mains like any other Scotsman, those who came from foreign parts still learning the language and customs, all of them praising God, if not His vicar on Earth who had brought them to this fate.

As that first village thrived and prospered, the knights spread out around Loch Fyne to found other settlements. Their ships were long gone—sunk, sold as merchant or fishing vessels, rotted away; likewise their fair white mantles had felt the moth's tooth. But the long straight swords were still put to old uses: the knights kept the blades bright, raising them to strike in battle or to kneel before in prayer.

What their wives thought was never to be known. Doubtless they were glad of the strong arms their husbands brought to their homes and to their king, but none knows what else they may have felt. What those husbands brought to the marriage-bed—well, as onetime monks, belike the knights were no worse mates than other men of their time, perhaps even better. Still, there was not a woman in the tiny Templar settlements but knew that this life, and she herself, and her children if child she had borne, had not been the first and longed-for choice of her spouse; the Almighty Himself was her eternal and undefeated rival. Perhaps it rankled; perhaps each strove to make it up to the other — and to those children that had come of them — out of duty or chivalry or loyalty or pity, or even out of love. Who can know how it may have been for them; or knowing, who would say?

But for those cross-hilted swords, in time one final use: traced on plain stone graveslabs, their images were set above the mortal remains of those who once had lived to serve as swords themselves. Monks though they had been, they were human also, and perhaps in the end they found they could not entirely forgive; so that, not caring to have upon their graves in Scotland the sign of the Church that had betrayed them in France, they still needed the sign of the One who had never betrayed them and never forgotten them and never failed them, as they had never betrayed or failed or forgotten Him...

And that day came when King Robert Bruce lay on his last bed, attended by his kindred and his captains and his friends. His queen had gone before him two years since, his daughter two years after Bannockburn; the child prince his son stood silent by. Yet none but Lord James Douglas heard the last words of the king, as Robert plucked with strengthless fingers at his friend's sleeve, and James bent low to hear.

"Take my heart to the holy land...Jamie...the blessed land....you know what land I truly mean..."

And, though the others were much gratified by this surprising display of piety—the dying wish of the once-excommunicated Robert Bruce, that his heart go on pilgrimage to, as they thought, Jerusalem—knowing very well what land his king did mean, James kissed him on the brow and promised, and knew also that he would obey.

The white light of Andalusia struck like a drawn sword through even his closed eyelids. Never had James dreamed there could be such heat and dryness and brightness. Skin used to Scottish mists and cloud-veiled sun was drawn tight as a drumhead for the sun to pound upon, and his own head was the drum itself.

And it is but March! What must it be like in high summer? Palestinia itself can be no hotter or drier than this—how the Templars could have fought there all those years, in armor and garb, I cannot imagine...

"This" was the field of Tebas de Ardales, hard by Tebas castle. Lord Sir James Douglas and Sir William Sinclair and the rest of their noble party found themselves on a battlefield that day, fighting against the Moors of Granada for the Christian king Alfonso of Castile, even as the great Cid himself, Rodrigo Diaz de Vivar, once had fought against Moors for another royal Castilian Alfonso, not so very long ago or far away...

Battle had not been part of their plan when they left Scotland. Reaching Spain, they had left their ship in Galicia, near the great pilgrim city of Santiago de Compostela—

where to the imposing cathedral and shrine of his saintly patron James had made awed and eager pilgrimage. Then they had come riding down through Castile, intending to continue on across to the coast, taking ship again from one of the Mediterranean ports that still served the Holy Land seaports of Acre and Jaffa. But, receiving them at his court in Burgos, King Alfonso had indicated he would be glad of their help against the emirs; bound by chivalry, they could do naught but oblige.

"It is in no way inconsonant with our errand," Sinclair had argued—he of the Roslin Sinclairs, an old Templar family that had its seat in that tiny Pentlands village looking out on those splendid blue hills. "Our king commanded us to bear his heart against the infidel, and here we have a chance to do so; he will approve and understand."

Indeed Rob would, and likely did, reflected James. *Though how my true errand is to be accomplished, and without the others twigging, I am sure I do not know. To get my king's heart to Keltia, as he did charge me—the only way he, or I, can now get there, unless…*

All the long and weary way from Scotland—even as he had knelt in farewell beside Bruce's coffin, in the dimness of Dunfermline abbey church—James had cherished the hope that somehow the Kelts would know his need: that their science, or their magic, could find him wherever he might be; that the Cabarfeidh would once more shadow the upper skies; that he and Connla mac Nessa vhic Dhau might sail together to wars among the stars; that his tall, bright-flashing lady greet him again under a different sun, and so he had never wed another.

But hope had dimmed the souther they had gone. *A lad's hope at best…Still, I did believe they would. And perhaps even yet they shall…*

On the field of Tebas, with clear eyes the Scottish knights beheld the steel wall of Moorish cavalry, many times their own numbers, that cut them off from Alfonso's army. Then they looked at one another, and their thought was all the same thought: *This is the fight that for us shall end all fights forever; we will not make it through this one alive…*

James found that he was fiercely glad, wondered if every soldier recognized the moment when it came for him at last. *If it cannot end the other way, then this is how it should end: if not that, then something else. For everything happens somewhere, as I have come to learn; more, as I have come to trust and believe…*

On his right, Sinclair straightened in his deep war-saddle, raising his head and lifting his visor, and the others kneed their horses closer so that they might hear his words.

"They will find his heart where we died for it, where we lie for it, and they will know that it went before us to the end. Belike they will return it to Scotland, enshrine it in some abbey, where it belongs—a heart of home on the ground of home. And I daresay that will serve. We have lived with and for a legend—now let us die for him as well, and forever live in legend ourselves like the heroes of old."

And James, looking at his friend's smiling, sunburned face, knew that Sinclair was no more afraid than he himself was, nor regretful that this was the way it would finish. *It will serve indeed…*

"Fitting it is that today is the observable day of our dear

king's crowning, twenty-four years ago at Scone," said James. "A good day to die; indeed, a better day than most." He leaned from the saddle to grip Sinclair's arm, feeling the strong pressure of an answering clasp, and the old wolf-grin scythed across his lean dark face. "And if the Low Road is the way we must travel to get home, be it so. It is not so far or so terrible a journey, and we do not go alone. So long as the heart be right, no matter where the rest shall lie—nay, nor the heart neither."

He reached within his mail, under his linen shirt, and drew out something on a leather cord, and seeing it Sinclair and the others instantly bared heads and crossed themselves. James held it up to the sun, and it flashed like a mirror in the slanting light of Spain: clasped in a fine gold lattice, a small silvery orb—the steel case, made of the blade of his own sword, that held the heart of Robert Bruce.

James kissed it, then passed it silently to Sinclair, who followed suit with equal reverence and passed it on, to Sir Simon of the Lee, to Sir William Keith, to the brother knights Sir Robert Logan and Sir Walter Logan and all the rest. When each man had touched his lips to the royal reliquary and crossed himself, receiving it back James kissed it again, and bowing his head over it he spoke words to it in a low voice that no one else did hear.

Then, standing in his stirrups, Lord James Douglas raised his arm above his head, and with all his strength he flung the little case from him, deep into the midst of the oncoming Saracen force, and spurred his war-horse at the foe, followed at once by the others. In the voice he used in battle shouting above the fight, his words rose over hoof-thunder as the charging destriers hit stride.

"Go first in the fight, brave heart, as thou hast ever done, and we shall follow as we ever did!"

And drew his sword, and did what he did best, and as he did so there came—even as he had hoped and prayed— from high above him, out of the heart of the sun, a great and welcome shadow falling like a cooling darkness...

Cool dimness within walls, voices eddying like rapids in a cold Highland burn. James tried to focus, but his glance was strangely misted, so instead he turned his attention to the one voice he could hear clearly—a man's voice, deep and pleasant, oddly familiar.

"You yourself trusted we would find you, brother, wherever you might be. Surely you did not doubt! We are come to keep our promise, and to bring you home."

He felt his heart give a great leap within him, and he smiled faintly through the pain. "I knew that you would, Connla mac Nessa vhic Dhau," he whispered. "As for promises, did I not say that I would call you friend in Keltia? I do so now, if it is not too late..."

And heard the smile in the answering voice, so close by him now as to sound within his head itself. *Everything happens somewhere; and no time is ever a time too late...*

"My lord of Douglas—to whom does he speak?" asked one of the Castilian doctors who stood by, helpless to stop the bleeding from five mortal wounds.

Through blinding tears Sinclair, himself near death where he lay on a pallet beside his friend, made him no answer; and then James spoke no word more that any in that chamber heard, nor did he hear the words they spoke to him, in their desperate need to reach him.

For he was not there. He was gone from them: gone from the castle chamber, gone from Spain, from the planet, from the world. Alive amid the heavens, he was back aboard the Cabarfeidh, outward bound. Surely no living man of Earth had seen such sights as now he saw: his home world shimmered blue and white behind him, Mars burned for him, Jupiter blazed its ruby eye, Saturn spun its shining rings as he passed them all. He seemed to be lying on that low couch upon which he had sat with Connla so long ago, the vast window beside him giving now a view onto the deepness of space; was a vague memory that he was wounded, and that it was the death wound, but it mattered not.

Too long a warrior not to know; and for all their skill and knowledge, even these starfolk could not stop it, nor even much delay it. Even if this were real… When the Low Road opens before you, there is naught to be done but ride – the swiftest way, and the surest, to come to the heart's true home. But perhaps…

He twisted lithely onto his side—there was no pain now—and looked out at the bluefire net of stars streaming past. *I am glad to have come to see this; perhaps there will indeed be time enough. For no time is truly too late…*

Yet though he was dying, and he knew it, somehow he was also walking alive in Keltia, with Connla his friend under a sky full of strange stars that bloomed and pulsed with light; and riding over far green plains with his lady beside him, knee to knee on matched grays, she fair and brave in Douglas colors…and laughing in a cold Highland rain with Rob, and standing back to back with Walter, sword in hand, at Bannockburn, and in the chapterhouse in Paris, Templar brethren thronging round with joyful greetings, blessed Jacques de Molay rising from his Master's throne to take him by the hand.

Truly, then, no time was too late: all times were one time, and at the same time no time at all, for a fair ringed planet that was circled by double moons, the loveliest thing he had ever seen, loomed now beyond the window. And it seemed to James that he would not be needing the ship nor even his body any longer, and so he floated down close to the surface of the world beneath.

His sight, always keen, had miraculously lengthened; and though through the great welcoming shout in his ears he heard no other sound, he saw below, as the light began to grow and spread behind him, a white stone building on the shores of a shining sea-loch; sensed the peace of the place, saw Templars in unfamiliar new blue robes walking and praying in cloister and garden. Then he caught his breath, and tears burned his eyes, for he saw, he Saw…

The stone building had been raised in form of a cross: not the cruel Latin cross nor yet the eight-point Templar cross but the suncross, the balanced Wheel, the circled equal-armed cross of the Celts and the Cathars and the Celi Dé and so many others—the symbol that points the four winds of the world and the four seasons of the year and the four elements of creation and the four sacred festivals of the sun, and the four Archangels and the four forts of the Danaans and the Four Chief Treasures of Britain; and ringing it round, the seamless, endless circle of Eternity that is the same for all and ever will be.

And seeing that—knowing that though all was indeed one, that "All" was not the same one—James was well content. He had left Connla and his lady behind when he left the ship, if ship it had been; now his spirit pulled back to soar up into that burning heart of light and Light. And those presences he had loved and missed and longed for were there to greet him; and someone else, someone he seemed to know well, and was glad of meeting once again—or for the first time, he did not know and it did not matter in the slightest—was taking his hand and conducting him, with honor and solemnity joyous enough to break his heart, except that his heart did not break but was healed and made whole, to a place, and into a Presence, that he had known always and longer still...

Next day in Tebas castle church they sang to holy Santiago a Mass for the repose of the soul of his namesake—a warrior's requiem, and a pilgrim's also. That night they boiled the bones clean for transport home, reverently lapping the strong, smooth ivory whitenesses in thin leaves of lead, tenderly robing the skull in Douglas colors, sealing the grim long package with the cross of the Temple and the scallop shell badge of Compostela—*campo stella*, "field of stars"— though they were never to know the full truth, or irony, of that last.

Sinclair too, who had died in the night speaking the names of Bruce and Douglas, received the same honors, and the other slain Scots as well, who had been found on the battlefield in a ring of dead Moors many times their number. With somber respect, the emirs had returned them, along with the little gold and steel reliquary, to honor their courage and their end; and the flesh that had been cleansed away in water was solemnly buried in the earth where they did fall.

But the heart of Bruce was borne on the bones of Douglas home again—a Crowned and Bloody Heart would grace the Douglas heraldry ever after—and laid to rest in Melrose Abbey in the Scottish borderlands. Though strange tales sprang up soon thereafter that it did not long remain there: that on a wild night of storm and thunder, it miraculously vanished upwards into the heavens in a great flash of light, and was not seen again on Earth.

James himself was laid to sleep forever in Saint Bride's church in his home country of Douglasdale, over the hills and not so far away, with Bríd herself—long a Celtic goddess or ever she came to be a Christian saint—to keep watch over him, and to keep safe in death and the life-after he who had never once been safe in life.

On a world circling a star that Earth astronomers call Delta Orionis, but which is named otherwise by those who dwell beneath its light, a bearded man clad in a dark-blue robe girt with a red cord and a plain longsword comes out of a low stone building. Standing on the foreshore of the sea-loch, he glances keenly around, as someone will quarter to all airts who has heard or sensed somewhat but knows not what or where or who.

Finding nothing, he raises his gaze to the heavens, and the hilt of his sword with it, and kneels briefly. His lips move silently, in prayer or chant or blessing; then he rises again, a faint puzzled frown on his broad brow.

Surely someone called? Who is here?

But no one is to be seen — at least not by any sight short of Sight. Still, true to his oath of chivalry and the rule of his Order and the faith of the folk of his much-loved new homeland, he will not chance letting any traveler go unblessed or unprotected, still less a stranger on such a voyage, a pilgrim on the Low Road, going home...

He smiles now, and turns away, and speaks aloud — to whomever, or whatever, might be near enough, or have ear enough, or heart enough, to hear — in words of a prayer newly learned a benison from of old.

"May your journey thrive."

TOUCHSTONE

touchstone: a means used to prove the quality
and true nature of something of excellence

May 3485 in the Common Reckoning,
3030 Anno Celtiae Conditae

"TIME TO WAKE, my brightness!" The old nurse's voice
sounded cheerful in the cool, sunny summer morning.

Too cheerful by half. Aeron turned over and dug deeper
into the pillows. "I *am* awake—"

Ten minutes later, sterner now: "You said you were
awake."

And you believed me? "Oh Nessa, must I get up?"

"You know very well you must. Have you forgotten
what is to happen today?"

My test of magic. How could *I forget, with all of you dinning
it into my head for the past sevennight?* "I have not. But does it
have to happen so *early*?"

"The Magistra has said this is the auspicious time for
it. Do you not want all the favorable force that you can
get, then?"

Oh – I suppose... She was out of bed now and heading to the pool-room to have her usual morning shower. It was a lovely room, with a large tiled pool like an ancient Roman bath, but for her it was the shower over on one stone wall, carved from the living rock of the mountain upon which the ancient castle sat. It was like being under a small waterfall, and she loved it, was attuned to water like most Kelts, never needing to be bribed or wrestled into it like her year-younger brother Rohan. Bathtime in the prince's rooms was invariably a grim and damp struggle; even their sister, Ríoghnach, a year younger still and a terror in all other respects, was not as averse as he to being clean.

Aeron Lassarina Angharad Aoibhell was nine years old and a princess of Keltia, heir to the Copper Crown. Two autumns ago, when she was seven, she had returned to Turusachan, the great royal palace that loomed over the capital city of Caerdroia, and which was the only home she had ever known. Two autumns before that, at the age of five, and all in accordance with ancient Keltic practice, she had been sent away for fostering, as was the case for all families of any great distinction of rank or wealth, and for many who had neither. The family chosen for the signal honor of first fostering her, the future monarch, was an old and noble one, not so old or noble as the Aoibhells, who had founded the star empire of Keltia and ruled it intermittently ever since, but powerful and influential all the same: the Douglases, planetary princes of Caledon. The first of that clan had come to Keltia in Erith's early fourteenth century, in fulfillment of a promise made by a Douglas lord and knight of Scotland to a Keltic starship captain, in a thoroughly strange but fateful encounter; though the lord himself could not come, much though he desired it. He had had responsibilities and duties that kept him on Erith, as the Kelts called the planet that had been their home, and later he had died trying to fulfill them; but true to his word he had sent his grandchildren and others of his people and kindred, and the family had settled on Caledon, achieving at last the title and position of Prince of Scots.

Aeron had been linked in fosterage with the present Prince's only daughter, Morwen, who was exactly her own age, and with Arianeira, daughter of the Prince of Gwynedd and five years their senior—not ideal for foster bonds, but as Aeron's father said, when they were all women grown it would make no differ whatsoever, and in the meantime the two younger girls would benefit by the advice and protection of an older sister. So there it had been left.

Aeron and Morwen had their birthdays within a week of one another, so Morwen too would be undergoing the same test as Aeron, though not until her actual birthday, when the autumn gales began on Caledon and the red leaves flew. There were very particular reasons why Aeron's test had been advanced a full five months—though few would discuss them, and none openly.

It was tradition that children should be tested at their own homeplaces, if that was at all possible, so Aeron had been kept at Turusachan, where she had returned a fortnight earlier for the celebration of the summer solstice and where those very particular reasons had manifested themselves, while Morwen had been left behind on Caledon for the nonce. Many had been the tears and much the fury of both girls, when they had learned they would be separated, not to be reunited until Aeron's test had been completed and the results pondered.

Though Aeron was a bit skittish, she was not afraid, particularly, more peevish than anything. What could happen, *really*? What *would* happen was that the Ban-draoi Magistra, Kesten Hannivec, whom she had known her entire life, would ask her some stupid questions, and require her to perform some...some *something*, some stupid magic feat that would probably prove not so terribly arduous. It was only a test. Everybody went through it. Morwen had already declared laughingly that she knew for a fact that she had less magic than dirt, than a twig, than things that grew on a stone wall in a swamp, and it was purely a waste of time to bother testing her to begin with.

Morwen's parents very firmly did not agree with her airy self-evaluation, however, and were only privately thankful that their own child's test could await its natural timing. Arianeira, being older, had undergone her own trial five years since, and was soon to be enrolled at the great Ban-draoi school of Scartanore; as expected, she had shown herself to be talented—if not quite so talented as her elder twin brother, Gwydion, their father's heir as Prince of Gwynedd, who was exceptionally gifted indeed.

The test Aeron was going to be subjected to this day, the draoích-crutha, the "proof of magic", was one every Keltic child had to undergo, as a rule on their tenth birthday, whether magic had appeared in them by then or not. The purpose was simple: to determine how much, if any, magical potential the child possessed. The time frame had been suddenly advanced in her case, however, since just last week, in the midst of the summer solstice celebration being conducted by her father, the High King Fionnbarr, at the holy circle of Ni-maen, she had managed to frighten half her homeworld by making the sun dance.

Or *appear* to dance, as everyone was very careful to point out; she did not actually move the system's star, Grían, from its place in the heavens—as astronomers, nervously triple-checking their calculations just to be sure, were loud in their assurances to the populace. Still, that appearance had been observed far and wide; folk had had hysterics clear across the planet, and that was something, admittedly, that few nine-year-olds in all Keltic history had been able to achieve. So now, today, the draoích-crutha was to be administered, to determine what was going on with her, in hopes of figuring out how to keep such an event from happening again; and none other than the Magistra herself, in the presence of Aeron's royal parents and two or three other witnesses, was going to administer it.

They all seemed to expect something momentous, Aeron thought to herself as she dressed, resigned to her fate, now only eager to get on the far side of it and be done. Well, she would not go out of her way to either oblige them or disappoint them; what would happen, would happen, and nothing she could do would alter it—or so she thought.

It was the custom of the royal family to breakfast together whenever possible, and today even more so. When Aeron entered the small solar where private meals were taken, she found her parents there before her. She smiled and ran to kiss them, and they hugged her more than usually close. With senses that of late seemed clearer, somehow, or sharper, she could tell that they were nervous for her; they were also excited, pleased, comforting and anticipating, but the underlying feeling was apprehension, like a fine metallic thread laid into the weft of the day.

She felt a twinge of annoyance as she took her usual seat and immediately rearranged her place setting to her liking. *Well, what do* they *have to be nervous about? I am the one undergoing the test this day, not any of them...* Though she knew they feared for her. Well, not fear, really; it was not a matter for fear. She was merely going to be put to the test by the head of the entire Ban-draoi order, that awesome sisterhood of magic-wielders, to see what her sorcerous capabilities might be—nothing more. But as Queen Emer offered a platter of sausages, her daughter's favorite, hoping to tempt her appetite, Aeron weighed the grim possibility that she might not *have* any magical capability—something she now realized, dismayed, she had not yet even considered.

On the face of it, it seemed most unlikely—as her maternal aunt Keina, herself a Ban-draoi Domina, had reassured her—that she would prove to be untalented, or, somehow a worse possibility far, merely *averagely* talented. Her family line ran heavy with sorcery on both sides: there was deep magic in the bloodlines, even Sidhe magic, going back millennia, to the very founding of Keltia—to before that, even, when the Kelts were not yet Kelts and still dwelled on Erith. Additionally there was the indisputable fact that she had already proved she was capable of not merely the tiny magics any child could perform but major magic in no uncertain terms — that little episode last week. Though that could have been a fluke, a onetime flareup, like beginner's luck, and no more magic remained in her store. But no: she would *not* fail, and she would do well enough to confound them all and suit even herself.

And what then? She picked moodily at her excellent breakfast. There would still be more fostering first of all. The test notwithstanding, she and Morwen and Arianeira were scheduled to move to Caer Dathyl, Ari's home castle on the planet Gwynedd, before the winter solstice, for the third and last stage of their fosternship. It had been an unusual arrangement — generally a child would spend all its fosterage time with one family only, the six years from age five to age eleven, more or less. But the circumstances here were unusual, as were the three girls themselves: they were all princesses, one of them heir to a duchy, one of them heir to a crown, and their royal parents had thought such a split arrangement good for them all, to fashion stronger links between the families, personal and political both, though the kindreds had been close for many centuries.

It had been the Queen Dowager, Gwyneira, Aeron's grandmother, to first float the idea, and then had been the one to work out the details; now, two terms into the rotation — the first two years at Kinloch Arnoch, the second two at Turusachan itself — it had been proved to all three kindreds what a brilliant idea it had been. Though already Arianeira, being older, did not spend all her time with her fosterns; and two years from the coming winter solstice the other girls would go their separate roads as well, depending on what had been decided by their parents on their behalf. For Aeron and Morwen, as for all other Keltic children, it had been at first tutors and the basic schooling they were now receiving; then would come a general educational grounding at bardic school, and then finally they would move on to academies of the professions: sorcery school, warrior school, brehon law school, healer school—whatever they proved to have a gift for. Which was what today was in large part going to determine.

Listening to her grandmother's quiet encouragement from the chair beside her, Aeron munched thoughtfully on a piece of toast spread with bacon cheddar. If she did well today, she would be sent off to Scartanore, like her great-grandmother, the Ard-rían Aoife, who had been there almost three hundred years ago. Female royalty, historically, attended Scartanore, whose name meant 'Thicket of Gold', for their sorceress training: the ancient college on the planet Erinna was the chief Ban-draoi institution in all Keltia, and the school of choice for a future High Queen. If not—well, though she had not been told so in as many words, the possibility was nonetheless there: that should her magic prove uncontrollable, as she had demonstrated last week, it might need to be bound, whether she wished it or no, and she barred from learning altogether. She scowled: a disagreeable prospect, but she *had* brought it on herself, any road, even though unwittingly...

"Aeron? Do you worry?" asked her mother, concerned for her eldest child's sudden silence. "It will all be well, dearling; there is no cause for fear."

The child smiled and shook her head. "Nay, mamaith,"

she said. "I was just thinking."

Emer relaxed a little. "No cause for fear," she said again, trying to reassure herself as much as Aeron, and across the table Fionnbarr, King of Kelts, smiled at his heir, a little tightly.

"It does not matter how you fare, my lass: you cannot fail. It is not that sort of test."

"But it *is* a test, not so?"

Fionnbarr shook his head emphatically, reaching to take his daughter's stiff little fingers in his. She noticed, though she had seen it thousands of times, the huge emerald set in heavy gold that sat ever upon his hand: the Great Seal of Keltia, that many monarchs had worn before him down the ages, back through Arthur himself to its first owner, the High Queen Athyn Blackmantle. One day, though she prayed that day would be long, long in coming, she would wear it herself—a strange and disquieting thought, which she put instantly aside.

"Nay, alanna, not entirely. Not like an examination set by your mathematics tutor or your fencing master. Whatever you do, that is the sole success of it. There is no judging, no passing nor failing. This test is merely to prove, to us but more importantly to you yourself, what is in you."

And to the rest of Keltia as well, though that he did not say aloud for fear of upsetting her further. But in all truth, how she fared at the draoích-crutha would be a strong indicator of how she would fare or fail at other tests in her future as Ard-rían, High Queen of Keltia. And what kind of queen she would indeed make: Keltia had had many different sorts of rulers in its long history. Some had been sorcerers, and an aptitude for such was what today's events would show. Others had been brehons or bards or warriors, or all those together. There had been great ones, poor ones, indifferent ones. Some had been monsters; one or two had been saints. Apart from the monsters, and perhaps apart from the saints also, it did not matter overmuch, in the long run.

Seeing his daughter nod, Fionnbarr left off lecturing, even so lightly as he had been. But in truth her whole life just now was a lecture, and the learning that came of it: she was being trained for her queenship to come, and though she was allowed to be as normal a growing child as possible, that fact would never, could never, be scanted or forgotten.

He turned to talk quietly to his wife and his mother, and to his sister-in-law Keina who had just joined them. There would be several other witnesses, unavoidably, to Aeron's test, including the Taoiseach, the First Minister of Keltia, Fionnbarr's chief aide in governance, the Archdruid, counterpart to the Ban-draoi Magistra, and the Pendragon, head of the magical-military order known as the Dragon Kinship. The rest of the realm's High Council, and the Privy Council also, would watch on viewscreens from the Council chambers; this was a very important day, and naturally they wanted to be kept informed of the progress of the future High Queen, but Emer did not wish to distress her daughter with a roomful of gawkers, so the in-person audience had been kept to the barest minimum.

Aeron had lost interest long since, and now she yawned prodigiously and drank off the last of her cup of hot shakla, more to give herself something to do than out of any real desire for the chocolate beverage, to which she was otherwise passionately addicted. She had not received any special instruction or foreknowledge of the Proving, as was tradition; the young candidate must come unprepared, the better for the pure native talent to be assessed. Nor was her clothing any kind of ritual garb; the aim was for the one being tested to feel relaxed and safe, so that the findings might be both accurate and correct. So she had been allowed by Nessa to choose her own clothes that morning, and she had dressed herself in a soft blue tunic and black, slim-fitting trews, with brown suede boots to finish off the costume and a small gold owl brooch pinning the tunic's collar — warm, comfortable, familiar.

But now her parents were rising from their places at the table, and her father held out his hand to her, and with her suddenly cold little paw in his sword-callused palm, her mother's own hand protectively on the back of her neck, the three of them, king, queen and princess, left the room, and the others followed after.

"So this is Aeron." The woman looked down at her, smiled, and after a moment the child smiled back. "Do you remember me, Highness? It has been a long time since I have seen you."

Aeron glanced warily up at the priestess. Kesten Hannivec was tall and silver-haired, with deep-set dark eyes and unlined skin; her age was hard to ascertain. At some moments, she seemed years younger than Queen Emer, at others, centuries older than Queen Gwyneira. Aeron decided it did not matter, for although she was not going to give any sign of it, or any sign of recognition either, she felt she trusted this stern priestess. She had met Ban-draoi before, of course, often; her aunt Keina was a most gifted one, and even her mother had had some training. The sorceresses of the order carried themselves proudly and humbly at the same time, seeming to be ruler and servant both. Which they were, Aeron thought in a tumble of quick observation, even if they were neither by birth. Something formed deep within, a thirst and a longing, a resolve and a prayer: *Let me do well in this test, to become a Ban-draoi myself when I am older…*

"Aeron, make your proper duty to the Magistra," came her grandmother Gwyneira's quiet voice, reminding her, and she flushed, belatedly remembering her manners, and made a small bob. The priestess smiled again.

"She was thinking too hard, Majesty, for even the manners which I know you taught her to be uppermost in her thought just now. But no matter. It is a proper frame of mind." Kesten gestured, and Aeron followed her to sit at a carved oak table by the window. There were a few books and tablets and inkstands and other such miscellany on the bare polished wood of the tabletop, and in the cleared space of the center stood a globe of faceted rock crystal in a bronze stand.

Taking the nearer of the two chairs, Aeron found her attention caught and held by the glittering fist-sized orb. She wanted to reach out and touch it, but somehow she knew that she was not permitted, and sat quietly as the Magistra took her own seat across the table's width.

"Now, child. The way of your draoích-crutha is this, and

very simple: here is an ordinary criostall, a scryglobe, as you see it." The Magistra picked it up. "You know what it is for, Aeron?"

She nodded, transfixed by the sparkling facets. "It is for scrying, magical farsight. For seeing things that are happening a long way away, and also in the past or the future. I have looked into one before, when mamaith or Aunt Keina showed me."

"Good, and so you will not fear if pictures come to you. But I am not going to ask you to see anything in it just yet. What I want you to do first is to lift it."

Easy enough. She started to reach out for it, then froze as the Magistra spoke again.

"Without touching it with your hands."

Emer barely controlled a start, and her sister Keina scowled darkly. Levitancy was very advanced magic, something that a Ban-draoi novice would in the ordinary way of things not even begin to learn until her second year at a training college. And it was decidedly *not* the usual structure of this test: generally the candidate was asked to simply scry in the criostall to see what might be seen, if anything, and to attempt a few other small magics like the ones Aeron had already performed like any other child — just little pishogues, earthfasting, cloud-herding. For the Magistra to command an untaught child of nine to attempt to lift anything at all… Keina shrugged inwardly. *Then again, Aeron has already more or less moved the sun…why quibble at a ball of quartz?*

Keina's brother-in-law was frowning. "Magistra," said Fionnbarr the King, "is that wise? Or necessary? She is after all still but a child, and she has not been instructed in such techniques. Will that not strain her powers unduly and untimely?"

But the priestess was not offended. "Child she may be, Barraun, but she will be High Queen one day, and you will doubtless recall what was spoken at her birth—about her particular...possibilities. And what her great-grandmother Aoife had to say on her deathbed about her, long before she was born. And what has already been shown. But I promise to stop the test if she grows overtaxed."

When Aeron's parents continued to look disapproving, she reminded them further, in low tones so that the child should not hear and become distressed, of the prophecies made when Aeron was born, and the King and Queen sighed and bowed their heads.

The Magistra turned her attention again to Aeron, who was sitting there looking very bored indeed, staring out the window, longing to be out and doing, perhaps later she could take her pony Eirlys and ride up to the standing stones of Ni-maen...

"Now. Aeron. You see the criostall? Aye, it is there. Reach out to it with your thought. Do not touch it, just feel it in your mind. How it sparkles, how heavy and cold and smooth it must be to the hand, how akin it is to water and air, yet it was born in earth and fire, was it not... aye, just so."

Aeron felt herself drawn again to the dazzling thing. The Magistra's words came like a warm, trance-like cloud, so that she saw nothing but the clear flawless sphere before her. It did seem like water, almost, or ice—pure frozen light. Cold, refreshing, like a mountain torrent or clear-springing waterfall…the intricate pattern of the facets were almost like a snowflake, or a thistle, she could get lost in them… Her right hand rose an inch or two from the table, not involuntarily but as an act of deliberate will; she felt a strange pressure between her eyes, and at the back of her neck and in the pit of her stomach there was a slow tightening, as if muscles that she did not know she even had were smoothly flexing.

"Good," said Kesten again, in a voice even quieter than before. "Now — lift it. Make it rise. Command it."

The child closed her eyes, then opened them wide, reaching out, feeling the pressure building. Then all of a sudden her face lit up with what was to the watchers the most jubilant, the most joyfully astonished, expression any of them had ever seen on anyone's face; she seemed to find something within her, some kind of key, and all at once the intolerable stress and discomfort were gone. And the glittering sphere rose slowly and smoothly from its bronze stand, to hover a foot above the black oak of the tabletop, spinning lazily and showering the room with rainbow flashes as its facets caught the sun.

What no one expected was that everything else in the room, including the people and the books on the table and the table itself and even her wolfhound puppy whom she had asked to have there for comfort, rose right along with it.

"Not just the room! Oh, by no *means* just the *room*! That would be too simple! Nay, she lifted everything and everyone in the *ENTIRE CITY*!" shouted Keina, who had been receiving reports all morning from staggered spellworkers all across Caerdroia, and who was considerably staggered herself. "Anything that was not nailed down, she raised it a foot into the air. And set it all back down again, just as featly. And gently: no one was harmed, by all accounts, not beast nor person, thank all gods, and apart from a few minor accidents of broken crockery and the like, not to mention general widespread panic and terror, nothing untoward occurred. Except of course the utter untowardness of the thing itself."

She glared wildly at the others ranged round the Council chamber, who all carefully avoided her gaze. "Seeing the wolf fetch of the family at age four—I was there! I saw her with her arms around the Faol-mór's very neck and his paw on her shoulder!—making the sun to dance, mass levitancy…how many more such proofs do we need before we admit to ourselves that we are dealing with a prodigy, and perhaps even a danger? I myself, any sorcerer I know— even you, Pendragon—could not have managed such things without a spell of tremendous power and proportion, and maybe not even then, let alone an untutored child on the spur of the moment! I *think* that proves past a whisper of a shadow of a doubt exactly what we have here! This, *this* is why we should not put such tests to untrained children: their talent is uncontrolled, and it produces uncontrollable results. Bad idea, Magistra! And this is also why it cannot be allowed to continue—what if next time she does not raise merely the things and people in the city but the city itself? Or the planet? Or makes the sun *truly* move?"

Before Kesten had gently cast her into a magic nap, up

in her chamber under Nessa's eye, Aeron had had no idea, really, of the magnitude of what she had done. She had been assured she had done well, and that had been that, though privately she had thought it great fun to see everyone go up in the air and hang there sputtering helplessly for a few seconds until she brought them down again; she would never have harmed them. Of course, what she had done had rendered the rest of the test largely irrelevant, and it had been hastily broken off: magical potential verified, in spades.

For their part, the adults had been careful not to show shock or even surprise before the child; but now they were letting their emotions out, understandably. Keina had actually gone hoarse from shouting, and now sat seething in the chair where she had flung herself — furious with the situation, not with her niece. The Magistra Kesten sighed; although she had expected something dramatic from Aeron, given what had occurred last week, she had not expected anything quite so dramatic as *that*. A shattered glass, an exploded lamp — those were the usual achievements, or overachievements, of a particularly strong tested child. No Kelt had seen anything like this in living memory. Possibly not ever.

"I must check the records at Scartanore," said Kesten aloud. "Perhaps they can tell us something. I myself cannot recall from the histories anything even remotely like it occurring since..."

"Since?" repeated Fionnbarr, with quiet apprehension.

"Since Morgan," she said reluctantly, and braced for the outcry.

Which broke loud and immediate from all in the room, louder than before. Emer's voice finally dominated. "Are you saying that my daughter is...that she could be like — Morguenna Pendreic..."

"We do not yet know what she is, still less what she could be. That remains to be discovered." Kesten looked at her King and Queen, and, though unspoken among them all, the inevitably linked name of Marguessan Pendreic hung uneasily in the air, like a thundercloud. "It could be that she is..."

"Is what?" snapped Emer, protective of her child, feeling completely out of her maternal depth at the same time.

Kesten exchanged a look and a thought with Keina and the Archdruid, Teilo ap Bearach, and across the room the Pendragon Alun Corentyn allowed a small smile to curve his lips — if the Magistra was going where he thought she was going, this was about to get very interesting indeed. Though really it was nothing to smile at. The levitancy test was either a very inspired stroke on the Magistra's part or a very wrong-headed one indeed...perhaps both.

"You know how Morguenna raised the Curtain Wall," said Kesten after a while.

The royal couple looked impatient. "Of course," said Emer crossly. "Every Kelt for the past fifteen hundred years knows *that*. She harnessed all the extraneous stars and planets in our region of space and exploded them all to power the Wall, with every Keltic sorcerer then alive to help her. Even the Sidhe, and all other magical beings, lent their aid to her effort. It was the greatest thing ever done amongst us — a mighty and impenetrable shield in space, to hide and protect us and all our star systems."

"Even so." Kesten seemed to be choosing her words more carefully than the situation required, and Emer felt suddenly chilled to the soul. "What if...I say only what if... if Morgan had not had need of any of that help, and had done the work herself alone?"

"That would not have been possible," said Gwyneira flatly.

"Would it not? What if she had been not merely a great enchantress but—something rather more?"

Color drained from faces around the room, from the room itself, as people considered. Fionnbarr recovered first. "If Morgan had been...what?"

Ah, I knew we'd get there in the end... Corentyn stirred where he sat. "A siabhra," he said in his deep voice, and a shudder went round his hearers as the word hit them. "The Magistra is speaking of a siabhra."

"A siabhra..." repeated Emer, bewildered, then horror unspeakable dawned on her face as she leaped to the connection at which Kesten had been hinting. "You think that *Aeron* could be one? My daughter, a...a *demon*?"

Kesten stepped forcefully in to head off the horror before it spread to the rest. "Not a demon, never that! Besides, that meaning of the word is long outdated, it was a poor translation from the start—never even think it. Nay...but I *am* saying that she may well be something that even Morguenna was not. Or maybe she was, only no one twigged it, or dared say so. It is early days to even think on it, early days. But..." She let word and thought trail off alike, and the others fell to their own thoughts.

Fionnbarr Ard-rígh sat back in his chair, his hand over his eyes. A siabhra. He sounded the word in his head: *shiv-ra*. In Keltic history, siabhras, humans in form and all ways else, were beings of utmost power, from the oldest days on Erith, and even before. There was speculation that siabhras were magical mutations, genetic freaks or sports, random-descended heirs to the immense powers of the Kelts' original starborn ancestors the Núminôrians—the Atlandeans of Erith. Who had been hugely powerful indeed, and so Atland fell. By what they had done, some siabhras had been held to be demons, that was true enough; others, likewise gods. Either way, they had been hated and feared. And later, when the Atlandeans had become the Danaans, and later still the Kelts, they brought the tales—and the terror—of siabhras with them.

It was almost never spoken of, certainly not among the general populace. No siabhra had ever been reliably reported in Keltia, though there were stories. As Kesten had hinted, even Morguenna—Morgan, as she was commonly known—mighty sister to Arthur the King and trained by the Sidhe themselves, had had it whispered of her that she might be such a...creature; especially after she had raised the Curtain Wall and sealed all Keltia off, protectively, from the outside galaxy—herself perishing in the process. And Edeyrn Marbh-draoi, the Deathdruid, the great enemy, defeated at the battle of Nandruidion by the slimmest of margins...perhaps him also? Or Marguessan, Morgan's admittedly evil twin sister—Arthur's sister also—whom Morgan had taken with her at the end, to possible redemption. No one could say for sure.

But yes, a siabhra could indeed do what those had done, and far more, unassisted, under its own power. Trivially: there were legends of siabhras destroying continents, slaughtering millions, exploding planets. So—who could say what an infant siabhra might not accomplish all unawares? Make the sun dance? Lift her entire city a foot in the air? More? Worse? Unbidden, the image of Aeron in the circle of Ni-maen on the solstice morning, one hand upon the sacred stone and one lifted to the dancing sun, joy on her face as she gazed at him, came to Fionnbarr's churning mind...

"Rubbish," said the King at last, curtly, straightening in his seat and glaring around the room. "Rubbish and stories. If Aeron were truly this—*thing* you suggest, she would not have made the sun merely appear to have moved, she would have bounced it about like a ball."

"And who is to say that next time she does not do just that?" said Teilo Archdruid, quietly, and Fionnbarr, who had been drawing breath for another charge, let himself sink back into his seat. "We have never seen or known a siabhra"—the sorcerer's voice was steady on the word—"at least not to our certainty, so how can we say what one would or would not do? Are they born, and if so are they inevitable? Or are they made, and if so are they preventable? How are they dealt with? How are they—stopped?"

Teilo himself stopped at the look on Queen Emer's face, which could have exploded planets on its own account. *Best stay away from that line of thought, then...* "So far Aeron has made the sun seem to move, and now she has hoisted the population of Caerdroia and all its movable possessions into the air like flags at a festival. All this, I might add, without one single formal magic lesson in her life and years before such training is to begin. Not to mention seeing the wolf fetch of the Aoibhells, the Faol-mór, in corporeal form at the age of four, and treating it as her own puppy. We should have realized back then that we were dealing with no ordinary talent. I think we need to, we *must*, rightly concern ourselves with what Aeron might or might not do next. Kesten, is there any way of, well, not binding her powers for she will need them to grow in magic in a normal way, but limiting them?"

"I do not know, Archdruid. We are all many miles out of our depth here." Kesten picked up a fold of her blue Ban-draoi robe, began pleating it unthinkingly between her fingers. "When I get back to Scartanore, I will look into it. I would set novices looking before that, to save time, but I think it wise that we keep this to ourselves here present, lest we set off a general panic if the word 'siabhra' works its way around the realm in connection with Aeron."

"Magistra—" Emer's voice was small but clear, and pleading. "What do you think? Is it possible?"

"My Queen, anything is possible." Kesten was pitying but firm. "We would not know until it—she began to manifest. More than two incidents. Three. And we would do well to remember that sometimes siabhras are sent among us in times of great need, to work on our best behalf; they are not always come to do ill. But I think that keeping this secret among us is the best choice we have. Above all, Aeron must never know what we have discussed."

On that all agreed, with relief all round. After several

hours' further discussion, they dispersed, uneasy in their own minds but resigned that they had done all that was possible. Emer and Fionnbarr could not leave the room fast enough, to go to their daughter. But they would not find her where she had been left.

Having apparently passed her draoích-crutha with flying colors, though of that she was not entirely sure and no one seemed to care to confirm it, Aeron had been taken back to her room by her nurse Nessa. She fell under Kesten's sleep-spell for a bit, then suddenly found herself sitting up wide awake, and eager for some fresh air. She did not bother seeking permission to go out of doors — the grownups were still talking amongst themselves, she expected, and would not care to be interrupted for so trivial a request — and Nessa had disappeared so she could not be asked. In any case, she was nine years old, she was no longer a baby — if she wanted to run around outside for a while she should be able to do as she did please.

So she had escaped to her favorite little pinewood up the side of Mount Eagle, the mountain peak against which the city of Caerdroia, and the royal palace of Turusachan, was built. She was not allowed there alone, though she loved the place; but the day her grandfather the old king had died, when she was four, she had run away to the wood, very like today, and had seen...had met...well, she could not really remember, the memory was elusive. But she had had an encounter, and it had been a good one...she thought. Usually when she was outdoors, she would be trailed by her personal guard, Rochana, who was Kin to the Dragon, a member of the Dragon Kinship, who had been her guard since birth. But strangely enough Rochana too seemed to have gone missing—an opportunity indeed. Aeron seldom had real total privacy of any sort, so she was not about to let this unexpected gift go by—who knew when such a chance would, or could, come again...

She was admiring the way the spears of sunlight came splintering through the pine branches to strike upon the needle-covered forest floor when there came a sudden ripple across the golden light, and she glanced up, startled. But it was not a cloud or oncoming storm, nor any other natural disturbance, like the shadow of a beast or person between her and the light...she looked instinctively to Rochana, and remembered that the Dragon was not there. Again the sunlight flickered, and though she still saw nothing, she heard the almost-silent feathering beat of the wings of a hunting owl. Wondering—*an owl, hunting in broad daylight?*—she touched fingertips to the owl brooch at her throat, more perplexed than frightened. But the light grew stronger, until the little clearing seemed to be glazed in silver-gold brilliance, clear and sharp, like being inside the crystal of her testing; then a calm, deep voice came to her ears.

"There is naught to fear, Aeron. You are in no peril from us. We merely wished to speak with you privately, and so we woke you, my sorrow to do so. Then we set your attendants—and your parents—aside for a while, and called you here."

She looked across the little glade to see who it was who had spoken, who had called her by name, and startled a little. A tall man with dark hair, of great fairness of face, was standing beside a granite boulder that Aeron in her visits to the grove had often used as a seat, or a fort. Beside him, and a little behind, stood a darker-haired, milk-skinned woman of such surpassing beauty that the child stared in wonder. Looking more closely, she discerned the faint rainbowing gleam that clung to them both, betokening their otherness, and drew a wondering breath: these two were of the Shining Ones, the faeriefolk, the dwellers beneath the hill—the Sidhe. And judging from their bearing, they were mighty among their kind.

She did not feel fear in the slightest, for she knew she was of their kin from long time past, but she did feel awe mount as she looked upon them, and before she realized it, she had made them a curtsey—not easy to carry off gracefully, clad as she was in tunic, trews and boots. But it seemed that the effort was appreciated, for the two visitors smiled and returned slight bows of their own.

"The legendary courtesy of the House of Aoibhell," said the woman, still smiling, and her voice was a marvel of music. "It is not required of crown princesses to make obeisance even to the Sidhe; but thank you, Tanista."

'Tanista'... The sound of her formal title as Heir of Keltia somehow steadied Aeron, and she turned her attention to the man who stood still facing her.

"We came to learn how you fared in your magical Proving, it being a matter of some concern to us," he said then, not unkindly, and looking appraisingly upon her. "I think you fairly showed us, and just about everyone else too, exactly what manner of magic you have in you. Twice."

Aeron blushed. "I did not mean to, lord," she murmured. "It just—happened." She felt the amusement of the faerie folk, though she sensed they did not mock, and scuffed a little at the pine needles beneath her feet. "Who are—I mean, who might—"

"My sorrow, child, we have not yet named ourselves to you," said the woman. "I am Etain, and this is my lord Gwyn son of Neith, king at Dún Aengus, beneath the Hill of Fare."

On hearing the names of the high rulers of all Sidhedom in Keltia, the musical sound of those names—*gwin, eh-tawn, neethe*—Aeron gasped a little. But it only made sense that they would come to check on her magical progress—she was, after all, the High King's heir, and she would be High Queen over the Sidhe as well as over all other sentient dwellers in Keltia—humans, silkies, sunsharks, merrows, dwarrows and all the rest, even the piasts who lived in the seas of Gwynedd. All manner of magical creatures as well, not the Sidhefolk only. Still...

Gwyn—the king!—saw her hesitancy. "If it will help you trust...here is someone you have met before, I think." He beckoned, and there beside him stood a wolf the size of a pony, the powerful chest of its brindled blacksilver coat marked with a milky star.

Aeron's face was a blaze of delight as the memory came flooding back at sight of the magical creature, the spirit-animal of her House. "My wolf! My Faol-mór! I remember now! He was here with me when—"

Without hesitation, she ran forward and threw her arms around the powerful creature, and the wolf nuzzled her hair, its tongue rasping her cheek. She was taller now than she had been at their first encounter, but he still seemed enormous, and made her feel a small child again as she hugged him.

"There now," said Etain, watching fondly. "Your fetch, Aeron-fach, who met you here the day your grandsir died. He is yours, and you are his—it is your fated dán. Few indeed can boast such a friend or such a fate—not even in our midst. You do know that you are kin to us, lass?"

"Aye, lady," said the child, nodding. "My parents and tutors have told me. That our family comes in part of the Shining Ones, that we have faerie blood mixed with Keltic—this is a great thing."

"And so it is, for us as well. But more than that, you come of my own kindred. You descend from houses both high and ancient: the line of Nia, the line of Midna and Kelver Donn, my own line, all knit together in you and your kin, through Brendan the Astrogator, first king of Keltia, whom you call saint." Amusement flashed like merry lightning across her face. "My lord Brendan was many things, though saint perhaps not so much...yet through our children, his and mine together, you are my many-times daughter."

Aeron stared stunned; she had not made that connection. "You are *that* Lady Etain...Queen Etain...my forefather Brendan's wife? You were Queen of Keltia with him, after the Great Immram! Which you helped him lead... But that was—three thousands of years ago...I had not thought... and now you are—"

Etain stepped forward, lifting the girl's chin with one white hand, and looked down into her face. And caught her breath: oh, but he was there, was Brendan! Her lord before Gwyn, her beloved human husband who had founded Keltia and given it a royal bloodline compounded of mortal and sidhaun alike. She could see him in the child's eyes, and all the others she had known down the years of the House of Aoibhell; she herself was there, even, and those of the kin beneath the hill reaching all the way back to their blissful time upon Erith. Before the Immram, the great voyage to find a new home out among the stars. Before the White Christ's faith came to Eruinn. Before the monk Pátraic.

She controlled the bitter hatred that had risen in her at even the thought of the detested name; it should not sully this moment, or this child. "Truly I am, alanna. For my people live with a life many times that of even the longest-lived Kelt, and long centuries after Brendan died I found joy again with my lord Gwyn, and will live with him beneath the hill until it is time for us both to fade and pass beyond. But I have always had a penchant for younger men."

Gwyn laughed, meeting his queen's eyes in a way that the child did not understand. "And glad I am of it, too. But Aeron, we have yet to tell you what we have borrowed you for. Let us do so in a more pleasant place. Your wolf may come with us, if he so pleases."

She looked around her, astonished anew. She had felt no movement, seen no spinning sparkle of translocation, but they were no longer in the pinewood. Instead they sat all four on the side of a hill that seemed to be nowhere near Caerdroia, reclining at ease on deep soft grass at the edge of an apple orchard, the shadows just beginning to lengthen;

it seemed to be late afternoon, where at Caerdroia it had not yet been midday. Below them, summer-decked woods rolled on for miles in the warm air, and she could see the silver line of a distant river threading the green tapestry. Away beyond the river, the woods yielded to vast open plains, before all was swallowed up in blue distances and heat-haze.

"Now that your Proving has been—accomplished," came Gwyn's voice, and it sounded different here on the hill than it had in the little wood, "and your gift made sure of, we have need to speak with you of something. So we have brought you here."

She gazed at him expectantly. Strangely, her current situation alarmed her not at all. Partly that was because of the great wolf behind her, whom she knew would protect her—she could lean back against his warm, rock-solid form and let her fingers twine for comfort in his mane—and partly because of Etain as she sat to Aeron's left, poised atop a granite boulder as if it had been a throne, her long, dark-red gúna flaring about her. But chiefly it was because of Gwyn himself, lounging in the grass to her right, booted legs stretched elegantly in front of him, leaning back on propped elbows—most unregally.

And yet his royalty was clear and true, even more so than Fionnbarr's. No surprise, for it was older far... Seen thus, in full sun—*we must be somewhere eastaways from Caerdroia, judging by the shadows it is later in the day; let us hope the same day still, and that I have not been taken into the far past, or future*—his otherworldly beauty was plain to Aeron's sight.

A strong, sculptured face, softened by a beard of bardic

trim; a build both graceful and powerful. He was dressed as any other Keltic male, in a doublet over a loose leinna, close-fitting sueded breeches and polished leather boots. In the sunlight the king's shoulder-length hair, with longer braided strands in front reaching to his chest, was lighter than she had thought: a rich blend of oak and chestnut and mahogany shot with gold streaks, that looked autumn-warm next to the true ebony of his queen's. But however casually he may have been attired, he was still every inch a king.

In the palm of his left hand, that lay casually upfacing in the grass, he bore, seemingly under the skin, the glittering silver imprint of a triple spiral—the sign of Sidheanbrugh on Erith, latterly known as Newgrange; the sign that in Keltia is cut into the stone pavement that lies before the gates of the Sidhe palace of Dún Aengus, beneath the Hill of Fare. His right palm carried a similarly sparkling mark: a knotwork image of the great wingwide owl known as the ghosthunter, traditionally associated with the faerie king and his rule and power, and Aeron wondered if that was the shape into which he could shift at will, as most folk of his race were able to assume various shapes of their own choice or nature.

She stealthily touched the owl brooch again, and tried not to rudely stare at the images, with scant success. He gave no sign that he had noticed her attention; but though she could not say they vanished, suddenly the silver markings were strangely not visible any longer, and she blinked and wondered what she had been staring at. After a moment she realized that Gwyn's palms, unlike those of mortals, bore no lines of any sort; the smooth, pale skin was altogether unmarked...how strange. She would have thought that his palms would be netted full of stars, threaded and crosshatched to match his years and wisdom. Yet like all his kind, he did not wear those years upon his face or form, only in his eyes — dark, fathomless, unbounded.

Strangely, he had a look about him of — of all people — her father; not merely their shared kingliness or power or distant kinship but something more, something like to somewhat she could not define, and this too helped her be unafraid. But on balance, Gwyn son of Neith was unnerving: he was strange, he was unearthly, he was inhuman, he was royal, he was magical, he was altogether splendid — and she was filled with a sudden great admiring affection for him, as for a favorite uncle, but even closer. He was not looking at her just now, nor at his queen neither, but out over the vast sweep of country below.

"We are in the Hollow Mountains," he said presently, and grinned disarmingly at her squeak of surprise. "Aye, more than two thousand miles from Caerdroia; but do not worry, we shall have you home in time for supper. Your parents have not yet realized that you are gone at all. Though I have a sense that the Magistra and Archdruid, and certainly the Pendragon, have a pretty fair idea as to whose company you are in at present — they tend to know about these things. Most annoyingly, we shall have to do something about that," he added, and Aeron giggled.

He raised an arm and swept it over the valley, away north to where the hills rose into blue ranges of real mountains. "All these lands you see before you are Sidhe lands, Aeron-fach. Treatied to our people by Brendan of the Ships: when the first great sailing came, when the Hui Corra beached her boats in Strath Mór, we came too. But I was born here, in lands very like to these, long ago and far from here, midwived into this world by your great kinswoman Athyn Blackmantle, who raised herself to become Ard-rían and drove the Firvolgi invaders from Keltia. Would you like to hear the story, the way we tell it amongst my folk?"

The child nodded eagerly, sitting spellbound as Gwyn recounted the tale of how, on a dark autumn night of oncoming storm, a lord of the Sidhe had sought aid from a young mortal horsegirl, a humble Erinnach orphan adopted into a family not her own; of how that lord had brought her under the hill to a royal birthchamber, where she had assisted at the coming to the world of a baby prince — the prince who had grown to be the king who now sat beside her, and the young horsegirl had herself become High Queen of the Kelts.

"So you are a Kelt native-born," she breathed when he had finished. "Like me."

Gwyn nodded. "Very much so. Born of and bound to Keltia just as you are…" He abruptly shifted mood, as if he had said too much. "We are not far here from the palace of Dún Aengus; it is our chief place of residing — Athyn of the Battles herself, and her lord King Morric Douglas, often visited us there."

"Can we go there? Could I visit too?" she asked, then blushed for her discourtesy: one does not invite oneself to another's home.

But the two beside her only laughed indulgently. "Certainly

you may come to visit us," Etain assured her. "You will be Ard-rían, and you are an Aoibhell—either way you are more than welcome in all our dúns and brughs and maenors. But not today. Today we have much else to discuss. You were a busy young lass, I think, this morning."

Aeron's blush grew deeper. "I was, I did, well, I did something that perhaps, probably, I was not supposed to do. I didn't mean to do it! But it happened anyway."

"Aye so." Gwyn's mouth twitched beneath the beard. "And at the circle of Ni-maen, when your father took you there last week to celebrate the summer Sunstanding? You did not mean to do that either, from what I have heard."

"Nay, well..."

The king's mouth twitched again, harder. "We saw that little frolic, of course; half the planet did. And the result of your Proving today, even from the Hill of Fare it was felt, though at least *we* managed to remain on the ground," he added, still amused. "Very impressive. Not to say entertaining... Come, do not feel shame of it! There has been nothing like it since the days of young Morguenna Pendreic—you cannot think what havoc *that* one managed to wreak, whilst learning her magic of us."

The child's voice was full of awe. "You knew St. Morgan... well, of course you did. And her brother also—Arthur." Her voice caught and trembled on the name. Arthur of Arvon, King in the Light and the greatest monarch Keltia had ever known, her worshipped hero, almost a god; to speak with someone who had actually known him, had known his family and his friends... It was too much for her: this king with whom she was speaking so easily had spoken with

Arthur fifteen hundred years ago—he whose death had never been proven, so that by courtesy he was still King of Kelts and all sovereigns since his day held their crown in his name.

"You knew *Arthur!*" she breathed when she could speak again, with reverence and wonder.

"Oh aye," said Gwyn softly, from a great and sudden distance. "Aye, I knew Arthur." He came back from where he had so briefly been, smiled at her. "And I promise you that we will talk together of him one day and I shall tell you all of how he was. But as my queen has said, just now there is something else claims our attention ."

"My test," said the child, sadly.

"Your test," said the king, sternly.

In a very few moments, Gwyn and Etain between them had gently extracted the whole story, and even more that Aeron did not know she was telling them, or that she even knew at all. To say that the Sidhe monarchs were interested would be a severe understatement; but they kept that from the child, and let her speak of how she had done what she had done.

"I could see that my parents and my aunt and the Magistra Kesten and the others seemed almost—afraid," said Aeron candidly, when her telling was completed. "I did not like that feeling, that I had made them feel so. Why would they fear at all?"

Gwyn paused before he spoke, and she could see that he was considering his words, how to say this to her correctly. "We spoke just now of Morguenna Pendreic, Morgan Magistra. You have learned in your schooling of her deeds?"

Aeron blinked, as surprised as her parents had been to be asked such a self-evident thing. "Surely! Everyone knows of St. Morgan of the Pale. Arthur's sister. She herself raised the Pale, the Curtain Wall, to protect us from the outside…why do you ask?"

"It is because of her that your kindred are a little afraid just now, as you noticed. In all Keltia, since the days of the three Pendreic sibs, there has never been another Kelt who has shown quite the kind of magic they had. The kind of magic *you* now have shown, at the solstice and today at your test. They are all wondering just now if you will grow to command power equal to theirs, and especially Morgan's— she who was taught her magic by us, at Collimare in Loch Bel Draccon."

Etain took up the explanation, a little more bluntly. "More even than that. They are wondering if your power may lie rather along the lines of that possessed by her sister, Arthur's and Morgan's other sib."

"Marguessan!" gasped the child. "But she was evil! She was a destroyer, not a maker; in league with the dark lord Edeyrn, the Marbh-draoi, taking his teachings and his power. She killed her sister in the end. I could *never* be like her!"

"I do not say you could, daughter. And I think you never would. But remember, even Marguessan started out with white hands. It was only later, when she felt forced to it, that her hands were stained irreparably. She did not repent her of her deeds, though that might have cleansed them even at the last. But do not forget, she may have been the death of Morgan, but Morgan was her death also, accomplishing a mighty work in the event, a work that defends our worlds until this day."

Aeron was still deeply insulted that anyone, especially this royal couple, could for even half a heartbeat entertain the thought that she might possibly become such a one as Marguessan Pendreic of vile deeds and viler memory, or worse still like the Marbh-draoi himself, who had not been called Deathdruid for flattery's sake.

"Well, if I did turn as she did," she said sullenly, "I like to think that I would have good reason for it, and if I acted upon it to stain my hands, that I would be sorry after, and ask forgiveness, and forgive myself. Though only after I had atoned for my offense against dán, of course."

She sensed the approved surprise in the two faerie beings, did not look at them but turned her attention suddenly to cuddling the great wolf she leaned against, scratching his silky ears, and he licked her face consolingly.

"That is wisdom far greater than your years, Tanista," said Gwyn after a while. "Let us hope it will not come to that. But there is something beyond even Marguessan Pendreic that you might come to be indeed."

At the sound of her title, Aeron bowed her head, trying not to let tears of frustration spill over, her fingers digging into the wolf's coat. "Then what? What *am* I? What are they so feared of? For the love of Dâna, Majesties, tell me what is it that I am!"

"Not what you are," said Etain at once. "They fear what you might become — something they do not, perhaps cannot, understand, and certainly cannot control. And they do not wish you to know of the possibility. But it seemed important to us that you do know, should know, indeed must know; and so we brought you here to tell you."

"This thing I might be? That they fear?" Aeron drew a sharp ragged breath. "It fears me more not knowing... Has it a name?"

"It has." Gwyn's dark eyes caught and held hers. "The name of it is siabhra."

Oh. She had heard of siabhras, but only in those books of legends she so loved to read; it did not seem a very desirable thing to be, or even a very real one.

"But those are—evil. Worse than all other evil things there are."

Etain was beside her now, sitting in the grass like a child herself, putting a sun-warm arm round Aeron's thin shoulders. "That is part of what your parents and the rest do not understand, and why they fear. Nay, siabhras are not evil. Well, at least not all of them—not by their first nature. But they are all indeed powerful and strong beyond right reason. Beyond human and sidhaun alike. Beyond good and evil alike."

"I do not think I wish to be this thing, or even to be thought so," the child said presently, uneasily. "Was Marguessan a siabhra?" she asked after a while. "Or the Marbh-draoi—Edeyrn? Was Morgan?"

Gwyn looked startled. "Marguessan? No. The others—harder to say." He drew breath as if he were about to say something more, but at the last moment chose not to, and said another thing instead. "If Edeyrn was not himself a siabhra, still he was something not far off it. For one who was after all half human, his power was vast indeed. He took even Merlynn Llwyd, the great mage, and prisoned him in a crystal tree. Only the Four Great Treasures of Keltia and the joined strength of many—my own and Arthur's included—could bring him down."

"But he was slain at the last," said Aeron, staring unguardedly at the king's handsome face, the deep-set, intelligent eyes. "I have read in my books of the tales of Arthur, that Taliesin Pen-bardd wrote, Arthur's own foster-brother…"

"He was." Gwyn went far away again, returned. "I was there at that battle, with Artos and Talyn and Morgan and the rest. And even that was not the last of it… Edeyrn was— was bent. From the start he was not right in this existence, do you see, and when he began to study forbidden things, and grew darker and darker, crueler and colder, that was when Arthur was sent to the world to bring us all together to stop him. You have doubtless read of how that came to pass. It is a high and honorable story."

Aeron nodded, thoughts flying like rooks wheeling and circling in a great dusky wing, home to their roosts at twilight. "But you say, not—not a siabhra."

"Who can now know?" Etain shrugged. "If he was not, he surely did the work of one. It is possible that magical bloodlines combined with mortal ones in his case to cause a siabhra, or the next closest thing to it, to be born upon the world, even as other bloodlines combined to bring us Arthur and his sisters—for good or for ill. Power in the blood can do many things unforeseen and unwished for. As it may do for you also."

"Which is not to say that *you* are such a one, alanna, or might become one, as your kin and their counselors seem to fear." Gwyn bent sidewise to look into the child's troubled eyes with a gently paternal expression, tipping her chin up to catch her glance. "But because of that, I would put the mark of the Sidhefolk upon you; not that you need it to be known of our blood, for you bear your ancestry in your face. But for your protection."

When Aeron's fear and confusion showed at last in her face, as she had bravely kept both concealed all this time, his voice softened. "I cannot speak for your folk, but there are not many of my own people who would be inclined to harm you, not many at all. Most of those who might did not come with us in the Great Immram and perished in the launching of the ships, and what came after. But a few of the less, shall we say, seelie kind did travel here, being unaccountable and perverse, and these it is whom I fear may make themselves known to you, and in no pleasant manner. Particularly given what you have done, being so hard now to ignore or conceal. Or what you may come to do in future. This will not bind your power, nor control you in any way. But I need your permission before I put such guarding on you—*your* permission, Tanista, not your parents'. Even I, Gwyn, must ask to be allowed."

"What would it be, then—this mark?"

"Well, a mark like the one I bear."

She looked more interested. "Like an engrain? An inking? Many Kelts have those. My father has engrains, and my great-uncle Elharn and my aunt Keina."

"Not quite. But look."

He held out his left hand, palm upwards, and the silver spirals emerged again, as a drawing carved in the sand of a beach will emerge from the withdrawing surf. Aeron caught her breath, and looking up at Gwyn, and seeing his faint smile, she put out a single finger to brush across the sign, carefully, curiously, then quickly snatched it back again. It had felt cool and smooth, taking no warmth from his hand, and it had buzzed faintly as she touched it, like a hum of distant bees.

"It will not hurt, neither in the making nor the wearing. There is no spellcraft in it — well, not of itself. But two things will it do: firstly, it will mark you as one with Sidhe-blood in her veins, and that might come to matter much one day." *As the magic carried in her mortal blood shall also one day matter...* but of that he said nothing.

"You said there were two things."

Gwyn's face was graver now. "The mark will protect you from coming too soon to knowledge that could destroy you — the knowledge that might, or might not, confirm you as...that which we have talked about. I do not mean to fright you, but it has been Seen that you may do deeds that may look like, well, the deeds of such a being as we spoke of, dreadful deeds perhaps, though for good cause; you will likely not know how or even why you did them, and nor will anyone else. For the reason is hidden, as it must be. But this mark will keep that knowledge, and the truth of your nature, from you and all others until you are strong enough to bear it. For bear it you must, to save all at the last. That too has been Seen. There have been prophecies made, and many of them have filled, but some of them still await their time. To be a siabhra...it is not a thing to fear aforetime, nor even yet is it the worst thing in the world to be, though

many might say otherwise. It may not even come to pass."
Though it will; and that worst also...

"The last siabhra did mighty things," said Etain quietly, in a voice that softly chimed with peace and power. "As others did before."

"But evil things!"

"Some. Some. But humans too, and Sidhefolk, can do worse, and have done. Will do so again. And even mightier deeds of good also, do not forget."

Well, that was true enough. Still, the idea that she might grow into some unstoppable monster of unimaginable strength, hated and feared by her people, was not a pleasant one. But perhaps...

"Can you, well, can you *make* me forget? About siabhras?" The idea bloomed dazzlingly; her eyes grew wide, her face alight. "Can you make *everyone* forget? About—about *everything*?"

She was staring at the grass and so missed the look Gwyn exchanged with Etain, and the way the fetch wolf met their glances as well.

"That is...a very interesting question, " said the king at last.

"Does it have an answer?"

He gave a shout of laughter and reached over to ruffle her coppery hair, and the Faol-mór gave a little eager bark. "Oh, several, I should think! At the very least. But the one you want to hear... True it is I have the power to make *you* forget. Until it becomes needful for you to remember. As for others: anyone who witnessed the trial today can be made to forget entirely, whether they were there present or watched from another chamber or experienced their, ah, elevation personally as residents of Caerdroia, or even merely heard of it."

Aeron stared at him in wonder. "You could do that? *Would* you do that?"

Gwyn stilled for a moment, went away within, came back again, though he never moved from his place in the grass. "It is done." He seemed very pleased with himself, and with her as well. "Not trivially, but it is done. A rann of forgetfulness. It is an elegant solution, and solves a great many problems; you are a clever girl to think of it. Though I am quite sure I would have thought of it myself eventually, with no help from a mere lass," he said to tease her, and she laughed as he had intended. "Your test will simply be accepted by all concerned as having been passed with ease and distinction, as befits a daughter of your house, and recorded as such in any place that needs it so recorded. No more questions, certainly no memories of, let us say, inappropriate altitudinousness. For them, it has already never happened. As for my old friends the Pendragon and the Magistra and the Archdruid: it might be perhaps somewhatly otherwise with them, and a bit more might yet be needed. They are powerful in craft, as you know; even my magic is likely not quite enough to erase entirely from their minds and memories the word 'siabhra' and the sight of you blithely tossing Caerdroia's entire population into the air like a shuttlecock."

"So you altered time, lord?"

"It is not quite altering time, or even rearranging it; merely blurring it. Sending it down a different road for a — a small detour. Already your actual test has ceased to exist in memory, and a different outcome been placed there. As for those three, I can dim the knowledge of these events until it is no more than an uneasy feeling touching the backs of their necks, or a bad and persistent headache. But there will come a day when all folk will be brought to remember, you included; just so you are aware of that. Shall I do so?"

Aeron thought about it for a while, and they respected her silence. Presently: "Aye, then. I think it would be best. If no one remembers it is there, especially the most powerful sorcerers in Keltia, not I, not anyone, then I will not have to explain it or fret about it."

He looked aside again at this most surprising child, nodded solemnly. "I can do that. And..." — once more the merest flicker of eye — "it is done."

Aeron flushed, all at once uncertain. "For me? I am of no import, really—"

"That is not true," reproved Etain gently. "You are the future High Queen of all this realm, though that is not the only thing, or even the most important thing." She rose fluidly to her feet, Gwyn with her, and drew Aeron up after her, her voice clear as a war-horn in the spring.

"This will be dán many years in the making. But now I set that name and fate upon you that were deemed by the Alterator Himself, the Doomsman of the Worlds, in Annwn, in the Hollow Lands. Words spoken to Athyn and Morric themselves in the presence of the very gods, heard by Arawn and Malen, witnessed by my lord and myself and one other. When magic begins to die, in Keltia and in worlds beyond, the sword that could not bring magic down will be magic's savior. In that time the Gwerin shall ride again in time of greatest need. Mark you the Turning Tower, the Swan of the North. Comes then the Spinner of the Web, and the Wolves of the Gods to hunt him."

Gwyn laid a hand upon her head, spoke in a voice as deep and as solemn as the earth itself. "In that time I myself shall be Lord of the Hunt, and so be thou named Caradrúin, who shall ride with me to harry the Dark. Be thou siabhra or human, mortal or Sidhe, bear thou the name and the nature, the pain and the power, the glory and the grief. And now I bid you forget—the word, the name, the duty, all. It may color your deeds and even your dreams, though you will not know why. Those who fear your possible nature have already forgotten. But the knowledge will slumber until it is needed, even as Arthur, King in the Light with his knights around him, does slumber beneath the holy mountain."

They both saw the complete incomprehension on Aeron's wondering face, and the growing panic; and it pierced their hearts. Then, sighing inwardly for the necessity of her action now, in service of the need she Saw in the future, Etain the queen reached out her hands to touch her fingertips to the child's forehead. For an instant Aeron saw close before her eyes the silver spirals glinting on the queen's left palm, the dazzling imprint of a sleek sea otter on the other, knotworked like her lord's owl. She started to ask a question, but it died away in her brain like a snuffed candle, and she looked around, smiling up at her two companions.

Gwyn inclined a little toward her; it was like an oak tree bending. "Aeron Lassarina, of the House of Aoibhell and the lines of Nia and Midna and Kelver Donn, be sained and sealed of the Aes Sidhe, and bear our mark, in silence and in secret."

Etain bowed her head. "You are worthy to carry this sign, daughter. It will grow as you grow. And when it comes to the uttermost need, which will not be the need you think is uttermost but another, a deed more distant from today than that first, and more dire also, let the memory of its presence rise in your mind once more, and give you strength to call upon, free and unspancelled."

The king took Aeron's left hand in his, as her own father might, and with two right-hand fingers began to gently draw a spiral on the small and, it must be said, slightly grubby palm; three times round he traced it sunwise, linking one to the next. Feeling his touch tickle, Aeron nevertheless held still; this was important magic being done, and she must bear herself correctly.

In silence they watched as the triple spiral appeared upon her skin in silver swirls, as if it were being pushed out from beneath, a mystic flower blooming, reaching to the sun, or to something brighter. When it was completely formed, Gwyn clasped it to his own mark, briefly, folding her hand between both of his, then releasing it. Her new marking shone out once, even more briefly, and then sank like water into sand, down in below the lines of her palm, vanishing. She flexed her hand, astonished; she could *feel* it there, just under her skin, cool and a little stiff, like a thin silver ribbon or wire. Then the sensation disappeared even as the mark itself had, and her hand was as it had ever been.

Gwyn nodded, well pleased, and now he was fully king again. "So magic must go: man to woman, woman to man.

As you were tested today with a touchstone of magic to prove your quality, so too in time will you be the touchstone yourself, to prove the quality of all Keltia, and let that be the mark of it."

The monarchs each bent to kiss Aeron on the brow, as parents to a much-loved child — taking away the memories, as she had asked, though the kisses were bestowed more like an accolade of some solemn order of chivalry — and she received the light touches in silence. What would happen, had happened; but she could not now for the life of her remember what it might have been.

And then they were standing in the small council chamber of Turusachan, facing a score of frantic people, all shouting, all striding about, all with Aeron's name in their mouths and fear on their faces.

No one seemed to notice them for several long moments. Then Aeron stepped forward. "Mamaith? Athra? I am come home. Look, the king and queen have brought me. We were talking on the hill." And the room, first frozen silent, exploded with relief.

So much so that for at least ten seconds more no one beheld the two tall figures that stood in the shadows. Still fiercely hugging her daughter, Emer was first to notice them, and gave Fionnbarr a light swat to get his attention. One by one the others saw also and grew still, standing to respectful astonished attention in the presence of the faefolk, who appeared, as usual, irritatingly immaculate in all respects, not a speck of dirt or blade of grass marring their uncreased garments, as if they had not spent the afternoon lounging on a hillside in the warm sun.

"My friends," said the High King, with deepest relief. "Thank you for bringing home my heir."

The choice of words was not lost on Gwyn, and he spoke not just to the King but to the room. "Considering we were the ones who took her in the first place and put such fear on you all, it was the least we could do, Ard-rígh, and we are sorry for it. We had somewhat to impart to her, seeing how her test fell out," he added. "And forgive our liberty, but it went better that we did so away from this place." *Meaning do not ask why we did so, High King, or any of the rest of you either…*

Fionnbarr heard the unspoken message plain and clear, though deep inside him a tiny flame of anger flickered— how dared even the Sidhe rulers take his child from her home! But he kept it within.

"It is well, then. She is home and you are here, kinsmen and friends who never visit often enough for our liking. Will you join us for the nightmeal? There is a banquet prepared to celebrate my daughter's day of trial, and how well she did at her test; you both are welcome at our table, as you well know."

But Etain declined, with utmost politeness, and Gwyn nodded regretful agreement. "We have been too long away from our Dún, and must return. Another time, surely."

Such was the power of Sidhe glamour that no one noticed the magic that Gwyn quietly cast over the room before vanishing with his queen, so that none would remember their presence—it was not yet his wish or intention to appear among mortals, though that day was fast approaching. As for the greater spell of forgetfulness, for several days the Pendragon, the Magistra and the Archdruid had raging headaches and sore stiff necks that, strangely enough, neither willowbark nor spellcraft could cure; and a vague, persistent feeling that they had forgotten something important plagued everyone in Caerdroia for several weeks to come.

As for Aeron, she had no such feeling, though the magic had been made for her, at her asking. She sat quietly at the banqueting table with her elders, ate all her favorite foods, almost in a trance—well, she had a great deal on her mind, though not so much as she might have had— and went all unbidden up to her tower rooms, a most unusual occurrence. Nessa, though longing to paddle the little bandit until she could not sit down for a week, for frightening everyone like that, on sight of her charge's small, thoughtful face thought better of it, and instead gently helped her to a soothing hot bath fragrant with lavender and sea-rose, and thence into bed.

The wolfhound puppy, delighted to see his person after a long, lonely day, finally stopped licking her hands, though he was shy of the scent of magic that clung about her, and even more so of the shadow of the enormous wolf that had seemed to follow her into the room, a shadow that the clueless humans seemed not to notice—and not just any magic or any wolf, either. The young hound watched carefully as the great shadow yawned and took up a guarding position on the hearth, nose on paws, watchful; reassured, the puppy curled up at the foot of the bed, where only Aeron ever let him stay, and tonight no one chased him off the bed.

As Nessa quietly closed the chamber door and set the usual wards, Aeron slid away into sleep almost at once—it had been a long, strange, confusing day. But in the darkness there came a faint gleam from the pillow upon which her left hand rested, arm flung out palm up. If anyone had been around, or awake, to notice, they would have seen three spirals glowing silver in the center of the child's palm. They glittered for a time, spilling their clear brilliance over the bed, illuminating the dim chamber beyond the bedcurtains until the glow shone from the windows; then they faded away, and were not seen again for many long years.

And upon his crystal throne in Dún Aengus beneath the Hill of Fare, far off in the Hollow Mountains, as night fell upon Tara, his queen silent beside him and her hand resting on his arm, Gwyn son of Neith, king of all the Sidhefolk of Keltia, sat brooding. None dared trouble him, and the spirals upon his own palm were sparkling in the light.

ALEMBIC

alembic: in alchemy, the vessel in
which a thing is purified and refined

3485 ~ 3488 in the Common Reckoning,
3029 ~ 3033 Anno Celtiae Conditae

THE PLANET GWYNEDD is a fair one, the only settled world of its system and one of the most important of all Keltic homeworlds, second to be founded after Tara, the Throneworld itself. Since the first establishment of Keltia it has been ruled by the line of the Princes of Dôn, and, as with the other Ruling Houses, there is in that kindred a significant admixture of Sidhe blood joined with the human.

The Aes Sidhe came to Keltia when the Kelts themselves first did; or perhaps a bit sooner, even—opinions differ and history is silent. Whatever the truth of it, they are there and have been from the first: they have no official position—their king rules his own folk, absolutely, although he and they pay at least outward courtesy to the High Crown—but they are citizens and subjects just as much as any others, and they make their influence known, to and through those whom they choose to notice, or, indeed, influence. Human Kelts are of at least two minds about the Sidhefolk: either they respect and admire them, even love them, or they envy and resent them. But no one ignores them; they are far too fascinating for that.

The respect and admiration speak for themselves, the love also: sidhauns are enthralling creatures, in every sense of the word — beguiling and captivating, beautiful and dangerous, hugely appealing to many mortals who ought to know better. The envy and resentment are built mostly around the fact that for all intents and purposes, the faefolk are immortal; or at least so long-lived as to make mortality irrelevant. Power comes into it as well: the Sidhe have magic as a matter of course, a simple birthright, and though mortal Kelts too have magic at their disposal, it is usually lesser in scope, except for exceptional gifted individuals. As a rule, most Kelts have to work hard to achieve magic, and some cannot manage it at all. Hence the resentment.

On Gwynedd, the Sidhe hold themselves a bit more apart from the daily life of the people than they do on other worlds. There are several reasons for that, chiefest among them being that historically the Gwyneddan sidhauns and the Gwyneddan humans have not always seen eye to eye, and there have been rulers on both sides who actively discouraged personal dealings between the two races. Conversely, when Gwyneddans on both sides *do* connect, they do so in the warmest and most basic of ways: deep friendships, affairs, love and even marriage — hence those familial admixtures down the ages.

But envy and jealousy have been beaten like ingredients into that mix, and humans are not the only ones doing the coveting. Though mortal Kelts often wonder why the faefolk could possibly envy mortals, the fact remains that they do. Many reasons have been put forth, but perhaps the simplest is the truest: mortals can change, and change is revivifying; mortals can die, and death can be a blessing—at least if one feels that virtual changeless immortality is a curse. The Aes Sidhe are not truly immortal, of course; only the gods are that. But their lifespans come as close as makes no differ, and though they can be slain before their time, by accident or in combat, as a rule they do not die of any other cause, and in the end they age and draw to a close in much the same way as mortals do, though many, many times more slowly.

Still, before that comes to pass, they seem to enjoy all sorts of benefits merely by grace of being immensely powerful magical creatures, ever young and beautiful, and there are always those mortals who will begrudge. But there are also those humans who can be trained to near-Sidhe powers, some of whom carry Sidhe bloodlines and some of whom do not. Young Keltic children are tested early for magical potential, whether such innate aptitude has shown yet in them or not, and even those who prove unsuited for further study can still be taught minor household workings or useful small pishogues. Those who show proper gifts are sent to religious schools for training, as magic is a manifestation of faith as much as a natural flair: girls to the Ban-draoi academies, boys to Druid colleges. Such institutions are scattered across Keltia, and all are excellent, but two there are that stand above the rest: the Ban-draoi convent of Scartanore, on the planet Erinna, and the Druid seminary of Dinas Affaraon on Gwynedd.

Down the millennia of Keltia's existence, both schools have offered places to students of humble and noble lineage alike—Scartanore has regularly taught Keltic princesses, and future High Queens also—but Dinas is special, for there it was, fifteen hundred years before, that Arthur of Arvon, Arthur Pendreic, King in the Light, received his druidical training. And apart from the unparalleled Morguenna Pendreic, his own half-sister, latterly known as St. Morgan of the Pale, Arthur was perhaps the greatest sorcerer Keltia has ever seen.

Until now.

Dinas Affaraon is stunningly situated in the north of Gwynedd's main continent. Built into the deep stone of a long knife-edged mountain ridge, it enjoys a dramatic overlook to an actively volcanic valley full of fumaroles and lava pools and steam fountains—the Long Valley, the ruins of a chain of vast craters that had exploded all at once, vast geological ages ago, before ever the Kelts had come there. The volcanism that still simmers and rumbles beneath the tortured crust is kept under control by master Druids who have made peace with the local place spirits, and the school is by their mutual agreement kept safe, though it is always a thrilling time when a carefully managed eruption is allowed by both authorities, to relieve pressure on the earth, and many come from all over Gwynedd to watch.

For all its antiquity and historicity, Dinas is by no

means the first Druid installation at this spectacular site; previously it had been known as Bargodion. Under that name it had seen as students Arthur himself, and the great bard Taliesin, his future brother-in-law, and their other close friends, in those darkest days of the Theocracy, when the school was hidden away against the Marbh-draoi Edeyrn, the Deathdruid, who held all Keltia in his evil grasp. In those times, all such establishments had had to conceal themselves, moving constantly to keep safe pupils and masters alike, and after Arthur and the others had left, inexorably headed for their fated appointment with dán and legend, Bargodion too had left. It had been replaced at that location by a Druid supercollege called Dinas Affaraon, run for and by those masters of masters known as the Pheryllt, and had provided a main seat of power in the war against Edeyrn and the rebuilding of all Keltia after.

Now, fifteen centuries after Arthur's time, Dinas has evolved to a middle ground: still a research college where the highest of magics are pored over by the highest of Druids, the college also serves to teach students who have completed their first training as sorcerers and wish to continue as graduates, striving for the rank of Pheryllt themselves. Sometimes too, Dinas admits those prodigies whose inborn talents have enabled them to skip directly there, with no precursor schooling required. Either way, it is an exciting place to learn exciting lessons, and most students who are sent there are very grateful for the chance.

He was not one of them. Oh, he loved his studies, no question of that, and he was greatly gifted, likewise no question, and he loved the school itself. But though he had spent so far a whole year at Dinas, he loved very little else about the place, and was firmly resolved to keep his head down and do what he must to get through the remaining years of his magical education.

He had arrived there in not quite the usual fashion for a Keltic youth, even one of great promise and high rank. Tested early and then home-schooled by the palace Druids his parents employed, Gwydion Penarvon had been pointed for Dinas Affaraon as soon as he passed his ten-years' testing, which he had done in spectacular fashion—though not quite so spectacularly or dramatically as the way in which Aeron Aoibhell would pass her own, five years after him. As a result, directly he had finished his first-degree bardic training, he was packed off at the age of fourteen, heading straight to Dinas as a bajand, a graduate postulant, brilliant enough for early admission. Why bother forcing him to dawdle through the basics at an ordinary school? his parents had asked; quite reasonably, as they thought. He already knows all the essentials, not so? He can do all the basic magics required, and easily? Well then, let him be challenged at his own speed; he will be bored silly otherwise and all too likely to cause trouble if held back to the plodding pace of less gifted fellows. So they had said; and no one was about to argue with them.

With good cause: those parents, Arawn and Gwenedour, were the Ruling Prince and Princess of Gwynedd. When his eldest son had been determined to be the possessor of Druidic talents, promising great future skill, Arawn had been delighted. He himself was not that way gifted, and a

Druid prince as ruler of Gwynedd after him he considered to be an excellent thing; indeed, Arawn had spent much time consulting with his chief druidical advisor, Cadoc ap Rhosgan, as to the best way to teach the young heir in the meantime. Gwydion's bardic education at Seren Beirdd came first, of course, as not only the boy's own preference but the basis for all other learning, and of course warrior training at the Fian war college, Caer Artos, would come later, when he had reached his full physical growth. But as for his magical tutelage, it had been decided to skip over the usual sequence because of his raw talent, and send him straight to train with the Pheryllt.

It had all worked out admirably, at least on parchment. By the time Gwydion was done with his fostering and his first basic stint at Star of the Bards, he had formed such a bond with magic, and it with him, as few of his years could boast. "It seems he merely needs to be reminded, not taught," said Cadoc, proudly, to Gwydion's equally proud mother, and indeed this did seem to be the case. Even complex spellwork that by rights only a full Druid or Bandraoi should be able to bring off came easily to the boy, and he appeared to merely need to glance at a rann to know how to cast it.

The extent of this gift, perhaps not so unexpected in one of Arthur's direct bloodline—Arthur had changed his surname when he became King, from Pendreic to Penarvon, for reasons that had seemed good to him—had been kept quiet by the family, and later by Gwydion himself, once he had left home. Few beyond the walls of Caer Dathyl, the enormous castle-capital of the Princes of Gwynedd, knew of their future ruler's magical proficiency, and Arawn and especially Gwenedour wished it kept so.

"It will be difficult enough for him," his mother said whenever she thought it good to remind people, including herself, "without everyone looking to him for instant solutions to all their difficulties. A wizard prince will show himself soon enough; leave tomorrow's dán to tomorrow."

So Gwydion spent his years of boyhood and early youth delighting in his gift, unworried; if it would come to be a burden for him in future—which it would, and then it would come to be a gift again—he did not seem to know it, or to show it. His twin sister, Arianeira, was talented as well, though nowhere near so much as he, and would be taught accordingly; as the future Prince, he had much more to learn and concern himself with. He passed his fosterage years happily enough, with the scions of other royal houses: his fosterns being Galvard, son of the Prince of Dalriada, and Pryderi son of the Prince of Dyved; one would be a true brother in time to come, the other—something else.

By family agreement the two had gone with him to Seren Beirdd—Star of the Bards—the great seat of bardic instruction at Caerdroia, in the shadow of the royal palace of Turusachan. Many youths and maidens, of noble and humble estate alike, were sent there to be further educated after their fostering. There were numerous other bardic schools, of course, but Seren Beirdd was the finest; the only criteria that counted for admission to so selective an institution were high intelligence and deep inclination to learning. The curriculum did not consist of music and literature and poetry only but many disciplines of instruction: history — of Keltia, Erith and other star-realms like Fomor and Firvolgior and the empire of the Yamazai and the Cabiri Imperium; all Keltic languages and many foreign ones, including the Erith tongues Englic, by now a galactic trading vernacular, and Latin, tongue of diplomacy; genealogy, brehon law, astrogation and mathematics and chemics and all manner of sciences, and such other general learning as would serve young minds best — specialization would come later.

But neither of his fosterns had followed him when he left for Dinas Affaraon, and Gwydion had found himself unexpectedly lonely. It was proving hard for him to make friends: his name and title and future position, and the power and stature of his ancient family, set him apart from the other students, many of whom resented and envied him for that alone; and now his gift, having deposited him directly here to begin with, had begun to set him still farther apart than that.

"What are you reading, little princeling? Are we so deeply boring that you would rather have your nose in a book than talk with us?"

Gwydion calmly turned a page of the book he had brought to the common room with him, and sighed inwardly. To be harassed so was nothing unusual; generally the same pack of louts did the taunting where any student was concerned, but this particular oaf had chosen to make a particular target of Gwydion, for reasons that went back well beyond their shared terms at Dinas.

"Since you ask...," he commented absently, never even looking up.

The offender scowled, annoyed at being so drawlingly dismissed. "Let us have a look at what so enthralls the future ruler of Gwynedd. Some of us at least will be fortunate enough not to live under his governance, so this is our only chance to learn."

The oaf in question was called Kyttifer Errwyn, and from the very first day that Gwydion's year's intake had arrived at Dinas and settled into the dorters assigned them, he had been the bane of their existence. A magistrant, or senior student, who had already spent three years at the college and had but this final one to go, Kyttifer was the scion of a middle-ranking, prosperous house of traders from the planet Kernow. Clearly not untalented, or he would not have been at Dinas to begin with, he was not unattractive, with bright red hair and a slim frame and a vulpine visage. But he was of a lazy habit, a mean nature and a bullying disposition, and Gwydion, though his prime target, was far from the only one.

Kyttifer had assembled a small clique around him of the like-minded—other, lesser bullies, or those who fawned on him for fear of being bullied themselves. His particular hostility toward Gwydion stemmed from an animosity between their two families, a perceived insult that went back several hundred years, when the Errwyns were supposed to have been called out by the Penarvons for cowardice in battle—a charge that held more than a grain of truth. The instant the two youths had met, Kyttifer had been consumed by the need to carry the old grudge forward and visit it on Gwydion, and the latter, though he had tried at first to overcome the hostility with friendship and reason, had finally resolved to merely ignore it.

A policy which, however prudent its enactor might have found it, only served to incense Kyttifer all the more. Concentrating his venom on his target, he had escalated the harassment as much as he dared, though, if only he had known, the Pheryllt masters were well aware of it from the start, and had been keeping a weather eye on the situation lest it turn into something graver than mere unpleasant hazing, which all the students were expected to learn to deal with themselves. They were adults, or near-adults: they must fight their own personal battles or else they would never prove fit to fight magical ones.

Still, Gwydion took comfort knowing that after this year Kyttifer Errwyn would trouble his life no more. It was possible, of course, that their paths might cross at some point in the future, but it seemed rather unlikely. As Ruling Prince of Gwynedd he would not need to concern himself with Kernish merchant traders; he would have people to do that for him—rank did indeed have its privileges, for which, for once, he was grateful.

At the moment, his usual strategy of regal disregard was in full effect: he coolly kept on reading, despite the muffled laughter of his peers, as many of which were approving of his studied ignoring as were in support of Kyttifer's childish pettiness. But Kyttifer only grew more and more annoyed at being so coolly mocked by a mere bajand in front of other members of his own senior rank, and especially his particular little coterie. He was totally unaware, as such people always are, that he was regarded by masters and students alike with deep contempt that he should behave so to a fellow, and one so much younger at that. But the school's policy of watchful noninterference unless things reached dangerous levels—these were young sorcerers, after all, capable of serious disruption—left Gwydion to deal with Kyttifer himself, and Kyttifer free to annoy.

"It looks a very *boring* book, does it not, lads? How sad that our dear little princeling must slog through it. Perhaps this will improve things for him."

After glancing around to make sure most of the nearby students had heard his deliberately loud declaration and that their eyes were on him, Kyttifer then magically caused the pages of Gwydion's book to be soaked with wine, so that they were instantly reduced to sodden purple pulp between the leather covers.

His lackeys roared with mirth, and a few of those watching, covertly or openly, snickered as well, though most refrained, exasperated or disgusted or both. None of them, however, expected Gwydion's reaction: without missing a beat, he vanished the damaged book and conjured another identical copy into his hand in its place, and kept right on reading.

Sudden silence on all sides: that was transport or replication magic, either one well beyond the capability of most of them, even the magistrants, and they were sharply reminded that someone who could so carelessly toss off a spell of that level, tremendously more complex than the one Kyttifer had used, might well be someone it was wisest not to antagonize. With a few final half-hearted sneers, and uneasy looks to go with them, Kyttifer and his little band gathered their own belongings and quitted the hall.

When the common room was empty of most other students, Gwydion stretched elaborately. Glancing around, and seeing no one near or watching, he tapped the book lightly with a finger, bringing back its original wine-sodden appearance, then watched, satisfied, as the pages knitted together and restored themselves, clean and dry, free of the purple liquid that had soaked them. With satisfaction, he began to read the volume exactly where he had left off.

It had not been any spell the thuggish group had thought it to be, but pure illusion: the book had been the same damaged volume all along, except he had made them all see something else. The magic he had just employed was nowhere near as effortless as he had managed to make it appear, but neither had it been as impressive as the beholders had believed. Or perhaps it had been impressive in a different way: it had not been summoning or replication, Gwydion did not yet have such skills any more than the others did, but he did possess a great natural gift for illusioning—a different magic, and in its way quite as remarkable. True, the original book had been ruined and then repaired; that much was fact, and indeed, modestly complex spells had been used to achieve both Kyttifer's marring and Gwydion's mending.

The rest was very different. Over the past year at Dinas, Gwydion had developed his skill with and talent for glamourie, the art of casting a magical illusion so convincing that it looked and felt in all ways real, and such a spell was what he had cast in the hall just now. There had never been a second book at all, merely the appearance of one, produced to discomfit Kyttifer and his creatures. Clearly, magic had uses Gwydion had not even begun to consider...and though he did not yet know it, his skill with glamourie was destined to serve himself and Keltia well in time to come.

But no matter his skill, such a conjuring still took a great deal out of him, and presently he found himself weary enough for an early bedtime. Picking up the volume that had started all the trouble, he headed up to his dorter, a small private chamber tucked away in a turret, with precious access to the battlements. Once safe inside, he collapsed bonelessly onto the wood-framed bed; putting one arm over his eyes, he began to relax as he had been taught, muscle by muscle, from his toes on up, in an effort to recover himself and combat his sudden black mood. The treatment he had just received was not such an uncommon occurrence for him: he had expected such hazing from the moment of his arrival at Dinas, especially since he was so much younger than the rest and had been preferred so far above them, and his grim expectations had not been disappointed. But there, at least for now, everything was against him—though to the outside eye, surely it appeared that absolutely everything else was *for* him.

It was an easy opinion to hold. Gwydion Penarvon ap Arawn was of considerable physical beauty: tall for his age, dark-haired and gray-eyed, with promise of more height and a warrior's frame to follow once he filled out. He came of a powerful house, one of the wealthiest and most illustrious lineages in all Keltia; indeed, the House of Dôn had once held the Copper Crown itself, that ultimate power that switched back and forth between several closely related kindreds down the centuries. By grace of his half-hour's seniority over his twin sister, Arianeira—now off at Scartanore for her Ban-draoi training—he, not she, was their father's heir; the youngest of the three sibs, Elved, remained as yet in fosterage. So Gwydion would be the next to rule Gwynedd when the time came, as planetary prince and vice-gerent to the Crown, though Arawn being a man of prime years, and strong in mind and body, no one looked for such an event anytime soon.

Perhaps if his gifts and rank and talents had been less impressive, he might have had the friends he longed for, though never would they have been many, for he was discriminating by nature—too choosy, his mother called it, despairing at what seemed to be his overly fastidious standards in allowing anyone to be close to him, whether it was young men as friends or young women as sweethearts. But he had always known that if something did not measure up to the inner mark he had set for it, he would prefer not to have anything at all: second-best was never good enough, and he would sooner go without than settle.

There was also in his character a surprising shyness, and an impatience with lesser minds, and introspection too, all of which he strove to overcome, because as a prince he must; but chiefly his nature was one of clear-eyed perceptiveness. He could tell at a glance that whatever their rank or lineage, the ingratiating glozers and the court strumpets alike were simply trying to collect him, like some rare specimen of flutterby. Not for himself, his own quality and worth; but to pin him to a board, flaunting his acquisition for their own self-importance, fawning on him for his present title and future position; and so he held back.

On the other hand, those youths and occasional maidens of better breeding and conduct, whom he would have very much liked to have as friends or as flames, were far too shy in their turn to approach him, for fear he would see them as toadies or tarts, like the others; and so *they* held back.

But there his age too was a factor: his classmates at the school were still at a stage where someone five and more years their junior was not yet a prospect for close friendship, though when all were men grown it would matter not in the slightest. As for likely lasses, there were none to be met with in the immediate vicinity of Dinas, and so he must wait until he was home at Caer Dathyl and his mother arranged balls and banquets, or if he should go visiting during holidays, to the homes of his fosterns or others he had known since childhood. He was courteous to his handful of true friends, and chivalrous to all the young women who crossed his path — occasionally more than that, with some of those last, but none so far had caught his deep heart.

Strangely, as his fellow students thought it, he never sought to pay the bullies back in kind. He was far too proud for that; also, which secret he kept hidden closest of all, he was far too afraid to do so. Not in the sense of cowardice, for such a charge was never to be laid to his account, either in battle or in life; but out of a fear that once he lost his temper and unleashed power in anger, either physical or magical, he might not be able to rein it in, and great damage might be done; so that to swallow the petty cruelties and try to rise above it all seemed his best course. Still, the knowing that he did not, and probably would not, have a friend at Dinas of the sort he craved made him unhappy, adding a layer of distance and hurt to a nature already reserved, and much as he balked to admit it, he was lonely.

Only in his studies could he find any kind of pleasure, and that was usually enough to content him, though his excellence in learning merely gave his unfriends another weapon to use against him. It did not trouble him overmuch: apart from his craft and his studies, he had books, and sports, and training, and the little crystals that projected plays and music and other entertainment, and books again and always — all of which were firmer and more trustworthy friends to him than most mortals would ever be. But a friend or two who liked him for himself, or a young lady he could romance and be romanced by, would have been a pleasant thing to have.

It was the attitude to those who would serve his rule in future that was most problematic — a character trait that would have to be worked on. No one wanted a Ruling Prince who could not delegate to his counselors and commanders because he felt he could do everything better and more quickly and easily himself, however true it might be. He would need to be able to work with everyone he encountered, for the Ard-tiarnas, the High Crown of Keltia, as well as for Gwynedd — it would be most unfortunate if he could not.

The issue turned on trust: after all, he got on excellently well with those of lesser rank — the soldiers of his father's guard and the servants of his mother's staff, the citizens of Caer Dathyl he met in the streets and the farmfolk he encountered on a ride through the hills. He enjoyed the interaction, was in no way a snob; he felt no discomfort talking as an equal to any such, nor they to him, and ever went out of his way to act friendly — to *be* friendly. And the folk respected him, were glad he was one day to rule them; respected him, admired him, even feared his competency and his gifts. But they did not love him, or at least not yet, and this he knew perfectly well. Respect, if that was all he was ever to have from his people, was well and good; he did not seek adoration. But it would have been pleasant to feel a warmer connection.

It was in truth only humans with whom Gwydion had difficulty: he felt nothing but easiness when dealing with those who were not. The dwarrows and the merrows, the kelpies and selkies, the clurachauns and liobrachauns, the banachas and bonachas, the hoggarts and boggarts and hobs and cobs — he was friends with all the many strange and benign or even tricksy magical creatures that made Keltia their home. Often in the twilight he could be seen walking on the hills behind Dinas in their exuberant company, laughing as a troop of chattering little goblins bounced excitedly along beside him, or when other such small cheerful beings would come to keep him company should he pace sleepless in the owl-time hours, happily confiding in him stories of their own world just a breath apart from his.

One thing: despite their shared and ancient kinship with the House of Dôn, the Sidhe never came to visit. That was no real surprise, for no mortal Kelt had reported even seeing one of the Shining Folk for several centuries. But before that, matters had stood very differently.

In the long history of the Penarvons alone, there had been five weddings of mortal and magic kind, though the genealogies and relationships were so intertwined that those were by no means the only infusions of sidhaun blood, just the formally sanctioned ones—romances had there been aplenty, both casual and deep. In truth, every great Keltic family could say the same, could boast of being sidheanach, human kin to the unhuman fae: the Aoibhells, of course, current holders of the High Crown, who ruled over all Six Nations and seven planetary systems; the Douglases, the Penarvons' counterpart on the planet Caledon; the Kerrigans and the Grahams, the Ó Dálaigh and the MacKinstreys, the Trevellians and the Kervouaecs—so many families of equal and lesser distinction could count descent from such unions.

Not so much these days, though, and perhaps that was where the strain did lie. Since the days of Edeyrn Marbh-draoi, who had imposed his evil Theocracy over all Keltia, killing the royal family of that time and causing, though it had been by no means his intent, the rise of Arthur of Arvon to become Ard-rígh over Keltia, the Sidhe had gradually widened and maintained a certain remote distance from mortal Kelts. Though no one could say why, just so: the Sidhe were not communicative on the matter, or indeed on any other; and those humans who were in a position to ask were not asking, or not answering if indeed they chanced to know.

Some said this recent distancing had all to do with Gwyn, present king of the Sidhefolk, and with the way in which he had come to his crown. His father, the late and celebrated King Neith, who had led the Sidhe to Keltia in the Great Immram, and at whose behest Taliesin Pen-bardd had founded the mighty order of the Dragon Kinship, had perished almost three centuries ago as the result of some mysterious happenstance that the then crown princess, Aoife Aoibhell, had allegedly brought about, though no one apart from the immediate kindreds concerned was at all sure as to what this terrible deed had been.

It had been held out as an accident, which in truth it was, and Neith had indeed died; but the calamity had caused the young and stricken princess to run away and hide on a world far from Keltia, sinking her guilt and shame in worse shame still, and had likewise caused the Sidhe to withdraw from mortals, in sorrow or in anger none could say. Aoife had been tracked and rescued and brought back, of course, though by no Kelt, and had gone on to rule as Ard-rían, becoming the oldest monarch in all Keltic history and the longest to reign; but the damage had been done. And so Gwyn son of Neith had succeeded to the kingship of his race at a young and unheard-of age for one of his kind; there had been deep feeling on both sides, and many thought the last had not yet been heard of the matter.

In any case, though the great silent brughs of the Sidhefolk remained, no mortal Kelt dared approach them, and no one on any Keltic world had had even a glimpse of a sidhaun, much less any deeper or more extensive contact. But that was about to change.

In his eighteenth year came Gwydion's final tests of magical accomplishment, after which he would, if he passed, be confirmed by the Archdruid as a high master of the order — though there were still higher ranks to be achieved, should he be so inclined. His life had become far more pleasant once Kyttifer Errwyn and his swinish companions had left the school, going off to inflict themselves on the rest of Keltia. They left with no glory to their names and no high Druidic standing achieved, just a bare sorcerer's competency; they had not even succeeded in passing their final tests.

Likewise too, as new students had entered who were more of an age with himself and who had no problem befriending or admiring instead of resenting and despising, he had found himself growing out of his isolate habits to meet them in friendship, as they did him. So it had come about that Gwydion's last years at Dinas were far happier than his first, and he had come to enjoy his leisure as much as he did his schoolwork. And when his own time for testing arrived, he knew that this he could accomplish, with ease and contentment.

Continually evolving down the centuries, but remaining basically the same, the Druidical tests were similar in nature to those of the Ban-draoi or the Fianna or the bards: all involved a vision journey of some sort, and a test at the heart of it. For the Ban-draoi, it was an immram, a trance deep within Broinn-na-draoíchta, the temple known as Magic's Womb — a spirit-voyage so deep it appeared like death itself, and indeed was not far off it. The Druids had such a trance also, called the marana, and other ordeals as well, for achieving the lower ranks of the hierarchy; but the chief trial for a magistrant claiming his degree, his habilitancy, was the ritual of the Spiral Path, a pacing of one of those mystical labyrinths constructed to encircle certain sacred hills, or tors.

There are such mazes all over Keltia, and the one selected for any particular student Druid's test is generally the one closest to the aspirant's home or school — familiarity breeds ease of spirit. But the most famous and most sacred is sited on Gwynedd: Glaston Tor, named for its Erith counterpart. A rounded eminence that rises as isolated endpoint to Aller Edge, a hill chain that runs for some ten miles, Glaston Tor is situated in beautiful green country north of Caer Dathyl. Its isolation causes it to look taller than it is; its shape is that of a long oval, or a ship, its scarp steeper and sharper on the northern or prow side, the southern end trailing off like a comet's tail in a long, gentle slope that leads back down into Glaston village itself. Thick woods of oak, ash and thorn cluster round its foot, while above the trees, bare and grassy flanks show plain the terraced, undulating, labyrinthine path that gives the hill its mystery, though in its pre-eminence Glaston possesses nine levels, not the more usual seven. Such a labyrinth is called 'troia', which means among other things 'spiral', and the word is part of the name of Caerdroia — Spiral Castle — the great walled capital city on the ringed planet Tara.

No one can say for sure what stands on Glaston's flat summit: there are some ruins, certainly, of an ancient stone circle, like the ones that top many Keltic hills, everyone knows that; but that is by no means all there is, or all there might be. Whatever else is present there is a mystery: each serious pilgrim, habilitant or no, encounters something different. Some say they found a towering bluestone circle, an open temple like the famous ones on Tara, perfect and complete, where the stones sang to them and grew transparent and moved about as in a dance; others swear that they came to a shining castle crowning the Tor, with towers set foursquare to the Quarters and mortared with magic; still others say nay, a sacred grove of tall trees with leaves of silver and branches of gold, or perhaps the other way round. People even tell of an impossibly vast plain that stretches on for miles, or a cold, serene lake fringed by reeds, or even somehow, equally impossibly, the sea itself. Everyone who ventures up the Tor with purpose and comes back down again—for it must be said that some do not, there is always peril, and Glaston Tor is the most perilous place of all—has a different tale to tell, and perhaps all the tales are true ones, and all manifestations on that hilltop mere gateways to Elfhame, to the Underlands, to the kingdom of the Sidhe.

Glaston Tor is also renowned for the holy wells that stand among its mystic turnings, and the springs that emerge from deep within the hill to feed them. There are three: though ancient stories tell of four, that last one has never been revealed to the common run of folk, though it has on occasion been found by favored seekers. But the three that are known hold wondrous properties for healing, for knowledge, for wisdom — those two last being by no means the same thing. Kelts of all ranks travel many star-miles to make the pilgrimage up the Tor: they are free to pray and reflect and drink of the water at each of the wells as they come to them, or simply to wander the slopes for pure enjoyment's sake, nothing more than that. It is a peculiarity of the labyrinth terraces that different journeyers encounter the wells at different stages; some find the sacred springs quite quickly, while others have to pace through many more turnings of the Spiral Path, or so it seems to them, before they are able to stop and drink.

Once a well is reached, though, it is the same for everyone, whether dedicated pilgrim or casual stroller: the Red Spring, its rust-tinged waters rising in a fountain of roseate marble; the White Spring, a pearlescent torrent foaming in a broad, shallow limestone cup; and the Dark Spring, whose topaz-colored cascade, smoky with peat, bursts from a granite rockface and falls to fill a rough-hewn hollow in the stone. All the waters of all the springs drain away again through underground channels that they have bored through the hill; clean and unsullied, they emerge once more to foam and tumble through a small healing pool, through which folk may walk barefoot, to seek healing from the waters' chill touch. At last the waters cascade down and collect in a larger, serene, ever-replenishing pool at the Tor's foot, much visited by those disinclined to climb the hill itself. Thence they overspill into the river Brona, a stream that winds its way across the land thereabouts, carrying the waters' sacred qualities through the oldest settled part of Gwynedd, to the sea.

But the fourth spring, the Silver Spring, is different. Legend says that its water is the clearest and purest and coldest and holiest of all; that it rises up at the very top of the Tor in a basin carved from a single huge diamond as clear as itself; that only the most purposeful of seekers can hope to find it or even behold it—the most devout, the most fated, the cleanest of heart. None can even say where its waters find their way to, for no one has ever seen those waters mix with the rest. Those few who do achieve it never speak of it, though they are permitted ever after to return at need to drink from it or to carry a flask away. It is even said that the water of the Silver Spring is proof against death itself. Not true, but very close; and no surprise, for the magic that dwells in and around this place is powerful indeed.

For Glaston Tor is the home and haunt of Gwyn ap Neith, and has been since before his accession to the Sidhe kingship. He rules from the crystal throne at the heart of Dún Aengus, the palace beneath the Hill of Fare on the planet Tara, as Neith his father had done, but owl-haunted Glaston is his particular place, and those who seek him out, whether for noble reasons or merely desperate ones, look for him there before any other spot, for Gwyn is lord of wishes and ruler of dreams, king of visions and dealer of correct justice. Then again, none have recently reported finding him, there or anywhere else; yet it is known that those who seek him with an honest heart find their need mysteriously met or their wish granted—though perhaps not always in the fashion they were expecting.

There was never a doubt as to which tor Gwydion would choose to ascend for his habilitancy trial. Though there were other sacred labyrinths nearer to Dinas Affaraon, or even to his home city of Caer Dathyl, he had known from the first that he would go up Glaston; never any other thought in his mind but that it would be so, indeed that it must be so. Glaston being the most challenging of all the troias, it seemed to him the proper place for his testing; if he won, it would be a victory worth winning, and if he lost, at least he would know that he failed honorably in the place of greatest difficulty.

And thus, leaving Dinas on a night of his own choosing, with only a brief scrawled note to let his Pheryllt tutor know what he was about, he travelled as swiftly as he might to Glaston borough itself, a quiet, charming stone-built huddle of red-tiled roofs at the Tor's foot that promised homely comforts. Foregoing the traditional night's lodging in the local Druid priory, to which he was entitled as an aspirant about to undergo his test, he decided to cosset himself instead with a nightmeal and rooms at the town's best inn, which catered to wealthy pilgrims, and felt not the least pinprick of guilt for so doing. No magical tenet said one was required to suffer privation in order to secure a successful outcome to such a venture, and by all gods he planned on enjoying himself and not thinking in the slightest about the trial to come, with no higher aim than to be both well fed and well rested before he set out on his trial.

So he dined alone in his rooms, with a splendid supper of shellfish soup and planked salmon and grilled beef and salt-roasted porrans, finishing off with a lordly dish of sliced local apples and crumbled shortbread and sugared cream so thick a spoon could stand in it upright, followed by an unbroken night's sleep in an excellent bed. His trial did not start until just before sunset, so he luxuriously slept in until nearly noon. A full breakfast was followed by a pleasant, lazy day spent poking round the local shops, buying small trinkets for his sister and her two young fellow-princess fosterns, Aeron Aoibhell and Morwen Douglas, a silver and amethyst brooch for his mother, books for his father and his brother and his Pheryllt tutor.

He had eaten so much for breakfast and for dinner the previous night that he was not at all hungry, but he knew he would get no food again after sunset, indeed nothing to eat until he was on the other side of his test, at dawn the next day, and the demands of nervous energy would be great; best he started out full-fed. So he managed to stuff down a substantial early supper in a tavern beside the river Brona, whose peaceful banks were overhung by ancient willows where it ran through the middle of the town, and then returned relaxed and happy to his rooms, to meditate a little, have a ritual bath and clothe himself for his night's work.

He had chosen the twenty-ninth day of September, the feast of Fionnasa, as the day on which to make his attempt. Fionn, the High God known as Friend-of-man, was a special patron of the Gwyneddan royal house, and for Gwydion to seek his blessing upon the test was natural and well thought of. The preparatory actions were prescribed by tradition: the herbs and incense and candles that accompanied the bath, to cleanse his spirit as well as his body; the simple tunic of plain dark wool and the trews and boots and thick woven mantle; no jewel save the small Druid pendant at his throat; no weapons save a ritual dagger made of thunderbolt iron; no provisions at all. He was permitted to carry an empty flask of thick, heavy glass, cleverly constructed with three compartments and three necks; this was not meant to be drunk from but to collect the waters of the three springs as he came to them. Once filled, it would be carefully sealed and shown as proof next day to the Master of the local priory, who would set his own seal on the flask for Gwydion to bring back to Dinas Affaraon, and also send word ahead of the candidate's success or failure, to Dinas and to Arawn and Gwenedour at Caer Dathyl, anxiously awaiting.

He had been carefully monitoring the slow descent of the sun over the hills to the west, and when it had reached a certain height in the heavens, he slung on his cloak and slipped from his room. He had been, he thought, both cautious and discreet in his night and day in Glaston: he had used another name at the inn, paid in silver, not gold, spoken to few, and that sparingly, mentioned to no one why he was there. Yet they seemed to know him even so, and knew his errand, for as he left the inn as inconspicuously as he could manage, he was quietly wished well by everyone he passed, and by his proper name and title too.

So much for discretion, though it was far more likely that the townsfolk, who lived with, in and amid magic on a daily basis, had seen so many would-be Druid habilitants pass through that they could spot one at a hundred paces, and true it was that his face was not unknown on his home planet—he had not troubled with a glamour to hide his looks, not wishing to spend the magical energy to do so. He was usually made uncomfortable by such attention: but that night he found that he was strangely cheered and warmed by the friendly well-wishing; it seemed almost an omen, a sign for his success.

Not that he had any doubt of the outcome: he was not vain, but he knew himself and he knew his abilities. Nay; if there was to be any…difficulty, it would not come from any inner insufficiency of his but from outer and unforeseen circumstances. Candidates failed all the time on the Spiral Path; it was certainly not beyond the bounds of the possible that he too might fail. But deep within himself he knew, felt, trusted, that he would not; all that his mind was now set on was the nature the test would take, where the Path would bring him. It would not be for him as it would for anyone else, it could not be; that was as it was, and it was well.

In less time than he expected, he found himself passing the last houses at the edge of the town, along the broad white road that skirts the famed apple orchards; turning his head, he glanced behind him, half fearing that a silent and unencouraged tail had escorted him. But no one was in sight; the sun was falling down swiftly now beyond the hills, and the folk had all gone withindoors as the light drained and the air rapidly cooled. All was quiet; it seemed a perfect time for the task at hand.

Coming to the ancient stone-pillared entrance gate that stood on the edge of the little wood at the Tor's foot, marking where the ascent began, Gwydion took a deep breath and went to one knee, bowing his head. He lifted a burnished bronze oak leaf from where it had been lying on the autumn-carpeted forest floor, and a long curling golden ash leaf and a deep red hawthorn leaf as well, the trinity of sacred trees: oak for the God, ash for the Goddess, thorn for the Alterator—all signifying the presence of the Sidhefolk. Those three trees growing together, unplanted by mortal hand, always marked an entrance to a magical precinct, holy ground, and had done so since the Kelts had dwelled on Erith, before the great starship voyages began; that had not changed since Kelts had come to Keltia, nor would it ever. Something else caught his eye, and reaching forward, he picked up also, with even more solemnity, a small white and bronze-barred plume—an owl's fallen feather, sign of the king beneath the hill.

Be with me, Kernûn and Kerridwen, God and Goddess; be with me, Alterator, thou Unnamed who decrees the fates of all created things. And be with me, Gwyn son of Neith, whose place this is... He bowed his head reverently over each leaf in its autumnal perfection, and over the owl feather in its clean-edged purity, and carefully placed them back where he had found them; then he stood straight, hands uplifted, and spoke aloud the customary formula of invocation, offering greetings and asking permission.

"To the king of spirits, and to his queen—Gwyn, you who are yonder in the forest, and above upon the slopes, and below within the hill, by grace of your throne and power and presence, for love of your mate, in amity twixt your people and mine, permit me to enter your dwelling-place and walk your paths."

That, *that* was why he had chosen Glaston over all other

tors in Keltia. It was Gwyn's maigen: his palace and home ground, the sacred seat of his rule. Given the Penarvons' kinship with the Sidhefolk, and with the line of Gwyn in especial, it seemed neither presumptuous nor unreasonable to ask for the fae king's help. That such help would come at a price, Gwydion knew very well; that it might not be straightforward in nature, he knew also — the Shining Folk were famed for their love of trickery and illusion. Not deceit: it was likewise known that the faerie race could not lie; but sleight and ruse and subterfuge and games were part of their very being — he was prepared, and pleased that he was not unskilled at illusion himself.

Still, he had a small and secret hope that perhaps, should he complete his task and it be well done, he might come face to face with the lord of the Tor. It could happen... Gwyn ap Neith was king of the Underlands: the somber god Arawn might rule the Hollow Lands of death itself, but Gwyn had precedence and authority in the realm that lay between death's country and the mortal world. To all certain knowledge, Arawn Deathlord and Malen his queen, lady of battle, two of the high gods farthest removed from human existence, had shown themselves to no mortals in life ever save Queen Athyn and King Morric alone; while over the centuries, Gwyn and his queen, Etain, and others of their kind had often appeared to human Kelts, in friendship and even love — less remote than the gods, warmer, merrier, yet still high and strange and mighty, and very dangerous at whiles. He must be very careful what he thought and prayed and wished for, and how he carried himself this night.

But however he hoped, he had no reply to his greeting, unless the momentary breeze that blew around him, snapping his cloak, might be one, and making sure the empty flask was well secured to his belt, he stepped past the pillars and into the wood, just as the sun vanished behind the blue hills.

The first thing he noticed was the increasing chill that had risen as soon as the sun westered, striking colder than it should for the time of year, and made him glad of the warm hooded cloak he wore, woven of thick hodden green. The second thing he noticed was the music. Far it was and faint, just a fidil and a bagpipe and a small frame-drum; but his bard's ear noted that the playing was skillful and the tune an ancient one that the Sidhe were said to love. It seemed to have been going on for some time; perhaps he had only become able to hear it once he set foot on the upward way — somehow, as he began the climb with a long, easy stride, the music comforted him. He had a view now, out over the tops of the autumnal trees: from this height the sun was not yet below the horizon, and there was an overspreading golden glaze in the hushed west, a giant bonfire all the way up to the zenith that matched the blazing trees below, though behind him in the east the sky was already deepest blue. He was not concerned; he had all night to make the ascent, which was by no means arduous, and already he was coming to the first turning of the labyrinthine way.

Even as that thought crossed his mind, things all at once grew strange: though he knew well that the Tor's smooth sides were ringed by grassy green terraces, suddenly he came upon a gorge like a slash cut in the hill by a giant knife, a gorge which he knew did not exist in real life. *Very well, then...the first illusion...* Walls of rough stone lined and defined it, gray for the most part, in varying shades from dove to charcoal, with every now and then a thin stratum of cream-colored harder stone stitching its way through the darker thicknesses, like thread through tweed, laid down level and even. There was no stream in the gorge's dry, narrow throat, and he could not have drunk from one in any case. By the laws of the test, he could drink only from the wells, and only while he was at them; no water was to be taken away save in his flask, and that was untouchable.

But clinging to the gorge's gray walls were ancient, gray-green apple trees, laden with ripe fruit—a final enticement, for neither was he to eat upon the path. He smiled as he passed the trees, untempted in the slightest by the rich apple fragrance that filled the air—foresighted had he been indeed to come full fed to his testing. So he moved through at a steady pace, feeling the breeze in his face, then he was out upon the Tor's open breast, and drew a deep breath to see the gorge mysteriously vanish behind him as if it had never been there, leaving only a green sward behind. *First check passed...*

As he started to climb in earnest, at each turning he seemed to be drawn more and more into a deepness, sinking within the Tor, his steps moving not atop the earth of the hillside but somehow through it, though when he glanced down, startled at the feeling, he saw only his boots standing sturdily upon the chalk. The turf-cut maze path seemed to shine beneath his feet, the white chalk of the hill gleaming like snow lines between the grassy ridges. The sky had now grown velvet-dark, and the air was cold, with the haunting scent of a distant leaf bonfire on the wind; he could see stars overhead in all directions, though tonight there was no moon. It was Fionn's night, and there was power drifting about the Tor like a blue mist.

He did not know how long he walked the terraces of the labyrinth, circling the Tor, passing through the Quarters again and again, following the ancient route of the Spiral Path. Three times three, thrice round thrice, "thrice to thine and thrice to mine and thrice again to make up nine", as the old rann had it: he knew that there were but nine such raised ridges girdling the hillside, but it seemed to him that there were many more, intersecting and weaving with each other, so that he moved up and down the face of the hill as he circled it; seemed also that he had been walking several long hours at least, and had not yet come to even the first of the sacred fountains. But even as he thought so, suddenly he found himself standing before the Red Spring, and the surprise of it brought him up short.

It was exactly as it had been described to him, the easiest achieved of the wells, the friendliest, open to all who wandered the hill, as was attested to by the many little rags and tags of fabric tied to neighboring low thorn bushes by wishers and hopers. He bent to carefully fill one of the flask's compartments with the red-tinted waters bubbling into the red marble fount; then, having sealed the flask again, he brought out his own small scrap of cloth and tied it to a handy branch, with an unvoiced wish and hope of his own.

Obedient to custom, he bent to the wellhead; ignoring the small stone bowl set there for drinking purposes, instead he let his cupped hands fill straight from the fountain.

After letting that first double palmful drain away on the turf as libation, an offering to the spirit of the spring, he was then free to drink himself. So he filled the stone bowl, raised it to his lips and eagerly drank. A little slurpingly perhaps, but he was very thirsty; no one was around to chide him, and he had a feeling that the power that ruled the Red Spring would not mind—though he apologized inwardly all the same. The water, pleasantly cool to the mouth, smelled and tasted very faintly of the dissolved iron that gave it its color, and Gwydion scoffed inwardly: what idiot had bruited the tale that the Shining Folk could not abide the touch of ferrous metal? One had only to see them in battle to know the lie of that—their steel cut as keen as any Kelt's, and to be struck down in combat was one of the only ways they could be slain. And also there was this spring of theirs—nay, if iron truly troubled them, it would never be here serving the purpose it did.

He paused for thought as he drank, suddenly struck: perhaps that story was no idiot's tale but rather a trickster ploy—something the Sidhe had put about themselves, to make their kind seem weaker than they truly were, for purposes of their own. True it was that they loved games and riddles and all things that were not as they appeared. It was their nature; and though they could tell no falsehood outright, they could, and often did, mask the truth by any other means they chose, for any reason and no reason, for deep purpose or for sheer delight in mischief. But that was a mystery not destined to be solved this night…

By the rules of the test, he was permitted to drink as much as he pleased while he rested beside any of the wells, and he took full advantage, not having realized until that moment how thirsty his climb had made him. After a dozen more deep drenches, he felt considerably restored and refreshed, and once his thirst was fully quenched he cupped another double handful and splashed it over his face. Instantly his sight seemed to clear, and he beheld the path before him lying plain. The twists and turns of the labyrinth went up and down, and this turn of the spiral saw him in fact lower than the last; while the next circuit somehow brought him a mystifying two levels up. It was hopeless to try to figure out the route in advance, but at least he now could see it in front of him.

As he gazed, he became aware of a white flurrying motion off to one side above his head, and instinctively he ducked, startled, as the motion drove right at him. Something with an edge like a sword brushed his cheek, then the whiteness took form and settled on the marble rim of the spring itself. He had thrown up an arm to protect himself while he was yet unsure of what it was might be; now he lowered it, and found himself looking at a pale and imposing owl, with snowy breast and bronze-barred back and wings, an owl that seemed to shine softly with a light of its own against the dark. A ghosthunter, that particular breed was called, Gwyn's creature, also one of his messengers: Gwydion recollected, as his rocketing pulse gradually quieted, that the vast wood surrounding Glaston's lower slopes was home to many such. He had heard them calling to one another as he climbed, though none had shown themselves; it was a ghosthunter's feather he had picked up from the ground, at the gate to the Tor.

But he recoiled, shocked, as he stared, for this particular owl was different from the rest, or so at least he fervently hoped: its pure white breast-feathers were soaked with blood that came welling through from underneath, as if from a deep and unseen wound, and the drops fell into the red marble fountain and upon the fountain's lip. Strangely, the beautiful wild thing showed no sign of pain or distress, but stared back at him with a fierce, outraged golden gaze, proud and somehow challenging. And he startled anew, for in an instant the gleaming creature, amid another flurry of feathers and talons and wings, had vanished before his eyes, and Gwydion realized that it had been but a vision, another illusion.

Yet it had touched him: the owl's wing, in passing, had brushed his face with one of its pinions, and now he raised a hand to his cheek where it had touched. Unsurprised, he gazed at his fingers, to see them tipped with blood, from the thin cut the razor-sharp pinion had left. What the meaning of all this was, he could not say; save that meaning it must assuredly have. For two things he knew for fact: the ghosthunter was sacred to Gwyn himself, who, it was said, did sometimes take that very form; and nothing encountered on the Spiral Path was ever met by chance. He therefore took no chances, and made a reverent bow towards where the owl had stood, and touched his bloodied fingertips to the water-damp stone.

I have as yet no spirit-animal, no personal fetch to guide me;

perhaps the ghosthunter is sent me to be my own? I would not mind that in the least — it would be a great honor, and a strong guide... But no answer came. Still shaken, he gathered his cloak around him; giving thanks aloud to the Red Spring's waters — and, vision or no, expecting every moment to feel the bite of steel talons piercing his back — he set out again, going upward, going round.

Despite the refreshment the well had given him, and the shock the vision owl had, it seemed to Gwydion that he had entered some kind of trance: his feet moved without his brain's participation, seemingly, and time was strangely stretched. He was not weary in the slightest, neither in body nor in mind, and as he walked he pondered upon the historical nature of the labyrinth beneath him, as he had learned at school.

The twisting form of it was thought by folk of Erith to have originated with the royal labyrinth at Minoan Knossos, on the island of Cretia, near Hellas in the eastern part of the Midearth Sea; but all Kelts knew it came from longer ago and farther away than that. Indeed, the labyrinth was not of Erith at all, but of Atland, that mightiest island-nation that was whelmed in the waves, and before that of Núminôrë itself, their people's original home among the stars. Beyond all other purposes — and there were many — it was a spirit path, sacred and sacring, and if he walked it with the proper intent it would bring him where he needed to be.

Not for the first time, he wondered about the Atlandeans and their starborn forebears. Incalculable ages since, the death of their sun had forced the Núminôrians to leave their distant home, and an ancient prophecy had brought them to Erith, where they had settled the great island-continent that stood in the smaller, more turbulent of the planet's two seas. Long years had they dwelt there in peace and freedom, employing their science and their magic, exploring their new home, living in friendship with the native races, many of whom regarded them as gods from the distant stars. Then corruption had set in, and in the end Atland had been destroyed, though survivors had managed to make their way to the closest sea-lands, and so had the Celts come to be, who would later go back to the stars and become the Kelts — a long tale, full of pain and glory...

Coming out of his reflections, he saw to his pleasure that he was now considerably higher up the Tor's flank than he had thought, and was approaching the second fountain, the White Spring, on the far face of the slope. There was a low bench standing before the basin, and he took that as permission for him to sit down and rest for a bit. And he would, he would, once he had performed his task; but for just a moment he watched the spring's waters pulse and pour from the white marble fount, slightly hypnotic, very faintly milky from their underground passage through deep-lying strata of white limestone. He glanced at the sky: no moon, but he could see by the wheeling stars that he was moving well within his allotted time, so a brief respite here was possible.

Before he could allow himself that, though, he dutifully filled the second of the flask's three compartments with water taken from the spring, and then poured another libation and thirstily drank again as he had done before. As he gratefully collapsed on the soft, springy turf, his arms propped behind him on the marble seat, his booted legs stretched out before, he thought he heard the distant music again, this time coming from somewhere below him, as before it had come from above.

Then it was that he heard the voices.

Whoever the speakers were, they seemed unaware of his presence; or perhaps merely uncaring of it. Though he could not distinguish their words, they sounded pleased and happy, and there were two voices in particular that came clear, though behind them was a murmur of many more, and again the music. A ball, perhaps; a merry evening for the folk beneath the hill. It was after all the feast of Fionn: no surprise if the Sidhe should revel this night in Gwyn's halls, and no cause to be alarmed.

Gwydion stretched luxuriously but warily, leaning back against the bench. Fionn the Young was the most human of the High Gods, the one who most concerned himself with the well-being of mortals, often in his own form and person, and so had Gwydion chosen the night of his feast to make his attempt; it seemed to him he could be only helped thereby. If the oldest tales and records could be believed, when St. Brendan and the Firstfarers, coming from Erith, had set foot in the valley of the Avon Dia, Fionn had been there before them, and had come to welcome them. It hardly seemed possible, but it had been so recorded. Well, and why not? Gods would scarcely need starships to come to Keltia with their people...

Some said that the gods still visited the high places on

such nights as this, their nights, to revel with the Sidhe who were their close kin, and even with such humans as might be honored enough to be invited, or brave enough to seek them out. In Seren Beirdd he had read in the ancient texts of mortal Kelts who had had friendly commerce with gods and Sidhe alike: among them Brendan of the Ships, and Athyn of the Battles and her lord Morric Fireheart, and Taliesin Pen-bardd, brother-in-law to Arthur, Arthur whom some had held to be himself an avatar of Fionn...Arthur, King in the Light. Gwydion shivered involuntarily: those great heroes were his own kindred, their blood was sidheanach, blood of Arthur and Brendan as well, passed down to him and others — might not like call to like? But those times were gone now, or at least they lay long asleep, and people did not these days enjoy such privilege. If privilege it were...

"Two parts his quest achieved, and still the youngling doubts!"

Gwydion sat up so swiftly he almost fell over. The voice — in the air — was it addressing *him*? Surely not!

It seemed the voice's owner had heard his thoughts, for now it was lightly mocking. "Ah, ever the note of disbelief... whatever might be said to convince him?"

He found his own voice, if not his self-possession. "Do you bespeak *me*? But — who are you?"

Laughter like the fountain's own music; now a woman's voice sounded, and a lovely one. "Did you not call upon us, son of Dôn? Have you not come here this night to listen? You are of a blood that hears, to be sure."

Gwydion was recovering himself; had he not been taught how to speak with magical beings, and were these beings not clearly magical? Aye on both counts… "When there is something worth the hearing, true enough. But what has my blood to do with it?"

The first voice sounded again, still amused; a man's voice, resonant as Gwydion's own bardic tones, which had finally hit their true depth and polish. "As you know, cousin. All the ruling families of Keltia have Sidhe blood, do they but choose to admit it. Some have more of it than others, true enough, and some have better blood than others. There is even blood of ours in many families who do not rule at all."

Gwydion spoke without thinking. "Very true, the Sidhe do get around…"

"Well, when one lives as long as we do, one must find something to relieve the tedium, and mortals are so *good* at that!" The woman's voice was openly teasing, and Gwydion was in no mood to be teased, especially by one whom he could not see. But he controlled his temper and bit back his impatience, though he could not forbear a snipe or two himself.

"Glad am I to know that there are *some* things my folk excel at, lady…it *is* 'lady', I assume? Difficult to tell—"

The owner of the voice did not seem offended; if anything, it seemed that her amusement grew. "Oh, some have called me so. Though of course a lady can hardly answer for her own gentility. Perhaps you will see for yourself. Perhaps even, one day, for today's doubting, you will be bound fast in a difficult place, and a woman will speak for you in my presence. Perhaps she will even be a lady. Or perhaps—"

Her voice trailed off just as the harp music swelled to a particularly lovely passage, a soul-call exalting his bard's ear and his bard's heart alike. But neither voice spoke to him again, and the music died away upon the wind.

He sat down on the bench, suddenly weary of all the strangeness, which he very well knew was far from done with and would only get worse before the end. Oddly, his thought was now running back to his first days at Dinas Affaraon, and the interminable petty torments visited upon him by Kyttifer Errwyn. He laughed shortly, unamused: perhaps it was poetic justice, or merely poetic, and unquestionably it was dán, but word had come to Dinas not long after Kyttifer's undistinguished departure that he had suffered the abrupt loss of all or most of his Druid powers. It sometimes happened like that: students of all ranks were continually reminded of the possibility by their tutors. There might be good reason for it, or no reason at all; it could be as randomly causeless as a chance fever of the body was, but generally it was thought to be the magic deserting what it considered to be an undeserving vessel. Perhaps Kyttifer's meanness of spirit had not gone unpunished after all, though Gwydion had had nothing to do with what befell his onetime nemesis—much as he might have longed to. Still, no doubt but that he would meet with worse far in his life to come.

But it was time he picked up the pace of his circuit... He shook himself, clearing his mind of all thoughts alike — yet still he sat on for some moments more, listening to the music of the water, longing to hear more of the glorious music from underground, hoping to hear the sound of the sidhaun voices that had bespoken him. But only the song of the falling water came to him; and at last, refreshed in mind and body both, he rose and set out again.

Now, for the first time, the way uphill began to feel as though it was ranged against him. There was a thickness in the very air, a resistance that he had to force his way through, like trying to run in the ocean—a struggle to gain every inch of the rising Spiral. But he sensed neither hostility nor unwelcomeness; merely that he was being made to work for his attainment, and the echo in his head of the mysterious voices was somehow carrying him along, guiding his steps. He knew he was very near to the top of the Tor now; there was no time restriction set on his endeavor, only that he should be off the hill by dawn. But how long till that should be he had no way of determining for certain—even the stars had blurred themselves, and he suspected by no cloud of the world.

Only one more spring to achieve, in any case: the Dark Spring, most difficult of the three to find, and the least visited by idle strollers on the Tor's slopes. He reflected why that should be so: true it was that darkness frightened many people, but there was no need to fear; it was a thing most natural—without the Dark there was no Light. The brighter the Light, the darker the Shadow, he recalled his first teacher, Cadoc, telling him, when he was a lad of no more than six and had asked why evil things so often befell good folk.

He smiled now, remembering that earnest young boy. The truth was far more complex, and more complicated, than that, though he was indeed still asking that same question, and no doubt would until he died. But it was also far simpler than that, and this the simplest of the great truths, and also the mightiest and most unsimple of all: the clearer and brighter the light in which you stand, the blacker and more sharp-edged the shadow you cast. And when you cannot see that shadow, or if you believe yourself too pure and perfect, too much a being of Light to even *have* a shadow, and do not think you cast one at all, that is the time to most beware it, for then the Shadow is right behind you.

And thinking so, he almost missed his next step with sheer surprise, and stumbled on the path. For the first time since he began his climb, he saw people moving around him—dim and misty, but people nonetheless. People tall and pale and elegantly clad, drifting along both sides of the Path some yards from him. Were these faerie guests on their way to the halls of Gwyn beneath his feet? *Visitors from the Otherlands, invited to celebrate Fionn's feast with the lord of the Underlands...*

Whoever and whatever they might be, they took no notice of him, but headed purposefully toward the top of the hill, which still he had not yet seen. But he knew it could not be far distant now: once the Dark Spring was reached, his task would be accomplished, and the elation of this thought caused him to quicken his pace.

And then he came to the last turn of the path and stood before the third well. A rough slabbed outcrop of shadowed and striated granite, man-high and thrice as long, reared out of the turf, above an irregular basin scoured from the rock by the water's action. The peat-infused waters of the Dark Spring burst out of the split stone; they were tinged a smoky transparent bronze in color, like a cairngorm stone, with a cold white ruffle of foam where the waters bubbled at the basin's edge.

He stepped forward and stooped beside the well-head to fill the third section of the flask, as he had done twice before, knowing that this was the last thing he had to do, careful that he did not fall at the final fence. He held the opened flask in the torrent that leaped from the rockface, and the achingly cold waters filled the final vessel. Corking it firmly, and checking the seal on the other sections, not failing to offer libation and to drink himself, he turned away with a sense of accomplishment and pleasurable pride, free to begin the ascent of the last few yards and come to the heart of the mystery.

It seemed strange to think so, when at last he did think of it, but Gwydion had given little thought or expectation to what he might find at the top of the Tor: whether his reward would be to behold the castle or the sea or the sacred grove, or perhaps something no one else had ever reported, something that was for him alone. And he was given little time to prepare for it, for no more than a score of paces beyond the Dark Spring was the summit of Glaston Tor.

He stepped from shadow into a broad, flat place drenched in moonlight, though as there was no moon that night he had no idea whence came the brightness. But he stopped short and gazed about him with dawning, piercing disappointment, for nothing stretched before him but the flat hilltop and short silvery turf, no visions of wonder or mystery or grandeur. Oddly, the stone ruins that were present in the everyday world were not now to be seen, though at that moment it did not seem strange to him that they were gone; nothing was all that was there.

Nay...nay, that was not so, there *was* something. Off to one side on the ground there was a huddled shadow that he had not noticed before, a shadow that did not move and seemingly was cast by nothing he could see. He blinked, thinking to clear his eyes; but the shadow remained. And then his sight sharpened, and the shadow resolved itself into a shape: a man lying on a bank of turf and mosses. He appeared at first glance dead, the turf his humble bier; then as Gwydion froze with the sheer shock of it, staring, he heard the man's voice, clear but faint with pain, and it spoke to him, just two words.

"Help me."

The words seemed somehow to break him free of his immobility: he dashed forward unthinking. It did not matter a pin's worth to him that such an action was strictly against the rules of the test: no habilitant was to have anything to do with any worldly interruption when one was upon the Spiral Path, and indeed great care was taken to ensure that a candidate was always alone upon the hill the night he made his attempt. How many times had he heard his tutors insist that even if he should find his infirm old grandmother lying bleeding on the side of the Tor, begging him to save her, still was he to ignore her and continue on his round? He had not agreed with their thinking then, and he agreed even less now.

Besides, was he not done with the Path, and therefore free to act as he would? In any case, it was not his grandmother collapsed there in her blood, but a man — or perhaps a youth of his own age or nearabouts, it was hard to judge, as his face seemed to flicker in and out of clear focus — who lay just off the track's edge upon the bordering bank. As Gwydion hastened to help, he saw with horror that the stranger had been grievously wounded — though he could see no sign of an injury, the fine white leinna was soaked with blood, welling through the shirt to cover his chest and side, seeping down to trickle into the turf below. He himself was not yet a warrior — that would come later — but he had seen blood and wounds before. Though as to how to treat it...

"Help me," the stranger said again, his voice fainter, and Gwydion found himself nodding fiercely as he knelt beside him. And got the shock of his life, for suddenly the face came into focus, and it was the face of none other than Kyttifer Errwyn himself. The red hair, the damp, freckled skin, the sneering mouth, which now was twisted not in a sneer but in pain — there was no mistake, and Gwydion drew back involuntarily in his surprise. The eyes, though: the eyes were different from those of his former bane, and Gwydion felt a touch of unease ghost across the back of his neck, a confused and wary thought.

This cannot be. That gaze seems far too clear for one as hurt as he seems. This is glamourie, surely; not truly Kyttifer but an apparant only, an eidolon, an illusion that bears his likeness. And no question that it does so because it means to try me to my limit: if I can heal and show compassion to the semblance of one who hates me, then I have proved myself as priest. But no matter; whoever it is, and whether his hurts be real or no, he has asked in need, and I can only answer in good faith, can do but what I may...

"I have little healing skill," he said honestly, setting aside his distaste at the appearance of his enemy and helping the other to sit up. "But whatever I can do for you, I will."

The Kyttifer-apparant nodded, with a certain remoteness. "Of your kindness, then, give me to drink from your flask. The power of the sacred waters is the only thing that can aid me."

Gwydion pushed aside the single flicker of dismay that he felt. The water in his flask was forbidden to be set to any purpose but its own...but surely for a higher purpose, to save a life? There was healing indeed at the heart of the Tor, but he had no way of knowing if he could come to it in time. That was the true center of the labyrinthine way, the place to which the Spiral Path and all its energies wound itself: the Spring at the Heart of the World, the Silver Spring that was the desired goal of every aspirant, and which so very few achieved.

But now, at need, not his need but another's, he did not hesitate even one heartbeat further to help the seeming Kyttifer drink from the flask; and when the first compartment was eagerly drained by the wounded man, Gwydion did not delay in uncorking the second nor yet the third, and begrudged not so much as a drop. This was the true test, he somehow knew. No matter the rules he had been given; the gift of healing from the wells was the only purpose that bore any weight here. That was what it was meant for; that was what this test was about. It was a gift, but it was not *his* gift; it was only his for the giving, the passing along, and the fact that the one in need appeared to be his erstwhile tormentor made no differ — it only made the testing true. If such a giving meant that he did not fulfill the trial, well then, so be it; better that than a life lost and he the cause...

"I fear that I have emptied your flask," said the eidolon then, lowering the bottle from his lips with a glance that might be called rueful, or perhaps watchful.

Gwydion shook his head impatiently. "Matters not; flasks can be refilled, and the water has served its proper use and need. Has it given you enough strength to stand? Shall you lean on my shoulder? Can you go forward now?"

The apparant smiled, as if some question for which he had sought a very particular response had just been answered to his liking, and rose to his feet, in one fluid motion that betokened grace and strength and power alike, giving no sign of hurt.

"Forward, aye; and farther still. But let us go together."

As Gwydion obeyed his companion's bidding and stepped out upon the open top of the hill, suddenly the Spiral Path appeared all around him, beneath and below, circling the hill like lines of silver fire all converging upon the labyrinth that he could now see stretched across the entire hilltop. The troia, the maze, the web of power, whatever name it went by—it was as if the Tor was crowned with a net of stars, and he looked on it amazed.

"You have reached the heart of the Tor," said not-Kyttifer then, and there was in his voice both pride and satisfaction. "Your actions have earned this for you."

Gwydion turned to question his companion's declaration, but the apparant was still speaking.

"You gave me to drink of the water of the Wells, prince of Arthur's line, and cared not that your flask was drained, that you had no proof to show your masters of your journey's success and completion. Let me refill the flask for you, then, as recompense. Not many come to the true test. Few reach it; still fewer pass it. And mine it is, happily, to reward those who do so. Come. See what your compassion has won you."

And the eidolon laid a hand on the young sorcerer's shoulder, and gently urged him forward.

Gwydion drew his eyes away from the face of the hated being that he had nonetheless healed, and looked around him, though where to look first he was sure he did not know. It was all true, he realized with an upwelling surge of the clearest, purest joy he had ever known; all the tales about this place were true ones. For, like shimmering colored mists that overlapped and layered themselves upon each other, the truths of the Spiral Way were all there for him to behold. The labyrinth on the hilltop replicated the one he had traversed to get there: it was still present, but now it was overlaid by other, even more splendid realities, pulsing within and around and against each other like magic's beating heart.

He saw the great foursquare towered castle standing strong against the stars, and the sacred Grove with its gold and silver trees, perdurable as oak, graceful as ash, vital as thorn, that soared like towers above his head, though from outside the magic precinct nothing of this could be beheld. Beneath his feet lay not wiry hilltop grasses but thick, damp, fresh green mosses that released clouds of glitter when trodden upon, like some rare pollen; the fragrance was dizzying, and yet also somehow clarifying and settling to his mind.

Too, there was the quiet crystal lake, edged with reeds that murmured in the wind, and the towering gray trilithons of the holy circle, even the boundless sea stretching away beyond the limits of the eye to follow; and other sights that he was far too dazzled to discern, though he knew them to be just as blessed. And he knew that no vision was more correct or more beautiful or more magical than any other.

But at the heart of it all was yet another spring, the greatest and the last. Surrounded by a small flower-starred lawn, a fount of water burst from an ancient bank of stonework, stone deeply incised with runes so worn that he had to look sidewise to see them at all. Standing clear of the stone was a small basin carved in the shape of two cupped hands, one plainly a man's, the other just as plainly a woman's, a right hand and a left; the hands were curved and held side by side to form the basin, so that the water, bubbling out of the rock, filled them until they ran over, letting the life-giving water spill into another, wider basin below.

That water was clearer and colder and purer than anything he had ever seen, like liquid diamonds, but it was somehow fitting that it should emerge from so humble a well-head — plain stone, not like the beautifully carven founts of the three healing springs he had already encountered. Nay — this fourth spring was altogether different; those other three were mighty and beneficent, true enough, but this...this was...

He bent to fill the cup at the stream where it bubbled free, but he did not fill it for himself. Instead, he turned to the apparant beside him, intending to hold the cup to the being's lips so that he might drink of the healing draught, but he startled to see that the man was gone, and that the humble stone basin was now a broad, sparkling chalice cut from a giant single rainbowing prisming diamond.

The icy shine of it cast a light upon his face, the gleam and glitter under the stars. It was a wide, shallow bowl like to that of the other springs, yet so different from them, and from its former self, that it tore his breath from him as he gazed upon it. Cold and dazzling and pure, the fountain stood before him, and the water that continually filled it and overflowed its edge was like molten frozen silver. It made a ringing music as it fell into the long conduit that led away, flowing in several curves and steps before vanishing over the edge of the hill, holding Gwydion entranced.

"This is the Silver Spring," came a voice then, one he had heard before, beside the second well, a woman's voice clear and low. "It is the heart of the magic that comes from the Tor for the good of all, though it can be achieved only by those who possess a heart to hold it. And so have you come here, Prince of Gwynedd."

Caught as he was by the glory before him, Gwydion did not turn to look at her; if he had, he would have seen nothing, for again she had chosen to veil herself from view. "I came upon an injured man, lady, and I thought to help him be healed. That was all. I would have done as much for any hurt creature." Unbidden, a picture flashed across his mind's eye: the ghosthunter owl at the first spring, blood upon its white-feathered breast—and a great, enormous question began to form within his own breast.

"Yet you forsook your test to help him, knowing well what

it would mean, stepping off the Spiral Path for any cause."

Gwydion shrugged. "It means what it will mean. If I fail, I fail. But if I had not stopped to aid a fellow being I had failed indeed, at a greater and higher test than this one. But where is he? What have you done with him, and why have you done it?"

"She has done nothing but what I have bidden her do," came a calm voice from his other side, and that voice too had he heard before. "As my queen, she was merely obeying her king's command."

"Not to make a practice of it, beloved—this 'obeying' that you speak of," said the woman lightly, amusedly, and the lord laughed. As he came forward into the now brilliant moonlight, Gwydion caught his breath. This could only be the ruler of the Sidhe himself; he knew the likeness from the ancient tapestries that hung in the royal palace of Turusachan at Caerdroia, in Gwahanlen, the hall that had been built for Arthur's legendary Companions, the hall that held the great round table…

"I am Gwyn," said the faerie king easily, standing before his rescuer. He had cast off the glamourie of Kyttifer Errwyn that he had worn and now showed himself in his true likeness. Tall he was, and young, but also older, far older, at the same time. His frame was that of a warrior, muscled and strong-looking; his hair was dark, his eyes darker, though a golden shimmer lay upon them, or within them, and a neat-trimmed beard outlined the clear-cut chin and jaw. The white leinna was spotless, no smallest stain of blood remaining; he moved not as a wounded man but as a king at home in his own place.

This was his true appearance, Gwydion realized, about as far from Kyttifer Errwyn, in all ways, as could possibly be. He might not even have troubled to name himself: in this time, in this place, surely he could be no other than who he was—king undoubted of the Sidhefolk of Keltia, who had not for long centuries made themselves known to Kelts. And yet he showed himself tonight to Gwydion, for what purpose was not yet entirely clear.

For Gwyn's part, as he studied his princely guest, studied him as closely and carefully as he had studied a young princess not long since, he could see strength of body and the promise of further strength to come in the young mortal; more importantly, the promise of strength in mind and spirit, and he smiled. *He will not fail at the test, when it comes to it. This is a branch cannot be broken, only judiciously bent, and he will choose the time and place of the bending himself...*

"I am no stranger to this place," the king said aloud, "nor are my queen and my subjects. And no more are you: though true it is that only seldom do we receive mortals as guests here, Prince of the House of Dôn."

Gwydion gave him the beautifully calibrated, respectful nod of equals that are not quite equals, the half bow that is given by one of lesser rank when "unsure of another's station", even though he was about as sure of their respective stations as he was of his own name. And he marveled, for he knew from the old tales that Athyn Blackmantle, that queen of great renown and mystical end, had midwifed Gwyn herself, brought beneath the hill to be present at his birth. Which made the faerie monarch not far off two thousand years old, and young for his kind; and yet they looked to be of an age together, such was the way it was with the Aes Sidhe.

But with all the wonders of the hilltop, it was Gwyn from whom Gwydion could not look away; he found he could do nothing but stare. The faerie monarch looked like no one and nothing save his own self: the strength and the beauty, and above all else the tides of power that rippled off him, like mist off the nearby spring. Feeling that his brief reverence had somehow not been enough, Gwydion dropped again to one knee, as he had before setting foot upon the Spiral Path, long hours since.

"Majesty."

"Gwyn, only," the faerie lord corrected him, pleasantly, "for you are both friend and kinsman. Rise then, and know that you have not failed your test. Indeed, you have accomplished it as few others have ever done."

"I trust I have not disturbed your revels, King of the Underlands," said Gwydion, rising to his feet as bidden, though he found he could not for any permission call the Sidhe ruler by his mere name. "I thought this night only to come to my testing as Druid, and the time seemed most auspicious."

Gwyn laughed. "The moment you asked my permission in the name of the love I bear my queen, you were a welcome guest here upon the hill. And within it, also, should you care to join us. For the revel, only, my sorrow to say," he added, still smiling. "Time has not come yet when you will join us here for more than a moment." He gestured royally, and Gwydion, no stranger to courtliness, was swept into the king's movement. "But first we have business to attend."

Taking the triple flask that still he held, the king stepped forward to the diamond fountain, where he filled all three of the flask's compartments with the silver water, and then handed it back to its owner. Which would utterly confound the Druid master when he came to uncork the flask next day, for only twice before had water of the Silver Spring been brought down from Glaston as fulfillment of a Proving.

"Drink now, yourself," came the king's word — whether invitation or command — and Gwydion, whose entire being had been yearning for but one sip of the sacred waters, and who would not have tasted a drop without permission if all Keltia had hung in the balance, bowed again, and cupping his hands under the torrent, obeyed.

The waters of the other wells, though each bore their own particular taste and magic, nevertheless were waters of the world. Not this. This was like drinking liquid stars: it tasted of thunderstorms and autumn and magic and frost, and it ran through his body like the Solas Sidhe itself, the Faerie Fire — every muscle, every vein, every cell all set alight with the spring's power. He felt as if he had awakened after a deep and troubled sleep that had left him listless and confused.

But the Sidhe king was not yet done. He held out his hand, and Gwydion, knowing what was required, instantly drew his ritual dagger and laid it hilt-first upon Gwyn's open palm. Smiling his approval, and showing not the tiniest flinch at the touch of thunderbolt iron, Gwyn stooped then, going to one knee upon the ground. Carving a small square of the mossy turf beside the fountain, he rose with unspeakable grace and pressed the damp grassy square into Gwydion's right hand, folded round the slim blade of magic iron.

"Now are you lawfully seized and possessed of the land you will one day rule. Sod and stone, turf and tree, the powers of the hill and the powers that lie beneath the hill — it belongs to you and ever has, and ever shall. This is your passport and token, which will never fade or dim."

"Lord," began Gwydion, then stopped, short of speech. Seizin — the ancient ritual by which a man or woman, be they newly crowned monarch or the buyer of a smallholding farm, was made rightfully possessed of the land. This was mighty magic... He began again. "Lord, you do me too much honor."

"I have not yet done with the doing. But for that you have always acted with goodwill to my folk, take that as gift of me," said Gwyn. "And this also." He beckoned, smiling, and out of the shadows beyond the well scampered dozens of tiny goblins — the hobs and cobs and other magic folk whom Gwydion had befriended over the years.

The king watched indulgently as the little creatures swarmed around Gwydion's legs, greeting him eagerly, and saw the smile with which the youth met their cheer and excitement, kneeling to greet them back, addressing many by name.

"King I am of the Aes Sidhe; but king too of these small ones to whom you have shown kindness and care."

"How would I not, for they have shown the same to me," said the youth simply. "When I had no one to befriend me, they were there."

"And for that you have always shown respect to my kin, who are your kin also." Again the beckoning gesture, and the tall, beautiful beings, solid now to Gwydion's sight, that had been drifting about the hilltop paused as one, in obedience to their king, and bowed or curtsied to Gwydion, who bowed back, bemused. "You will have need of all such friends in future, as you have been friends to them in the past."

Gwydion began to ask, for he was very full of questions, but Gwyn cut him off with a warning glance. "Not yet, but soon..." He continued conversationally, "Your compassion for an enemy, as you thought him to be, served to fulfill your quest. For quest it was, and always will be. Like metal refining in the forge, like the work in the chymist's alembic — you have become more truly yourself by what has happened this night. Your future will reflect this: nevermore shall you have such difficulties as you have had these past few years, nor ever be friendless again, though traitors mar your path. It has all been a trial, son of Dôn, and you will have further trials, and greater ones, in time to come, tests to match your metal. But my word to you is that you will prevail. And we will be there to see it.

"But come. Join us now for a taste of our revel. You have my promise you will lose no time thereby, and you have earned, I think, somewhat of a reward."

They walked forward together past the fountain, into the grove, or the ring of stones, or whatever it was, and between one step and the next Gwydion found himself in a vast hall with silver walls and a golden ceiling and a floor of shining marble — Gwyn's palace within the Tor. It was clearly beneath the hill and between the worlds: it seemed to go on forever, though it also seemed to stand open to the heavens. Perhaps a different sky and stars...all opened up to an endless distance and soft light everywhere.

He was within the Tor in truth: all round the hall were dancers clad in the richest of apparel — fair ladies, and lords no less fair. The music resounding was the music he had earlier heard, though now more musicians played it — fidil and pipes and drum were joined by harp and horns and other instruments to which he could give no name, and his musician's soul that had been trained at Seren Beirdd longed to join in.

"Ah, they are playing my song," said Gwyn, amused, and Gwydion fought a wild desire to laugh out loud, for the song being played by the fae musicians — an ages-old reel, and apparently a favorite of them both — was known as "The King of the Faeries."

But he managed to hold himself to a smile matching Gwyn's own, and they moved through the dancing throng like a sun-shark through water.

Beyond the merrymaking, there was a precinct at one end of the vast chamber from which his soul instinctively shied away. Raised and pillared, it seemed holy and deeply apart, and yet not forbidden; merely not permitted for now. Someone or something was there that he was not ready to meet; as he stared at what seemed to be a sparkling mist, concealing whatever, or whoever, was present, he received a sense of amused benevolence, and a quick glimpse of a red cloak and long feathering golden hair. Could it be? It *was* Fionn's night, after all, Fionn's feast... But his mind swerved away like a horse running out from a jump, and he turned from that corner to look upon the rest of the hall.

Which held perils of its own: a lady of such loveliness that surely she must be a queen at least, if not a goddess, came up to the two men where they stood. She made them a curtsey, and Gwydion gave her the graceful bent knee and bow she deserved.

The king bowed in turn, extending his hand to her, then kissed her fingers when she placed her hand in his. "I hate that test," he muttered, and she laughed.

"And so it is that I set it. But you have broken the Hills, prince," she said to Gwydion, smiling, and he recognized her voice at once as the one that bespoken him beside the White Spring, and again atop the Tor. "I am Etain," she said then, "queen to Gwyn, once queen to Brendan of the Ships."

Though Gwydion had known that—every child in Keltia did—and had guessed her identity as soon as she approached, he was dumbstruck all the same. Etain the White, of a high house of the Sidhefolk of Eruinn, had been wife to Brendan the Astrogator, the first queen of Keltia, wed to her mortal first lord on Erith itself more than a thousand years before Gwyn was born, and who knew how long she had walked on Erith before that. She it was who had helped Brendan plan and achieve the Great Immram, which had seen Kelts come to Keltia, full three thousand years in the past. She had loved and lived with Brendan until his death, in great happiness and glory, if the legends were true, and now she was queen again, to a mate of her own kind who was king of all the Fairfolk in Keltia.

It was too much. He was going to faint, or collapse, or weep. To give himself a moment's countenance, Gwydion looked around him, at the shimmering wrought-silver gates and the tall marble columns and the broad stairway that rose up to the top of the Tor itself, which he did not recall descending. Warm light, as if from crystal torches, spilled up the stair and out onto the hilltop; and from the festal hall's other side came the sound of the music he had been hearing all night as he climbed the hill; the sound of voices too, lifted in merry talk and laughter.

"It is the night of Fionn's feast," he said. "The Sidhe revel in the palace of Gwyn."

"So we do," agreed the young king. "And you shall join us. For a night, at least."

Gwydion gestured around him, helplessly dazzled, yet with a small reserved part of his inmost being held back, watching, wary. "So this is what lies at the troia's heart."

"It can be," said Etain. "And what is it, then, that lies at Caerdroia's heart? What lies there for you within Spiral Castle, and for all Kelts?" When he made no reply, she inclined her head to him, a thin crescented crown of sapphires sparkling in her black hair, and laid a gentle hand upon his sleeve. "These things that have troubled you— they are of no matter. Know that they are of the smallest and least significant. They will trouble you no more; you will find your powers, you will find yourself able to trust, to rule, to love. You will find yourself at the end of your testing, and at that end you will find yourself triumphant."

"Not by any merit of my own," he said sincerely, and she laughed.

"Not? Then whose, pray? Nay, Prince of Dôn, this doing tonight is yours."

"Mine?"

Gwyn nodded. "Yours, and perhaps some others'…" His eyes sought his queen's, as if confirming a thing they had agreed between them, then he fixed his gaze upon Gwydion again. "We are minded to come back into the life of Keltia, my folk and I. We have been too long away, and this our meeting tonight is the second herald of our returning."

Gwydion could not control the question. "The *second*? What the hells then was the first?" At the king's thrown-back head and shout of laughter: "I mean no disrespect, lord. We have missed you greatly. But surely if you had made even the smallest return amongst us there would have been such a welcoming outcry as would have reached at least the outer pale of the Curtain Wall. This is a huge thing. We have yet seen no sign that you and your folk are returned."

"We are back even so, Prince of Dôn," said Etain gently. "And to that end, we have already made ourselves known to your future High Queen."

His astonishment overcame his manners. "To Aeron? Aeron *Aoibhell*? She is only a child! My sister's fostern— surely she…"

"Child she may be," said Gwyn equably, though his eyes flashed warning, and seeing that flash, the unblinking firegold stare of a hunting owl, Gwydion instantly lowered his own gaze. "But nonetheless she it was to whom we chose to reveal ourselves, a small time since, and to set protection on her, a mark of our future shared—enterprise."

"The same mark we offer now to you," said Etain, and her voice was solemn. "For there will come a day when all of us must set our hands to a mighty work, my lord and I from the hill, you and Aeron from the throne." She smiled at the look of utter astonishment on his face: *the throne?* "Oh aye, and others also—other realms, other thrones, other magics. And so, if you would have it, we shall set the mark of our people on you as we set it upon her—for several reasons, one in especial that you will learn to know better in time to come."

"Take this guerdon of the Sidhe," said Gwyn, and though he was not smiling he was not stern either. "It will not be the first one we have bestowed. Nor will it, I think, be the last. And all shall be needed where they are given."

Etain held out her left hand, and Gwydion saw the triple spiral that suddenly bloomed upon her white skin, filling her slender palm like a silver thread, a labyrinth itself.

"It is the mark of our people," said Gwyn evenly, seeing his doubt. "Our people who are also your own. Or do the old tales lie when they tell of the great love borne by ladies of your House to lords of mine, and of two faefolk princesses who for love of two Penarvon princes wedded and dwelled with them until they died? I do not think those stories speak falsely."

"Nay, that they do not," answered Gwydion after a moment or two. The stories were true indeed, at least if the histories of his own House had been told aright; but though he had never thought to doubt the tales, still had he never expected to be confronted full on with the proof of them. The Sidhe were not human, and they were not *like* humans: it was not that they were not to be trusted—it was common knowledge that they could not tell lies—but it was equally common knowledge that they could certainly slant the truth, and often did. They were unaccountable in their ways and dealings with mortals. They had magic that even Druids and Ban-draoi could not match, and their gifts to humans with whom they came in contact were unexpected and sometimes perverse. If they had chosen to return to the everyday Keltic world, they had their own reasons for it; and that was a thing perhaps worrisome, and certainly one to be watchful of. He made up his mind, suddenly and strongly.

"Well, then," he said, and held out his hand to Gwyn. But it was Etain who took it, Etain who traced three circles upon his palm, Etain who set the silver spirals alight in a cool blaze. Gwydion watched, breath caught and held, as the spirals formed and glittered, and looked at her with wonder plain upon his face.

"Man to woman, woman to man," she said gravely. "Save from parent to child, magic must pass so, if it is to pass correctly. And most especially so, with greatest care, where mortals are in it. But sidhaun blood is in you as your blood is in us—blood of mine, blood of my lord's. You are sidheanachta, kin of the faefolk. This mark merely confirms it, and it will be of greatest aid and use to you in days to come."

Gwydion stared at the spirals as they melted into his palm, sinking down beneath the skin and disappearing like water in a thirsty land, like frost in sunlight. As Aeron had experienced before him, he felt the silver design sink beneath the skin and come to rest there, chill and smooth for a moment, before it became part of his hand and he felt it no more.

"Though it is made and set there for greater trials than this," Etain said with laughter in her voice, "do you but show *that* to the Druid masters and I think you will not have to worry about having proper proof of your test's achievement! In truth, though, you cannot show them; it is not theirs to see. You yourself will forget it is there, until it shows itself in need. In any case, you did not leave your trial unfinished. You reached the Spring at the Heart of the World, and you take away with you proof to convince a thousand Druid masters — the silver water of the Last Well. Few enough candidates have ever come to the crown of Glaston; only two others have achieved to the Silver Spring, and those long since. The main of them are halted long before."

"Where, then, do they come to?"

She waved dismissive fingers. "Oh, another place, an elsewhere place. They finish their patterns as they are meant to. As you did. Not as other candidates, maybe, but you did."

"Better than they have ever done," came Gwyn's deep voice, thoughtfully. "More than they ever did. But it is time for us to part for now. Though not for long, at least as we count it."

Etain nodded, regret plain on her face. "We must take tonight's memory from you, until such time as it becomes needful for you to remember it. But we shall not forget. You will come to us in a time of need, bringing a treasure for safekeeping, though you will give your greatest treasure into peril, and into freedom at the last."

Gwydion would have thanked them profusely, but his heart was too full and his voice failed him. Still, it seemed as if they understood well what he would say, and were glad of it. The king nodded once, and Etain stepped forward and kissed Gwydion lightly upon the mouth, and Gwyn kissed him upon the brow. Then all was enveloped in a shining cloud: the great hall, the unearthly guests, the royal couple themselves. The last thing that lingered in the air before him was the eyes of the ghosthunter owl, Gwyn's eyes, burning through the cloud like the fire of the rising sun...

When Gwydion awoke in the brilliant dawn, sunlight showing bright and red-gold through his closed eyelids, he found himself lying on the crest of the Tor. He was wrapped in his cloak, diamonded with the dew that glittered all over the turf, and he was alone.

Well, at least I can see no one here with me, which is by no means the same thing as being alone. Indeed, I may never consider myself alone again...

He stood up, shaking himself all over, experimentally, but he seemed to be unharmed, all parts of him safely present and accounted for, and the all-important flask was hanging in its place at his hip. He could tell by its weight and by peering through the thick bubbled glass that the water of the Silver Spring remained in it; it had been no faerie gift that vanished with the dawn.

Though — he took his hands out of the pocket-slit in his tunic into which he had pushed them for warmth — his palm seemed oddly cold. Had it been merely a dream, then? A

glamour put upon him by the faefolk? He could recall little
bits and pieces: a grave dark king, a lovely laughing queen,
a revel beneath the hill; apparently his hosts beneath the Tor
had thought it better to allow small glimpses of what he had
seen, rather than wipe his memory clean of all and take his
victory from him. He was not quite sure how he felt about
it, or not just yet at least. He recalled his own journey: the
Red Spring and the wounded owl; the White Spring and the
voices in the air; the Dark Spring and the — and the what?
And why did the troublous, treacherous face of Kyttifer
Errwyn keep swimming into his sight?

The flooding early morning light, rushing out of the east
across the green plains, was breaking in gold waves upon
the sides of the Tor, like surf running up a beach. He saw
the dagger of thunderbolt iron, and the mossy sod of seizin
that lay beside it, as fresh and green and damp as when it
had been cut. But now there lay upon the little turf square
the white and bronze feather of an owl, glowing like an opal
in the dawn.

*So...not only my quest fulfilled, but my fetch found, my spirit-
animal — that is the message here...* After staring stupidly at it
for a moment, he came to himself, and took a small piece
of cloth from his pocket. Carefully wrapping the feather
and the small square of sod in it, he tucked both into the
leather belt-pouch. As he did so, he saw a brief tiny spark
of brilliant silver flash from his hand in the broadening
brightness, but nothing was visible to his sight that seemed
to have caused it.

He rubbed his palm against his breast, thoughtfully; it felt
as if *some*thing was there, right enough, somehow beneath his

very skin. Not painful—just *there*, like something his hand was holding. But however closely he peered, he could see nothing. Still, as he settled his cloak around him and began the descent of the Tor, by the long, easy sloping trackway that led down the western face and would have him back in the town in a mere ten minutes, he had the feeling that something had indeed been there, a gift for a gift; and with any luck, or dán, at all, it would be there again.

He could wait.

CRUCIBLE

crucible: in alchemy, a vessel where substances
come together to bring about a desired reaction

*3512 in the Common Reckoning,
3057 Anno Celtiae Conditae*

SARAH ROSE HONORA O'REILLY had never not planned on
going into the Federacy Navy. She had been born in
Sandiangeles, growing up her whole early life in that
enormous city-state that stretches for hundreds of miles,
from the Saltonsea in the far south all the way to the Topa
Topanga mountains north and west, along the new coastline
and eastwards to the far rim of the verdant and orchardful
Mojave Plain, where the great starport now stands.

Once, fifteen centuries ago, at the dawn of space flight
and before the Greatquake, that plain had been a hot, dry,
barren desert. There had been a testing base there, where
the first space shuttles landed, coming home from their
brief hops up to low earth orbit where the giant rockets
had thrown them. Over and over again, she had watched
the ancient footage on viewing crystals, mesmerized every
time at how the primitive craft seemed both ungainly and
graceful, like great fat silver geese, as they glided down

to Earth unpowered, only the supreme skill of the pilots to keep them from spiraling wild—astronauts, those first spacefarers had been called, 'star-sailors'. Even now, fifteen centuries later, their courage and their dash were admired.

Now that early test base was a major starship hub: from her childhood, she had been accustomed to watch the sleek ships taking off and landing beyond the mountains—lightyears away, both literally and figuratively, from those earliest stubby little sub-lunar shuttles. Usually the vessels she watched so longingly were only local ferries, bringing civilians and fleet personnel out beyond Luna in geosynchronous orbit, to where the giant interstellar ships were parked in the skyharbors, commercial and military alike, that served the western coast; every now and then a larger ship would rise into the cloudless skies, and if she was very lucky she would catch a glimpse of it.

But even the ferries were impressive; as for the greater craft, they looked gleaming and dangerous and powerful even in skydock, or taxiing majestically out of their berths to move away from the station to a safe takeoff distance. And then, once the stardrive was engaged, they looked like accelerating comets, surfing away from Terra's grasp on a sparkling rainbow wave, painting the heavens with fire and snow.

So when Sarah's aunt and uncle the much-decorated starfleet commanders had sat her down on her sixteenth birthday and asked if she would care to try for a place at the Western Academy, on track for a future commission, and if she did they would see what they could do about a recommendation, she had leapt at the chance, and when it had come through she had been ecstatic.

She had done well at school, graduating in the top tenth of a particularly talented year, even with a demanding course load — all the usual sciences and maths and histories and languages, but some rather surprising other study choices as well. She had wanted to be as free as possible to pick her own assignment; and when she was asked in her second year to declare her field of interest, with a career path in mind, she had not hesitated in choosing exploration and diplomacy.

After her graduation, it had taken several years' apprenticing in postings to small, unglamorous ships — census sloops, geology survey vessels and the like — to start getting the kind of assignments she coveted. No combat starships: she had never wanted that side of the Fleet, glamorous as many of her classmates had thought it. Her secretly held opinion had always been that no space duty tour was ever dull; you were in *space*, you were traveling to distant stars, meeting alien races — *how* could it *possibly* be *boring*? So by grace of her diplomatic training and language skills, she had soon won short-term assignments to embassy ships, a few, and had done well; the promotion to lieutenant was honestly and early earned, a little ahead of schedule, even, and at last she made the roster to serve on one of the coldsleep vessels.

A plum assignment, her absolute dream; or at least *she* thought so, good-naturedly ignoring her friends' teasing ("Only Sarah could fix it so she can sleep on the job for five years and get paid for it!"). The ships were themselves computer-assigned to patiently fly gridded searches at superlight speeds through sparse, unexplored quadrants, sailing past undistinguished systems that the ministers for such matters thought should be explored nonetheless. The coldsleep program, only a few decades old, was already paying big dividends in new contacts and encounters; it was expensive, but funding was there, and even so it was enormously more cost-effective than if active ships with awake personnel were sent out to do the same job.

It had been carefully explained to her that the odds were overwhelming that she would merely sleep for the entire five-year tour and wake up back home none the worse for wear, not having appreciably aged—a coldsleep benefit— and not having seen or discovered a single damn thing in the whole term of voyage; and always there was the outside chance that she might never wake up again at all. Accidents happened in coldsleep, and ships far larger and better defended than hers would be had been taken out by meteors or swatted by the unexpected tail of a comet or blown to bits by trigger-happy aliens who shot first and asked later. She had not cared, couldn't sign on fast enough. Because you just never knew, and you just had to try.

Besides, if the worst happened, at least you'd never know what hit you.

The name of her ship was the Sword, a spacious six-berther with lovely, graceful lines, newly rebuilt from a small destroyer and equally newly commissioned for its first coldsleep run, and Sarah fell in love with it on sight. Its captain was Theo Haruko, an older and experienced commander whose last mission this would be before well-earned retirement; he was Japanasian by birth, with a reputation for cleanly honorable dealings and great fairness, like a samurai of old, and O'Reilly had liked him immediately. Sarah herself was communications officer and junior diplomatist, her training and language skills at the Academy having factored heavily into her selection for this voyage. The other crewmembers were her fellow Lieutenants Warren Hathaway, astrogator and de facto second officer, and Hugh Tindal, science officer; and Ensigns Athenée Mikhailova, technical officer, and Tarquin Gro, engineering and weapons. They were not all entirely congenial—Mikhailova was young and shy and a bit naïve, and could be a little annoying from time to time, and Tindal was a smirking, cynical boor whom they all pretty much loathed, though very good at his job, which was why he'd been chosen. But for the most part they got on well enough, and as Hathaway had privately remarked to O'Reilly, they'd all be asleep anyway, so what the hell difference did it make.

As it turned out, it would make a very great difference indeed. What the Sword was to discover, and then precipitate, would soon shake a goodly portion of the settled galaxy to its very foundations. But in those first blazing days of initial contact and the beginnings of interstellar diplomacy between Earth and its new and mighty friend, many things came unlooked-for to the birth…

The Sword's launch from Aristarchus skyharbor had been typically uneventful, and its crew's descent into the comfortable antigravity field of coldsleep equally effortless. The flight plan, tested many times by other crews on previous exploratories, was for all personnel to manually set the ship on course and then retire to their sleep berths, there to remain until, if ever, the ship gave them a wakeup call — a subcutaneous, microscopic alarm set to ping on the left mastoid process, the bulging bone behind the ear. This would normally occur, ideally, if the instruments picked up signs of civilization: a planet with intelligent life, or an approaching ship. The protocol was for the captain to be brought online, as it were, first; then, when he had been given his wakeup sprayshot by the medidroid and had assessed the situation, he would either awaken at least O'Reilly and Hathaway to discuss options or call the event himself. If consensus was that contact should be attempted, then the remaining crew would be brought out of sleep and the diplomatic mission would commence. If not, Haruko would go back to bed without troubling anyone else, and everyone would be left to slumber on, in the bright, vivid, complex dreams of coldsleep.

There had been a sad and unscheduled awakening about a year into the sail: Ensign Gro died in his sleep, totally unexpectedly, and the ship had brought all of them out of hibernation to attend to it. Mikhailova, who served as medtech in the absence of a full-time doctor, had declared as her official medical opinion that a congenital and undetected aneurysm had blown, and so quickly had it occurred that he had not even woken up to die. When medical emergencies occurred, the beds in which the crew slept were set to heal, if possible, the person involved, without waking him or her; if the bed could not cope, it was supposed to wake the crew so that the afflicted one could be taken to one of the more specialized and better-equipped medbeds. But on this occasion it had neither coped nor alerted, and Tarquin Gro had slipped painlessly from coldsleep into something longer and deeper.

They had finally been informed of the incident by the main computer that routinely scanned the entire ship; it had discovered the anomaly of only five live sleeping forms, not six, and had belatedly alerted them to the event. Clearly, there was no question of it being anything but a sad accident, a malfunction of both technology and anatomy. Such things happened with infrequency these days, but they did happen; hence the fearsome waiver that all coldsleep personnel signed beforehand.

Haruko had verified the death, along with Mikhailova as medical officer; and then, led by the captain and with Sarah serving as ad hoc chaplain, the five survivors had conducted a brief funeral service, in the age-old shipboard fashion. Gro had not been a practitioner of any particular religion, so the service had been both simple and nonsectarian. Mikhailova had taken care to make a recording of the ceremony to be sent to Gro's parents, who had been fleet officers themselves, on the monthly subspace carrier waves that brought status reports back to Earth; it seemed cold for them to learn so of their son's death, but it would be colder still to make them wait four years more for the tragic news in person. The late ensign's flag-wrapped body was placed back in his sleep pod, which was then sealed to form a casket and launched out into the vast burial ground of interstellar space.

Burial at sea, in the starfaring age: apart from the location and the technology, it was not very much different from burial at sea in the eighteenth century, when a sailor who had died aboard one of the wooden sailing-ships of that time was sewn into his sleeping-hammock, weighted with roundshot, and then slipped over the side from under the flag of his vessel, into the open arms of the rolling ocean. Now, in the thirty-sixth century, Haruko had followed the tradition as best he could. But he had been angry, though at what or whom he was forever after unsure, while the others were merely subdued and sad; they had returned to their own sleepbeds as quickly as they might, saying very little to one another. All of them thought of Tarquin Gro before closing their eyes.

When the alarm sounded again, a year further into the sail and almost at the point of turnaround, Sarah O'Reilly opened her eyes and found herself staring blearily at the bulkhead above her, where she had affixed photocubes of family, friends and favorite places. She smiled at the familiar faces and scenes, then suddenly it dawned on her. Awake. She was awake. The alarm had gone off. She had just gotten the sprayshot to wake her up. That must mean… *Oh please God let it be different from last time, let it be real this time, for all our sakes…*

She jumped up, pulling on her flightsuit over the light skivvies they all slept in—no need for a sonic shower or other physical needs to be attended to, the beds kept them all clean, fed and relieved—and dashed forward to find Haruko already there on the bridge. The others came stumbling in along with her, and Sarah could hear the footfalls gradually slow and still as they saw what she saw.

"There's not supposed to be anyone around here for parsecs," said Mikhailova in a hushed voice. "Who could they be, do you think?"

All the screens showed the same thing: a very sleek-looking black and silver ship, with no markings that they could see, at least from this angle, heading straight for them. Very, very swiftly.

Tindal muttered something, then, louder: "O'Reilly, say hello to them."

Haruko, annoyed, confirmed the order, which should have been his to give, not Tindal's, but O'Reilly had already seated herself at her communications console and had begun tapping out greetings and assurances of peace on the lightcoder, in Englic first of all, as the galactic common or trading language, then a few other likely tongues, then as still no answer was forthcoming, in the twenty-three other spacegoing languages at present known to the Federacy, plus a few wild cards of her own.

Suddenly the board blazed with an incoming coherent response; Sarah automatically translated, then let out a startled shout. "LATIN! They speak *Latin*! Oh my God—"

Her fingers danced over the keypad, and without even a pause more Latin came back at her. A look of delight began to spread over her face, though as of yet the other had no clue and she in her joyful transport was totally forgetting to provide a translation.

"Coming on visual," said Tindal from his portside chair, feeling irritated and left out.

As one, they all stared. Human, or at least humanoid. Very tall, lots of hair, rather strangely dressed. O'Reilly continued to shoot Latin back at them, verbal now as well as lightcode—all those language studies at the academy were finally paying off. The more the strangers spoke, though, the more bemused she got: maybe sometime soon now she would get something she could tell the others, because so far she was finding it really, really hard to buy any of this... Then the language changed, no longer Latin but a musical-sounding tongue, for all it seemed to be made up of nothing but consonants, and guttural ones at that.

I have not got a CLUE... Sarah, who hated to admit linguistic defeat, quickly cut in the computer, and suddenly sat back hard in her chair, stunned.

"Lieutenant O'Reilly?" The captain's voice had sharpened just enough to pierce her momentary distraction.

"Yes, sir. Sorry, sir. Gaelic. I mean that's what they're speaking. Gaelic! It's not possible, but there it is."

"Gaelic? You mean—these people are Irish? The Irish are in outer space?" Well, it was possible, he supposed, for there to be some pan-Celtic star exploration program he did not know about, though it seemed unlikely...

Feeling a bit at sea, and more at home in Latin, Sarah ventured a bit more, with a heavy interrogative slant to it, and received a long string of it back. Smiles broke out then, like a tremulous bit of sunshine, on both sides.

"No...no, they're from Earth. Earth! Well, originally from Earth. I mean, not this lot, but—"

It was all too much. She couldn't deal, and the strangers were watching her calmly to see what would happen next;

the feeling coming over the screens was amusement and not a little enjoyment at her befuddled state.

"Pull yourself together," murmured Haruko, and with a tremendous effort Sarah managed to compose herself.

"Sir. They *said* they are from an interstellar monarchy known as Keltia, and they, or their ancestors I should say, have been out here since Earth year 453 C.R. Not Celts. Kelts. They're — Kelts."

Now it was Haruko's turn to feel dizzy, and judging by the expressions on the others' faces, they were not exactly stable themselves.

"Do they speak Englic?" he asked presently, forgetting that that had been the first language sent out. It was a trading tongue, almost all aliens could speak a little...

"No, not these two. They're just scouts, on patrol from a destroyer in the area, and their sloop has no language computer. But they've sent a message to their ship; they say there are people on board her who do speak Englic, and down on their worlds plenty of people speak it too, so they don't think we'll have much trouble. Latin is their own diplomatic language, though, and they suggest we all sleep-study it intensively, and maybe a little of the Gaeloch, as they call it, too, before..."

Hathaway stirred for the first time, over at his own station across the bridge "Before what?"

Sarah gestured helplessly out the port, and on the other screen the Kelts smiled back at her. "Before whatever."

"Mother of poodles!"

Hathaway continued to swear quietly and creatively to himself; the rest of the crew of the Sword merely stared. It was barely a full ship's day later, and they were back again clustered on the bridge and staring at the viewscreens. Then they would all turn their heads aside in unison, to stare through the ports to see it for real, then back to the screens that magnified it many hundreds of times, for what they were gazing at was still very, very far away. But closing fast, faster than they had ever seen anything move outside of hyperspace.

Well, it was six things they were gazing at, to be precise. And one of them was bigger than anything any of them had ever seen in their lives. Haruko shook his head in wonder. A ship ten miles long and a mile and a half wide. *How the hell does anyone get around inside it? Unless most of it is engine room, or motiver space...maybe they use internal transporters, or plates, or jumpers...what's their motiving power, I wonder? Any ship that can move like that...matter/antimatter? Dark-matter drive? Black holes? White holes? Or something we've never even imagined?*

"I make her more than twelve times bigger than the Empress Elisabeth," Mikhailova was saying, in a voice she was trying very hard to keep matter-of-fact. "Four times the size of Leviathan! I don't even want to *guess* at her armaments." A note of outraged astonishment colored her voice: those two ships, commercial and military respectively, were the biggest starcraft that the Terran Federacy had, and she was feeling a bit indignant on their behalf to see them so outmatched.

O'Reilly, instead, was grinning with a kind of idiot pride. If the foreign flagship, for surely it could be nothing else, was going to be bigger than anything else around, how great that it was Irish, right? Well, Keltic. Her people, in any case. In the few hours they had been waiting for the flagship's arrival, O'Reilly had grown so eager to meet these strangers who spoke her own tongue and carried her own blood that she could hardly sit still. She had been talking to the two officers in the scout ship, and had learned more and more with every passing moment.

She had not begun from a place of total ignorance, the way her fellow crew members had. From childhood, she had done much reading on the history of her race, and she knew all about the legends of their heroic past: stories of warriors and explorers, kings and goddesses; and now she was calling up records of half-forgotten tales, reinterpreting them in the light of new knowledge. There were things called vitrified forts in remote areas of Ireland and Scotland, places where the ground itself had been melted into great shiny expanses of glassy slag, such as no little prehistoric campfires could ever have caused to happen. She recalled how she had pondered over those fascinating stories, as a child, and later at the starfleet academy: explanations, all wildly unsatisfactory, posited everything from miniature black holes passing through the landscape to the vestigial scars of siege weapons from ancient Atlantis, theories that had been relegated to loopy books and supermarket journalism, still somehow alive and well and not so loopy after all, in the age of star travel.

Now she stared open-mouthed at the small display

screen by her console, at the pictures she had pulled up, wondering if maybe those glassed-over places on the screen were indeed some of the original grounds from where the Kelts, as they now called themselves, had launched themselves into space. *Nothing like seeing a lunatic theory prove itself out...I will ask our new friends, just as soon as I can. I wonder if they know about the Loch Ness monster. Or Lemuria. But at the moment...*

At the moment, the small foreign fleet had now come to a halt beside their position in space, and unconsciously they all rose to their feet as the great flagship paused itself a safe distance away, smoothly and instantaneously. It looked like a dragon. A huge golden dragon ten miles long, hanging like a comet in the dark. A ship of war that looked like a work of art. What like were they, the race that had thought it and built it? Who were they, the race that now sailed it?

The same questions were in all five Terran heads, with answers not thick on the ground, nor, clearly, immediately forthcoming. There followed a brief period of spirited discussion, between Captain Haruko and his apparently Englic-fluent opposite number aboard the Keltic flagship—the Firedrake by name, they had been told. O'Reilly, lost in dreamy contemplation, startled suddenly at the sound of her name.

"Sir?"

"Prepare some kind of welcome speech, Lieutenant. Whatever you think appropriate and historic. You're going to have company."

'You'? Not 'we'? "And you, sir?"

Haruko smiled at his favorite crewman. "I have to take a

little trip." He nodded out the port. "Over there." And tried to ignore the look of deep and instant envy on O'Reilly's face.

The Sword soon took its visitor aboard: Gwennan Chynoweth, the captain of the Firedrake, who was making her own exchange visit of inspection to their ship, just as Haruko was doing aboard her vessel. She was courteous in the extreme, if rather less than informative. But presently the two visits were over; the Keltic captain had returned to her dragon craft, and Haruko had, with great relief, come back to his own, vastly tinier vessel. He looked deeply shaken, and though he did not choose to explain himself, his crew, who knew him well enough by now, had known not to press him. He had muttered a few things, then had ordered a relaxer sprayshot and headed straight for the cabin he used when not in coldsleep, and firmly shut the door behind him.

The four of them talked a little while among themselves, then headed for their own cabins. They all had quarters for use in waking hours, even though they were meant to spend most of their time in the pods. But it served no purpose to retire into the coldsleep berths when they needed to be awake for a prolonged period, as they did now, and a change of scene as well as consciousness kept them on an even keel in more ways than one.

They were all glad to avail themselves of time awake: Hathaway headed for the exercise room, while Tindal said he had some private experiments to look at and Mikhailova curled up in the library to entertain herself for a bit. But Sarah stared out the port at the giant golden ship, like a meerkat looking at a buffalo herd, eager and curious and a little wistful, a bit uncomprehending, a bit longing, a bit scared. Well, they were going to find out soon enough what they had unwittingly sailed into. But it couldn't come soon enough for her.

It had quickly been determined that contact having been made, political relations should speedily be established. To that end, the Sword followed the destroyer Glaistig to a nearby Keltic quarantine planet known as Inishgall, the Island of the Foreigners, about halfway between their former location and Keltia itself. There they were subjected to not only quite sophisticated quarantine practices but to a brief introductory course in the history of Keltia, their new temporary home. Their instructors were impressive: the charming Princess Melangell, cousin to the Keltic queen— yes, it was a working monarchy, which thrilled O'Reilly to her inmost soul and deeply annoyed Tindal—and a dark, inscrutable bard called Morgan Cairbre. Between them, they imparted to their Terran visitors all the critical information that they would need to know before arriving on the Keltic Throneworld of Tara, and the crew of the Sword received it and stored it gratefully away.

They remained on the quarantine planet for three days, adjusting to the situation and to their hosts, discussing what the reaction might be on the other end, whether the Keltic rulers were having as interesting a time adjusting to the situation as the Terrans were; the consensus was, more so. On the fourth morning, the bard Cairbre announced to them at breakfast that they would be leaving for Keltia as soon as the guests could finish their meal and gather up their belongings. Moreover, he informed them that they would be making this voyage not on the Sword but on the Glaistig, as the big destroyer was keyed to pass through some kind of defense called the Curtain Wall and the Terran ship was not. In fact, it would be towed empty behind the Keltic craft all the way to their destination — the safest course, according to their hosts.

As might be imagined, this did not sit entirely well with some members of the Sword's complement. As might be expected, opinion divided along previously and precisely established planes of cleavage: Haruko, Hathaway and O'Reilly on one side, Mikhailova and Tindal on the other. It had fallen out suchwise on all too many occasions, making pretty much all of them look forward devoutly to the peace they hoped awaited them at journey's end.

But first they had to get there. O'Reilly, her personal possessions already sent aboard the Glaistig, was in the shuttle before the others, hoping to secure herself a position away from pretty much all of them. She loathed Tindal, of course, had no feeling one way or another towards the wishy-washy Mikhailova, and though she liked both Hathaway and Haruko, just now she didn't want to be near them either. This was an epic journey, somehow solemn — a pilgrimage of sorts — and she wanted very much to do it alone, as all good quests were done. She huddled against the glass of the little porthole, looked upwards, and prayed to be off.

The quest was accomplished quicker than any of them could have expected: only a few hours later, and they were approaching something vast and dark and strange—a roiling, churning sea shot by lightnings and storms that no world had ever seen. It was a starless void yet the very birthplace of stars, visible even from Earth, where it was listed in the astronomy texts under a different name, and even there was regarded with suspicion and wariness, if not downright fear. Under whatever name, though, it was no place that anyone in their right mind wanted to be in the same quadrant with, and yet here the Kelts were sailing straight for it, completely unconcerned, if Sarah was any judge.

Melangell, who stood near her, smiled at the look of consternation on the faces of all the visitors. "Do not worry. It is many, many star-miles off. We do not go that way. Just nearby."

"But—what is it?"

"That is the Dead Sea of space, the Morimaruse. It has long been our first defense."

Tindal smiled derisively. "How do you figure?"

"For that it has been so ever since we came to Keltia," she replied, not offended in the slightest. "Lying as it does between us and the most thickly settled galactic regions, it serves as a powerful discouragement for any starfaring race to take a chance finding out what lies beyond, and so discovering us. For many centuries it was the only defense we had; then St. Morgan raised the Wall to be our good shield, and we were safe forever. Now, when a ship comes too close to the Curtain Wall, it is transported to the other side of the Morimaruse, unharmed, but no doubt very confused. And reluctant to try again."

Sarah dragged her eyes away from the rapidly approaching star-maw. "Okay, if you say so..."

Another Kelt moved over to O'Reilly's side, at a subtle inclination of Melangell's head, and the princess herself moved to stand beside Haruko. As the Terrans could see, each of them now had a Keltic protector, or companion. *And why might that be?* She looked up at the tall blond-bearded officer beside her, but before she could ask, he answered.

"It is a little difficult going through the Curtain Wall for the first time. Better if you have someone with you."

"In case I faint?" asked Sarah nastily.

He laughed. "Or worse! It has been known to happen, even to strong warriors. I am sure you will do fine enough, Lieutenant. Oh, my sorrow, I am Commander Ardan mac Galaher, bridge officer. But look on the screen — we are just now coming to the Wall."

O'Reilly looked to the screen he had indicated; and though she did not faint, she did feel a certain dizzying dislocation, a very definite nausea in the back of her throat, and she would sooner have died where she stood than let the Keltic commander see what she felt. The Morimaruse had been unsettling enough, but this... The Curtain Wall: as Morgan Cairbre had told them on Inishgall, this was the greatest achievement of the Keltic people, and it was beyond staggering. It looked like a vast sheet of white-blue fire frozen in place, unflickering and unmoving, and it went on forever, as far and far as she could see in all directions. But it did not appear outside the big windows, only on half a dozen of the main screens on the bridge.

"Why can't I see it outside the port?" said O'Reilly, very precisely, trying not to lose her already stretched grip on her personal composure, not to mention her breakfast.

"It was designed to appear so, or rather to not appear so. For the benefit of any enemy trying to get through — which is, I may say, impossible. Our defenses are unbreakable."

Yeah, right, and how many times have I heard that *in the course of my Navy life?* "We were told it was set up and run by magic," she continued, still in the precise careful voice, as if he had not spoken at all.

"True is that word," he agreed. "Centuries ago, by Morgan Magistra."

"St. Morguenna of the Pale," said Sarah vaguely. She shivered once. "So all that is *real*? What that bard told us?"

Ardan nodded. "Oh aye. She was the greatest sorcerer we have ever had, along with her own brother — Arthur. If anyone could have raised the Wall for our protection, it would have been she. She summoned to its raising every being in Keltia who possessed any sort of magic at all, from Druids and Ban-draoi to Dragon Kinship members to those who had nothing but small-magic to do household pishogues. Even the Sidhe helped, I have heard," he added in a lower voice. "The Shining Ones themselves, and all the sidhaun folk, the merrows and silkies and even the little hobs of the hills. It was our great work, and we all set our hands to it, to put all the magic of Keltia into it. And it was raised, at terrible cost, and it has lasted fifteen centuries, keeping us hidden from the rest of the galaxy."

While he was speaking, O'Reilly was not really listening to

him, and most of what he was saying was incomprehensible to her anyway. So she had merely watched with increasing dread as the sheet of blue light drew closer and closer. And then, with only the faintest of shivers, as though something heavy had punched the Glaistig's hull, they were through the Wall. O'Reilly took a step closer to the viewport, as if in a trance: in the vast expanse of space before her, seven stars now burned, and bright planets spun around the nearest.

"Our Throneworld," said Ardan mac Galaher, nodding toward a splendid ringed and double-mooned planet slightly bigger than Earth itself. "Tara."

O'Reilly looked up to where Haruko was standing with Melangell. "Welcome, Haruko," she heard the princess say. "Oh, welcome to Keltia."

Trailing behind her escort, a palace page in livery of the royal green, O'Reilly was too busy staring around her at the halls of the huge royal fortress of Turusachan to pay much attention to how they went. Her escort was more than willing to talk, being just as intrigued by the new arrivals from Erith, as they called it, as they were with their hosts; but both were finding it difficult to speak. Too many questions fighting themselves to get out, too many impressions to sort out. So they deferred to each other with such politeness and courtesy that very few things were said, though great goodwill was communicated, and many smiles.

At last they came to the end of a long hallway of polished light-colored stone. The double doors before them had intricate decoration on them, inlaid in oh my God could that be actual *gold*? Sarah wasn't sure, and didn't want to look foolish by asking. It didn't matter anyway, and it was already forgotten as she entered the spacious rooms. They were high up in one of the fortress's guest-wing corridors, and she could see through the windows across the sitting room the spectacular view that lay before her: on one side the sea, on the other side the great city through which they had just been triumphantly borne in open chariots.

Caerdroia — Spiral Castle — the capital and first-founded city of Keltia, lay upon the knees of a mountain range called, they had been told, the Loom; the city ran back from the valley floor up the slopes of Mount Eagle, and Turusachan sprawled across a broad flat ledge overlooking the sea, some fifteen hundred feet above the plain, the highest point of the city. The castle ran back further up, ascending the mountain in assorted terraces and wings and quadrangles, so that its highest tower was itself more than another thousand feet above the lowest courtyard.

We've seen a lot of stuff, but this is power on a scale we couldn't have dreamed. And what an interesting blend of the archaic and the grand technological this place is…they get around with horses, and horses pulling chariots, and yet this magic wall of invisible light surrounds their seven star systems — seven! — and hides them from the sight of the entire galaxy…oh, yeah, and what about that magic, too…

They had also been presented to the ruler of this place, the High Queen Aeron, and her ministers and councilors. It had been a rather intimidating event: thousands of people assembled in a hall whose ceiling was an arched dome three hundred feet high; a long, long walk down a carpeted aisle, at the end of which was a seven-stepped dais and a throne carved from cream-colored granite standing atop it. And on the throne…

She grinned and shook her head, scrambling up to kneel happily on the window seat, leaning out. She hadn't known what to expect, meeting a queen, but certainly she had not expected *that*. Her. Aeron Aoibhell. To begin with, she was so young, only a few years older than Sarah herself. And she was so composed, and so…well, so *royal*. She laughed then. What else should a queen be but royal? There were still kings and queens on Earth, she knew, but the titles they bore were purely honorific, denoting and acknowledging nothing more than a long and documented pedigree; no one in their right mind would have dreamed of giving any Terran royalty the smallest speck of real control, and in any case their countries had all gone over to far more democratic systems many centuries ago. Yet here was this young woman running an interstellar empire, with unimaginable power at her sole personal command, all according to a monarchical model long obsolete on Earth, and was a mighty sorceress to boot.

Keltia. Sarah shook her head. It still seemed incredible to her, that such an empire, though none of its inhabitants called it that, of seven star systems with all the vast and powerful reach of a protectorate consisting of many systems more, should have managed to remain completely hidden for so long. *Hidden only from Earth, though. From us…* The Kelts were well known throughout many quadrants, their trade — and wars — being, as someone had told them, outward from Earth, and their paths, and those of their friends and enemies, unlikely to have crossed Earth's just yet.

O'Reilly frowned, and leaned her chin in her hands as she looked out over the stunning view. Her people had learned from other exploratory voyages that monarchy and even empire were both alive and well, and in many cases flourishing. But here were all sorts of new affiliations that Terrans had never even heard of, all of them sounding pretty nasty: the Cabiri Imperium of the Coranians, for one, apparently a major thorn in the collective galactic side and particularly in the Kelts'; the loose affiliation known as the Phalanx, led by Fomor, another difficult system; Firvolgior, a single world, but vastly influential in trade; many more doubtless as yet undiscovered and undealt with by Earth.

O'Reilly barely heard her escort bidding her a good rest and informing her that he would return in four hours to show her down to dinner, as she would never find the place herself. She roamed around the chambers in a haze of fizzy delight: bouncing on the bed, a monstrous fourposted affair curtained with tapestries and wide enough for six people; admiring the fur coverlet and the gold-framed portraits adorning the paneled walls and the huge marble fireplace; marveling at the vast bathchamber, where a tiled pool large enough to swim in was steaming gently away, heated by the thermal springs that rose from far beneath the Loom, gift of remnant volcanism.

As to the implications of their arrival, it was all too much to think on. She decided she would let Haruko do that, he being the captain and all, and Hathaway as second officer; she was only third in rank, though as junior diplomatist she was second to the captain alone. Either way, such matters were far above her pay grade. But since she was after all the communications officer, she planned on doing some serious communicating, and was looking forward to it. These Kelts were courteous enough to speak to them in Englic, and that was fine and helpful for now, but you couldn't expect them to go on doing so forever.

Back aboard the Sword, she had resolved that if the effort killed her stone-cold dead, all five Terrans would be reasonably fluent in the Gaeloch, the standard and mellifluous Keltic speech—an amalgam of all the Celtic tongues of Earth, with some new linguistic permutations added over the last three millennia—by the end of a fortnight. It could be accomplished easily enough, and it was only courteous. Latin too, if she could whip them into it. It was also only prudent: if secrets or comments were being passed right in front of them, O'Reilly was damn well going to know all about it. True, the Kelts probably had many regional vernaculars that they could employ to speak freely in front of the Terrans and still keep their own counsel, and there was really no help for that, she couldn't learn *every* single dialect; but she would do what she could, and she had done quite a bit already.

And, she realized with a shiver of delight, it was going to be *fun*.

At the formal feast that night in their honor, held in the huge and impressive royal banqueting hall of Mi-cuarta, O'Reilly found herself, for the first time in her life or even her imagination, seated at table with royalty and asking them to please pass the salt. Well, actually there was a solid gold salt dish and spoon at each place, so no, that wouldn't happen, but still. Excellent food and wine too, no weird horrible exotic native dishes, fish's eyeballs and the like, that she would have to choke down a decent helping of, just to show willing and not offend anyone; diplomacy could often be really, really painful, and so could the cuisine. But this food she could have dined on in any elegant restaurant at home: several different soups, platters of shellfish, roasts and stuffed fowl, assorted vegetables and rice dishes, luscious desserts, even a course of assorted savouries.

She glanced around, trying not to stare. Her fellow officers had all risen to the occasion, and she was so proud of them: Haruko, seated beside the Queen in the place of honor, was listening with genuine interest to that lady's undoubtedly well-practiced tabletalk, while Hathaway seemed to be regaling his neighbors with entertaining stories, as everyone in his immediate vicinity was roaring with laughter; Mikhailova had gamely set aside her shyness and was speaking volubly to her dinner partner, and even Tindal was conversing amiably with those near him. Sarah felt prouder still: all that high-speed sleep-speech language learning had obviously paid off — her associates were acting like the diplomats they had been trained to be. And their table manners, which had also been enforced by a crash course in etiquette, were perfection itself.

She turned her speculative gaze on her hosts. All the Kelts seemed equally pleased with their guests, so that boded well; they were looking quite splendid in robes, or gowns, or tunics and breeches. Thankfully, the organizers of the sleepship program had been foresighted enough to stow aboard all levels of uniform, so at least the five of them were suitably clad for dinner in their best dress kit, awards included; Haruko looked especially impressive, his formal samurai kimono befitting his warrior heritage, though he did forego the two swords for the occasion. But eyeing the far more gorgeously appareled Kelts, with equal parts envy and admiration, Sarah resolved to go shopping for clothes just as soon as she had the chance, and not have to wear a dreary old uniform at every banquet. If dinners like this were to be a regular feature of her immediate and indefinite future, then by Dobeis, New Cretan god of merchants, she was going to look the part and honor the table.

Her gaze was drawn again toward the center place at the long polished board, where Aeron sat beside her consort, Gwydion, the Prince of Gwynedd and First Lord of War, with Haruko on her right and Morwen to partner him. Sarah had a feeling this was not the usual arrangement, but diplomacy invariably prevailed and she likewise suspected that few occasions could have been more diplomacious, or indeed more historic, than this one. She was only a few places down from them, with the Queen's heir-presumptive, Prince Rohan, as her own dinner partner, and some other royal she remembered meeting, briefly, on her other side.

Pushing her food around her plate, Sarah covertly studied the Queen. Aeron Aoibhell, Queen for only the past three years, was very good to look at, as the Terrans had observed that afternoon at the formal reception in the Hall of Heroes; but so were most of the people in the hall, royal or not—obviously a superior gene pool. She was tall and elegant, athletic-looking, like a dancer or a fencer, with long, long dark-red hair, pale skin, the grass-green eyes that so often went with that coloring. At the moment, she was laughing heartily at a story that Haruko was telling to her and Gwydion and Morwen; though O'Reilly was seated a place or two beyond hearing range, she could still observe. Morwen had a pleased and pleasing appearance to her, with dark-gold hair and blue eyes like the rest of her family, the aspect of an amused lioness, while Gwydion bore more the look of a hunting hawk, dark and alert. As for Haruko, he had not looked so free from care, O'Reilly guessed, for many months; certainly not since their encounter with the Glaistig, perhaps not since the death of Ensign Gro, and it pleased her very much to see it.

Sarah continued to watch them, until her attention was reclaimed by her own table partners and she turned back to converse with them. Still, she cast her glance out over the rest of the huge chamber whenever she could. She had been told that the diners here tonight were not the usual ones — the people who called the fortress home, or worked there, or were stationed there — but instead carefully chosen guests from all over Keltia, of rank or powerful position or other such importance as to have merited an invitation. Several hundred of them, probably, and Sarah was all too uncomfortably aware of their gazes, whether those were covert glances or cheerfully open stares.

Mercifully, Aeron did not keep them long once the meal was finished; she left the table rather abruptly, bidding her guests good night and vanishing, presumably, to her own rooms. Which set the visitors free to do likewise; O'Reilly, skipping the music and merrymaking, hauled herself upstairs in company with Mikhailova and Haruko. Bidding her colleagues goodnight, each outside their own quarters, she collapsed on her bed, so glad to be there, staring up at the blue-frescoed, star-bespangled vaulted ceiling.

That was probably the longest damn day in the whole entire damn history of days. You might well think that local time and space were rearranged strictly for our benefit...

She kicked off her boots, pulled off her dress jacket and trousers and burrowed under the coverlet, hearing nothing but the crash, far below, of waves rolling in to break against the cliffs, listening to the familiar sound and finding herself strangely soothed thereby. *Yeah...and just what does that say for time and space to come?*

In the days following, O'Reilly found herself much at leisure to wander about Caerdroia. At first a Fian guard had accompanied her, and she supposed this made sense: she didn't have a clue as to where she was going, and they were after all honored guests and perhaps needed to be protected, against the curious crowds if nothing else. But after a week, when she had gently made it plain that she preferred roaming around the city by herself and was familiar enough with local geography to be trusted on her own, she had been allowed to do so — though she suspected that her guard had merely been ordered to make itself invisible, not absent.

"You are not prisoners here, Lieutenant," Morwen Douglas had said, smiling — the Taoiseach, the Prime Minister, who despite her highest office, or perhaps because of it, seemed to be the Kelt chiefly responsible for the Terrans' welfare. "You are our honored guests, and you may do as you like, within the confines of your own duties. Be sure that if we need your presence, you will be called for; and if there is anywhere we do not wish you to go, for any reason, you will not find your way there. But I cannot think of any such place in this city, so feel free to wander as you please. Anyone will help you if you get lost; you have but to ask."

Indeed that had been true, and even something of a problem. On her first venture out unaccompanied, she had gotten seriously turned around in the charming, twisty lanes of the ancient section known as the Stonerows; a timid inquiry as to how to get back to the castle elicited not only a flood of easy directions but friendly questions and invitations alike. She was running out of polite excuses to decline supper, and was no nearer her goal, when she caught sight of Hathaway strolling down the street in her direction, looking far too much at home for his own good, and she almost wept with relief as she hastened up to him.

"Well, of *course* I look at home, silly girl, because, unlike you, I studied a map or two before venturing out. As I always do," he said loftily, when she taxed him with it. "And therefore I am prepared. As I always am. But come on, let's go shopping. Didn't you say you wanted to buy some new threads? The palace steward changed our trading currency into local and also gave us code cards, to draw upon the royal bourse if we ran short. He also warned me that we probably wouldn't be allowed to pay for a thing anyway."

"Better and better."

Though O'Reilly and Hathaway agreed on their way back to
Turusachan that they were still being prudently kept watch
on lest an incident, or an accident, befall them that might
have unfortunate interstellar repercussions, or even just
local personal ones, they and the others accepted the fact
with a good grace and did not let it trouble them, though
Tindal, predictably, grumbled about it until the rest of them
were ready to bash his head in with a poker. It did not matter
to her, as long as she could wander around the endlessly
fascinating streets. Sometimes she did so in company with
her fellow officers, usually Hathaway or Mikhailova. Tindal
was not a favorite with her: she had no idea how he spent
his time, or with whom, and could not have cared less; and
Haruko was generally busy with diplomatic chores, which
meant he was frequently closeted with Aeron and Morwen.

Perversely, once she had established her preference
for being alone, Sarah suddenly decided she wanted local
company, and had let it be known. No one had batted an
eye at her change of attitude, and her newly assigned guides
changed from day to day. Most often she was companioned
by Slaine Aoibhell, another of Aeron's apparently
inexhaustible cousinage, or else a sharp-witted young
woman named Sabia ní Dálaigh, who had been with Aeron
at warrior-training school and who remained close friends
with her, knowing much of her mind and mood. More to
the present point, both young women also knew all the
best markets and craftsmen in the city, and were delighted
to share both their knowledge and their enthusiasm for
shopping, and so it was that O'Reilly became the proud
owner of more Keltic merchandise, and that of other worlds

as well, than the rest of her comrades combined. She did not worry about it: Sabia had told her that anything she wished could be sent home to family or friends from the Kelts' trading planet of Clero.

"We have regular post-ships that can get to Clero in less than a day, and dispatchers who will be happy to send on anything you wish, under the royal frank. What? Nay, of course there is no fee; you are ambassadors as well as guests. Post reaches Erith in less than a fortnight; we can send non-sentient items more speedily than we can get people there, though not of course faster than messages."

They were both admiring Sarah's purchases to date, spread out on her vast bed: things for her family and friends back home, and of course a tidy few items for herself — beautifully crafted jewelry, knotworked leather, gold- and silver-shot brocade tunics trimmed with fur, a set of cups in various gemstones, lovely artworks, even some enchanting toys for her young nieces and nephews. And, of course, the Keltic clothing she had coveted from the first: the graceful dresses called gúnas, so reminiscent of medieval Earth garb, some with wench-style bodices; for more casual occasions, tunics and breeches and boots, full-sleeved shirts and leather doublets.

She had tried her best to pay for it all, but as Hathaway had warned her, just about every bit of it had been gifts, pressed upon her by shopkeepers eager to boast that they had had the custom of the foreign visitors and the honor of serving them, and all — canny merchants to the core — rightly suspecting that not only would those visitors come back, to actually buy stuff this time, but many times more customers would be drawn in by the reflected glamour of association, or the power of advertising.

"Yes, the rechtair told us...my God, I *did* get a lot, didn't I?"

Sabia laughed. "You do realize that you need not make up for a three-thousand-year trade deficit in the first fortnight you're here?"

An embarrassed scoff. "If you think *this* is a lot, you should see what Warren has bought. Well, I say 'bought', we've been allowed to actually pay for pretty much nothing. We felt bad about that, so really it's only shame that has stopped us shopping for more." She glanced up at the Keltic woman, a little diffidently. "What do your people really think of us? Only, I was wondering..."

Sabia curled up in one corner of the overstuffed sofa nearest the fireplace, toying with a goblet of ale. "I would imagine, much the same as your folk must be thinking of us. You are the first formal contact we have had with Erith — Earth, Terra — since we left there thirty centuries ago. This is a very big occasion — reunion, rather."

Sarah's quick ear had caught the shading. "You say 'formal contact'. Have there been informal contacts, then? That might explain a lot..."

"I daresay it might," said Sabia, laughing. "And I will not deny it. Aye, we have been back on numerous occasions. Mostly, at first, to keep an eye on the lands and folk we left, and to take away those who still wished to depart, and for whatever reasons could not leave with us in the first going, the Great Immram. Those voyages continued on for a very long time, until it was decided that the emigrations were done. It was becoming too dangerous: the risk that your people would notice us was far too great. Indeed, we *were* noticed on too many occasions, resulting in some extremely creative explanations of what and who we might be. After that we returned only at long intervals, a few times a century, perhaps."

"Really? To what purpose? If everybody was gone and no one on Earth knew of you any longer—"

"Oh, again, just to keep a general watch on things, and to steal good ideas."

"To *steal* things! What things, pray?"

"Good things, of course. Symphonic music, thoroughbred horses, fine wine cultivars..."

Sarah felt unaccountably annoyed on behalf of her home planet. "Music and horses and wine? Nothing else? You didn't think anything was good enough to steal?"

"Well, only consider," said Sabia, with an apologetic grin. "What else *would* we have taken? Technology? We have goleor of that already, and, no offense, far in advance of your own for far longer. The same with healing, and our work in that area has only become more sophisticated. We had much for ourselves, and no need to steal yours. But horses, now..."

And they were off on their favorite topic of discussion. It was only later, when she had bidden Sabia good night and closed the door and was floating luxuriously in the warm, steaming pool-bath, that it occurred to Sarah that the Kelt had never really answered her question as to how her people saw the Terran visitors. At all.

By the end of the third week O'Reilly was wandering alone, with confidence, resolved to tread every single street in Caerdroia. To that end, she was tracing day by day a purposeful pattern back and forth boustrophedon-style, through the stepped and terraced streets, quarter by quarter, from the imposing governmental buildings like Star of the Bards and the high temples of the Druids and Bandraoi and Turusachan itself, to the elegant family mansions of the aristocracy, set on the broad ledge called Highfold, down into the most ancient parts of the city, the Stonerows and other residential quarters. Many of the houses still dwelled in dated from the first founding of Caerdroia; she found to her great surprise that the inhabitants, seeing her pass and knowing her for one of the Terran embassy, would compete amongst themselves to invite her in to share bread and cheese and ale, or a more elegant repast of creamcakes and wine.

But by far her favorite pursuit was to go for a leisurely ride in the nearby countryside, whenever she was able. To her delight, once her hosts had assured themselves that Sarah knew what she was doing, she had been allowed up on the towering, amazing Keltic-bred horses, twenty and more hands high, the biggest of them, to suit the Kelts' greater stature, but built like the ancient Gypsy Vanners of Earth, spirited and enduring, with feathered hooves and luxuriant manes that swept almost to their knees and flurrying silkfloss tails that touched the ground.

She had mentioned to Sabia that at home she had loved

riding, and missed it; the Fian had immediately arranged for a horseback excursion down to the beaches below the City, where the Avon Dia, the broad and mighty river that flows through the Great Glen, meets the sea, and the outing had become a regular occurrence, several times a week. Sometimes they were accompanied: Aeron's cousins or sibs, the bard Morgan Cairbre returned from Clero, even on one occasion the Queen herself. Sarah had repeatedly invited her shipmates to join them, but they had all begged off, in no uncertain terms.

"We may have mastery of the stars, Sorcha," Sabia had told her on that first ride. "But we love the old ways also. And for our people, horses are a great part of that. Once we had a High Queen who grew up as a humble horsegirl, an orphan, and she ended by not only ridding us of the occupying Firvolgi but founding a royal stud bred from horses of the Sidhe themselves. My own family are well known down the centuries for raising horses, with bloodlines from that same stud; in fact, not a few of our beasts are housed in the castle stables. Would you care to see?"

After an interested walk-through of those facilities, Sabia providing expert commentary, dispensing apples and sugar lumps as they went, playing no favorites, O'Reilly had at last judiciously chosen from three handsome animals selected for her approval a beautiful dapple-gray, with black mane and tail and stockings. She had been informed that there were horses even taller and larger, as many farmsteads still preferred to use massive giant draft breeds to work the land, and had been introduced to the pride of the stables — Brónach, Aeron's own horse, a fiery black mare who had been a coronation gift from Sabia's kin.

That first ride, just the two of them, had done much to clear Sarah's head. They had clattered through the streets and out of the Seagate, the nearest portal to the ocean cliffs that edged Caerdroia to the west, and then down the long slope of the land to a vast, empty beach that ran up to the Avon Dia—a gleaming white-sand crescent bordered by wiry machair-covered dunes and then green turf.

Today Sarah was enjoying the usual thundering gallop through the edge of the surf, foam flying from under the gray's hooves; then, pulling up, she breathed deep of the cold fresh air and patted the horse's curving neck. It reminded her of similar gallops along the beaches near her home, when she had been growing up. Those beaches were not what they had once been, long ago: the rising ocean, over the centuries, had carved away at the Californian coastline, and earthquakes too had vastly altered the Sandiangelan landscape.

The San Andreas Fault was largely responsible for that, having let go at last in the cataclysmic landshift of 2578, measured at a shattering and utterly unprecedented 15.4 on the venerable open-ended Richter scale, which had had to be updated to accommodate the catastrophic earth movement—so that now the reshaped and renamed mountain ranges stood with their feet in the surf, and to the south a whole new bay and archipelago had formed. Indeed, if all the remaining buildings had been swept away—as they nearly had been—and the remnant coastal mountain ranges raised a bit higher, the lands where much of Los Angeles had once stood would not look very different from these round her now...

A wave of sadness swept over her, and she slumped a little in the saddle. Earth's great breakthrough in tectonic stabilization had come three hundred years too late: after grim and feverish work and with the assistance of several alien races, such uncontrolled seismic horrors were now, thankfully, things of the past on her home planet. Even tsunamis had been effectively tamed by modified sound technology that could stop them in their tracks mid-ocean — a huge blessing. Billions had died in the Greatquake, as it was called, not only in California but all around the globe, from triggered tremors and volcanic eruptions as well as tsunamis a thousand feet high, which had rolled from one side of the Pacific to the other and in places a hundred miles inland, covering whole countries. The entire planet had rung like a bell, disarranged by the sheer size of the landshift; so huge had been the impact that Terra's orbit had actually shifted and the length of the day and year had been observably affected.

It had taken many centuries to recover and rebuild: the lesson had been harshly learned and the reconstruction thoughtfully and carefully planned. Now there were wide floodplains to hold off any possible waves that could not be otherwise coped with, and cities had been rebuilt well above and away from the coasts and the faultlines. There were still people who lived beside the oceans, that couldn't be helped — though not so many, nor so heedlessly, as in time past. But the beaches and hills that remained had a sense of being well used, a kind of spent airlessness; here, there was only freshness and vast openness, although the lands had been settled far longer.

"We planned it so," said Slaine, when questioned. "And Brendan made sure of it. All the same, Caerdroia outgrew its walls thrice in his own lifetime; you can see the oldest battlements down in the Stonerows, those massive stone arcs dividing the streets. Then St. Nia, Brendan's mother, who was full Sidhe, raised the outmost defenses that you see over there. That is no work of construction, but natural: a single enormous sill of stone, seven miles long, that she summoned out of the ground, by magic. Once the wall was in place, she caused the Wolf Gate to pierce it, and for many centuries that was the only gate. That was where the city stopped, by choice. For all those confines, though, sometimes the place has been half empty, as it was when Edeyrn Marbh-draoi, that evil creature, ruled Keltia. Little by little, once Arthur Ard-ríigh reconquered, folk crept back, and today it is pleasantly populous. Not that we could not find room somewhere for, say, a few folk from Erith," she added with a smile, "should such folk care to choose to live here."

Sarah, who had been gazing awed as ever on the walls of Caerdroia, smiled back and decided to play along. "What would such folk do for paid work, if they did come to live here, do you think?"

"Oh, goleor of things. You might care to join our own star navy. My father Prince Elharn, Aeron's great-uncle, is Admiral of the Fleet—well, Master of Sail as his correct title is. I am sure she would put in an official royal word for you with him, or I could too, of course, if you wished to remain in active space service—your experience would be immensely valuable. If you chose to stay planetside, you might go into commerce: with your background and skills, many would seek to employ you in trading ventures, either here or on our trade planet Clero. Or you could set up your own import-export shop."

O'Reilly grinned, remembering a sign she and Hathaway had seen hanging outside a shop in the Stonerows. "I could get a license to sell weasels and jade earrings..."

Slaine raised delicate brows in bemusement. "Indeed? Well, there are very many things that you could do. Aeron would hire you in a heartbeat if you wished to remain here at Turusachan. You have good training as a diplomatist, we have all seen it, and you speak many languages, Erith tongues and others. You could be your world's consul here, or on another of our home planets. We would have good use for you at court, doubt it not. Especially if..."

"If there is a war," finished O'Reilly with some heaviness. "Oh please, you don't need to skirt the topic, I've been hearing about a possible war ever since we got here—how my world linking itself to Keltia would tip over certain balances of power. Do you think it likely?"

"I do not see how we can avoid it." Slaine stared out to sea. "It has been brewing for at least a generation, and come to the boil in the last three years—since Aeron's accession, in fact, and the manner of that accession did much to further the bad attitude. And in all honesty, though I mean this never in blame, your arrival has made war more likely than not...there are galactic thugs and belligerent factions who would do anything to see that we did not unite with our old homeworld, and I daresay there are other factions who feel the same about you. But not to fear: we are very well protected behind our Curtain Wall, as you did see for yourself when you came through. In the many centuries since its raising, never has an enemy broken through it to come at us here."

She reined her horse around to head back to the city, and Sarah's mount turned unbidden to follow. "Still—no defense is perfect, and no safety lasts forever. If it comes to pass that we are put to fight, then we will do so. We have done so before, and no doubt will do so again."

There was so much else to do to occupy her, besides helping Haruko in whatever she could, that O'Reilly had little leisure to dread the possible advent of interstellar conflict, though she did report Slaine's words to her captain, who merely nodded. No doubt he had been informed by Aeron or Morwen of the possibilities at the earliest opportunity. She did a little research on the chances, and who the likely adversaries might be, and was not cheered at what she learned. She and her crewmates discussed it every now and again, including what would be their own chosen course of action should battle come to pass, and Sarah kept to herself the resolution she had already made that she would not be returning to Earth with the others, not even if it meant deserting—though she hoped it wouldn't come to that.

But in the midst of her duties and her worries, she still had time for her own pursuits: one morning she made her way to the Hall of Heralds in Seren Beirdd, Star of the Bards. Directed by an encouraging suggestion from Gwydion, she had gone there to try to trace her ancestral lines. Her parents had always boasted that they came of pure Irish descent on both sides, which was unusual in these times when most folk of Earth were well and genially mixed in their family genetics. She had spent several pleasant days in the record chambers at the bardic headquarters, assisted by helpful heralds, and as the lines were painstakingly traced back, crossing and recrossing, multiplying with the countless generations, she was startled and well pleased to find that not only were her parents' claims correct ones but they, and she herself, were far-distant kin to Aeron and Morwen both, from connections in Ireland and Scotland, long centuries ago.

"It justifies me," she confided that evening to the table at large, at the nightmeal in Mi-cuarta. "It gives me a feeling of rootedness, that my feet have a right to be upon this ground and under this table. The research bards told me there have been O'Reillys in Keltia since the earliest days," she added, all puffed up with understandable pride.

"Indeed there have," said Morwen, waving a servitor to bring more wine to the guest. "The name was spelled differently then, of course: first Uí Raghallaigh, then Ó Rahillagh, and differently again now—O'Rahilly. O'Reilly, as you have it: still the same, and all the same, and pronounced the same. You might choose to return to the old orthography if you like. It would look very well blazoned so, below a shield of your own arms, if the Ard-rían in her wisdom sees fit to grant you such: Sorcha ní Rahillagh."

"Very elegant," agreed Aeron, not rising to Morwen's teasing. "As for a grant of arms, that is easily done, and well deserved. You may discuss yours with the Master

Herald, Caerdroia King of Arms, whenever you care to, under my sanction. I will have the authorizations sent over. You may want to use a variation of the arms of your cadet branch, or have a blazon entirely your own, as the first of your house in Keltia."

Her own coat of arms! "Thank you, Your Majesty... Ard-rían, I mean. One of the bards even told me that the O'Reillys have their own banshee," said Sarah in wonder. "Though I hope to God I never have to hear it. No offense, banshee!" she added in apology, looking up, and the others laughed.

"No surprise there; the Ó Rahillagh are of the very oldest sidheanachta," said Gwydion. "Did they not tell you at Seren Beirdd?"

Sarah shook her head, still a little overawed by him. "If they did, the meaning escaped me. What is that, then, First Lord?"

"Merely a word we use of those families with blood of the Sidhefolk in their veins. I doubt not you have heard that the Sidhe themselves, and other magical beings, are collectively described as sidhaun?" He sounded the word out—*shee-awn*—and O'Reilly nodded. "Saves us having to say 'Sidhefolk' or 'Shining Folk' or specify every kind of magical being every time. Which can only be endlessly irritating to those folk themselves: would you care always to be described as 'daughter of Earth' or some other such pompous label?" Gwydion smiled to see O'Reilly laugh and shake her head. "Just so. Well, humans with faerie bloodlines are called sidheanach—*sheean-ach*—or of the sidheanachta, for the same reason. It is largely a matter of short-hand."

"Matter of laziness, more like!" said Aeron, laughing. "Though it does carry a certain, m'hm, significance. You will see, Sorcha."

Sorcha... O'Reilly had been given the Gaeloch version of her name before she had even arrived in Caerdroia, and most of the Kelts now called her that. It was not a translation: in Englic, and its original Hebraic, "Sarah" meant "princess", while in Gaeloch, "Sorcha" or one of its variants—Sorsha, Soracha, Sorca—meant "brightness, clear light". Good enough, though O'Reilly deeply longed to use the equally unrelated "Saoirse", *seer-sha*, which she had discovered in an old namebook and which meant "freedom", and sometimes, secretly, she thought of herself by that name, wishing she had the nerve to insist on it publicly. Seer-sha, sor-sha...names were fun, like putting on different clothes. Haruko often called her Sally, which she did not personally care for but would never dream of correcting him, as she liked him, and Hathaway occasionally called her Saro, which she found rather pleasing. But now she made Aeron some smiling reply and attended again to her plate, a little more thoughtful than she had been earlier.

So she herself was sidheanach; Gwydion had said so. Well, maybe that wasn't so very surprising after all: it was true that her parents and her other relatives had told stories around the holiday dinner tables for years, wild and grand tales of how the O'Reillys and their associated kin had been mighty warriors and bards and rulers in the unimaginable days of Ireland long past. And true it also was that she had felt it in herself, this strangeness that perhaps had come down to her from the Sidhe and perhaps had not. It would explain, maybe, why she had felt so immediately at home here, why she was totally at ease now seated at the high table in Mi-cuarta dining with the people who ran this place, why she was clad as she was in a graceful floor-length gown with a gold-wrapped silk torse set upon her hair, why she felt as comfortable wearing local dress as she did wearing her fleet uniform—maybe even more so, though that she refused to admit to anyone, her captain least of all.

Except for full-dress formal occasions, Haruko himself had kept resolutely and stiffly to his own regular uniform, as had Tindal and Athenée, though Mikhailova was wavering, or so she'd told Sarah. Hathaway had been happily experimenting with Keltic garb from the first. O'Reilly was of the opinion that Warren did it as much to wind up Tindal as to be more comfortable and less visible to public notice, as he claimed, though his smooth, milk-chocolate-colored skin certainly worked against that last, and local dress only made him look all the more handsomely exotic in this remarkably homogeneous nation.

However friendly as it was meant, it had begun to grate upon them all—the constant public attention and curiosity, to the point where Mikhailova had burrowed herself away and seldom left Turusachan at all, and Tindal went out early of a morning and was gone sometimes all night; no one knew where he went, though if he had ever been urgently needed the Sword's comlink could have located him easily enough. But although no one was discourteous or demanding, the pressure was slowly beginning to bend them, like wood being shaped under steam.

They were all changing, more than they knew, or could tell; whether it was themselves fitting into Keltia or Keltia working upon them, they could not say, but despite their orders not to engage with locals or get involved with local politics, they were by no means the same as they had been when they had arrived. Sarah had only to look at the Captain, or herself; even Tindal had changed his usual spots, or some of them, at least. For the most part, she was comfortable with it; it would be a problem only if the change became more general. Or would it? Over the past few days, she had been thinking about what Slaine had said, her off-hand speculation about the Terrans staying here in various capacities—maybe that was something they should all be giving more thought to, in case that somehow came to be no longer a choice.

She stole a glance over the vast feasting-hall. How would that *be* for them, for her—to be here by right, to have this as her home? They would have interesting, important work to do, a comfortable place to live. They all had Keltic friends now; maybe they would even find themselves something more than friends, something more than a home. It needn't be exile or banishment from their own homes, not forever— unless they chose it to be. If ever she had seen a place she could wish to stay in always, it would be this place, with these folk. She just wondered if she would have the free choosing of it, or if the choice would be made for her, by force.

Letting out a long delighted sigh, O'Reilly looked around her, turning in a full circle to make sure she didn't miss anything. *How unbelievably beautiful it is here...* She was standing on a flat stone viewing platform high up on the side of the Loom, on the long craggy mountain known as Llwynogue, the Young Lion, and indeed it resembled in profile a couched lion, ready to spring. Mere feet from her, a raging waterfall, a force as the Kelts called it, was racing away down the mountain's flank to join the Avon Dia, miles away: the Falls of Yarin, which marked the eastern boundary of Caerdroia, where it met the extreme edge of the great wall that circled the city.

She sat down happily and tiredly, flopping boneless and all askew in the warm dry grass; it had been a bit of a scramble up here, and there was more to come, as her plan was to trek the full length of the trail Sabia had told her about, until she reached the stone circle of Ni-maen just above Turusachan. It wasn't a particularly long or arduous hike, a mere seven miles, and she was eager for the exercise, as she had not been able to get out of the city for weeks now, except for her daily ride.

But she didn't want to miss a single vista, and truly there was much to see. Above her to the west reared the splendid stone palisades known as the Painted Cliffs, great frozen swathes of multicolored stone — a sill, she knew, in geologic terminology, like the one that St. Nia had called out of the earth, lower down, to form the city wall, a great lava lip that had obtruded itself into the granite and sandstone and granodiorite of the Loom, ages ago, as the mountains were being formed. *Orogeny recapitulates morphogeny*, she thought with a giggle. *See, those courses at school in world-building came in handy after all…*

It felt like lunchtime: reaching for the small pack she had brought with her, she pulled out thick slices of cold chicken and ham, crusty bread with butter, a cheddar-type cheese. The palace cooks had also packed some other things that she had no idea what they were, but the alien foodstuffs proved very tasty when she cautiously nibbled at them: sliced tomatoes, or what looked a bit like tomatoes and were far less slimy; a container of something resembling duck confit—presumably, or hopefully, made from something resembling a duck; a purplish-red fruit that looked like a giant plum and tasted like nothing she had ever eaten, meltingly light and sweet; something banana-ish in appearance but pear-like in taste; even several large slabs of the dark chocolate called shakla that the Kelts favored.

She was feeling ravenous after her climb—Slaine had transported her in one of the little aircars the seven miles across the City to the beginning of the trail, and told her cheerfully that as for coming back, she was on her own—and now she stuffed her face, saving most of the lavish supplies in case she later grew peckish along the path. Caerdroia was thousands of feet below, but she would hardly starve before she got to the end; there were easy paths downward every mile or so, and if she needed help, Slaine had also provided her with a silvery crystal that seemed to work as both a beacon and a comlink. All she had to do was speak into it, or hold it up and it would send out a great beacon of light; the Fian sentries on the walls would hear or mark it, and someone would be dispatched to rescue her.

But she was resolved not to need it; that would be far too embarrassing. She had hours and hours of daylight ahead of her—the longer day on Tara was finally something she had gotten used to, and she was well on pace to reach Ni-maen before sunset; it was only seven miles, after all. Bags of time to get there.

Leaning back on her elbows, Sarah looked out over the vast view with an equally vast contentment. She truly loved it here, felt utterly and completely at home. So much so that now she felt a sudden pang: how was she going to bear it if, when, inevitably, she had to leave? She was still, as Haruko had not unkindly pointed out, a Terran serving officer; it was her business to obey orders and go where she was sent. And if Keltia was going to be plunged into interstellar conflict, war with the Cabiri Imperium and with Fomor, as looked hourly more and more likely, then the scout mission would have to head home, inevitably; it was in their orders.

She shifted in the grass. But would that really be their best course of action? They might do better to stay here, might well be safer here even if it came to war, rather than trying to make their way back to Earth in the tiny and massively undefended Sword. Such armaments as they had were designed for repelling a single attacking ship, perhaps two or three at most, so as to allow them to escape by superior speed and maneuverability. They had not a hope of evading anything greater, certainly not the kind of vast armada this Jaun Akhera she had heard so much about was clearly going to throw at Keltia. She had read up on the Coranians and the Fomori since Sabia had first explained the political situation to her, and it did not look good.

Ever since Aeron's accession under ghastly circumstances, three years ago, this had been building; everyone said so, Morwen and Rohan and all the rest, anyone she spoke to. It had been monstrous: the Ard-rían's parents, Fionnbarr and

Emer, and her first consort, Morwen's brother Roderick — *only 'consort', not 'husband'*, thought Sarah, curiously — had been savagely murdered by King Bres of Fomor, while outside the Curtain Wall on a diplomatic mission, and most of the civilized galaxy had been appalled. They were soon even more appalled by the stark vengeance Aeron took, when she went out alone and used her magic to destroy the Fomorian military planetoid from which the attack had been launched.

Sarah rubbed her arms as if chilled. Bellator — the name had become a byword for terror and vengeance, and no one discussed it willingly; she had had to practically twist Sabia's arm to get the information. Not a soul had survived, and the planetoid itself had been melted down to clinkered bedrock. The High Queen had had her revenge, true enough, but she had also almost died of her own reaction to the deed, and only the care and devotion of friends and family, and, ultimately, Gwydion's love, had brought her back.

When she got to Gwydion, O'Reilly smiled. The Prince of Gwynedd had become a good friend, to her and Haruko alike; sure, he was still an imposing and intimidating figure, but they had managed to get behind the mask of sternness he wore, and had come to know the person. She was glad that he and Aeron were together and so clearly madly in love; they would marry soon, as most everyone she had spoken to had told her — obviously a match that the people approved of. Though if war came…but she put that thought firmly aside. However furious and hating the Fomori king and his ally the Cabiri heir might be with Aeron, surely war on such a scale was not something they would lightly undertake. Perhaps they would let vengeance be set against vengefulness: call the score settled and no more blood need be spilled.

And perhaps pigs will captain starships... Since their arrival in Keltia, the Terrans had not been allowed to see much of a military nature, but what they had seen had shown beyond any doubt that Keltia was a very formidable power indeed, both in offense and defense, and the Kelts were far from alone—they had protectorate systems all through this quadrant, and the treaties were mutually defensive. If any system was attacked, the others would defend. What Earth would make of the whole situation when the latest dispatches reached there, O'Reilly had no idea, and Haruko, if he had any thoughts on the subject, was keeping them strictly to himself. Though she knew that both her new home and her old one wished alliance. It was just that everyone might well have run out of time...

But she had dallied here atop the soft turf long enough; any longer and she would doze off and probably end up sleeping there all night. Finishing her lunch and her sobering inner dialogue alike, she rose and re-shouldered her pack and took a long drench of water; going to the very edge of the thundering force, she carefully and precariously leaned out on a slippery granite slab and thrust the flask under a little sidespray to refill it from the icy torrent. Then she turned to follow the clearly marked path that led along the side of the Loom.

As she walked, she could feel her mood lightening with every step. It felt so good to stretch out her muscles, and this was a well-kept and popular trail along the Painted

Cliffs, though so far she seemed to be the only hiker upon it today. From here, she could look out over the city and the plains beyond, far down the valley of the Avon Dia to the east, while northwards, the snow-crowned giants of the Stair looked near enough to touch at forty miles' distance, and the beaches where she had ridden along the bay made a white coral necklace below the City on the west. Hard to believe that this peaceful vale had witnessed battle and strife in centuries past: Sabia had told her, on the short flight here, that an old prophecy said that there would be yet more great battles, at a place not too far distant, a place called Nandruidion.

She shivered a little in the strong cold breeze pouring off the sea seven miles away, troubled and reassured in almost equal parts. This very mountainside beneath her boots had seen war before: Arthur of Arvon, the one the Kelts held in almost godlike regard, had in his epic bid to reclaim the city and the throne sent all his cavalry and half his foot soldiers this way, downslope beside Yarin — a steep and dangerous descent — while he himself, with the rest of his forces, had made their way through a tunnel called the Nantosvelta, that ran under the entire mountain range. It had been a brilliant strategy, and he had succeeded with equal brilliance.

For a moment she pictured it in her head as she had read about it: the gallant, desperate army poised to fall like an avalanche on the heads of the enemy occupiers; the brave invaders streaming out from the cavernous tunnel like grim warriors in ancient sagas who had slept beneath the mountain for a hundred years, leaping armed and death-eyed into the throne room itself, led by the young king and his sorceress sister...whatever else they might be, clearly the Kelts did not lack for courage. But that was not the way it would be this time. This time, there would be battle out among the stars long before it came to fighting here on this ground, and maybe even her home planet would be dragged into it before it was done...

As the long afternoon began to shade toward dusk, Sarah came at last, glad and a little puffed, to the bright secret valley up above Turusachan in which lay Ni-maen, Daughter of Stone. Many had told her of this great bluestone circle, one of the three most sacred in all Keltia, where solemn ceremonies took place; it reminded her of Stonehenge, back on Earth, still standing proudly upon Salisbury Plain even after eight thousand years. It was primarily a royal site: Aeron and all other Keltic monarchs had come here to Ni-maen to be crowned, royal marriages and the saining of royal babies had taken place here, the four chief holydays of the Keltic year were celebrated here by the ruler and the highest clerics of the Druid and Ban-draoi orders. But anyone at all could just walk up here, to have a picnic or get married themselves, or merely to contemplate in spiritual silence. To the stones, it was all one.

    Ni-maen served also as a burying ground: lining the walls of the valley on both sides were rounded green barrows with flat stones set atop them—the resting places of Keltia's royal dead. Some of the stones were worn and lichened, clearly dating from the earliest days of Keltic habitation; some newer, with bright engraving on them. Plenty of room for future use, she noted somberly to herself, and maybe sooner than anyone would like, given what was coming. She could only hope that none of the ones she now counted as friends would be among the valley's new inhabitants.

O'Reilly looked around in the slanting afternoon light, feeling the peace of the place, but also feeling suddenly lost and lonely for her home planet, thinking how very far away Earth was, thinking of her own little home high in the coastal hills amid the orange groves, high above the tsunami line. *Can I really give that up to stay here, I wonder?* She shook herself crossly, touching the necklace she wore, a chain of little enamel-on-gold shields bearing Aeron's sword-and-crown personal device. The Ard-rían had taken it from her own neck a few weeks ago and fastened it around Sarah's, and the latter had been so stupefyingly thrilled that she had barely taken it off since. *What the hell is wrong with me today? I'm a sloppy, self-pitying, sentimental mess. Knock it off, Saoirse!*

She looked up quickly at a movement just beyond her vision's focus: an owl skimming silently overhead, above the ring of stones. The sight gave her a pleasurable, cozy feeling of night drawing in, though it was still full light—owls here came out to hunt around dusk, just as they did at home, and it was comforting to see that some things did not change. This one seemed a bit early, or maybe it was just extra-hungry; perhaps Keltic owls were Terran owls by long-ago origin, and had come here with the first ships. The owl swept by again, closer, letting a bronze and white feather fall a few yards away, but she was too lazy to go and pick it up just yet; she'd do it later, and would ask Sabia or another of her friends what kind of owl it was...perhaps even Aeron would know.

The air was much cooler now than it had been as the sun moved behind the valley walls; the western sky was beginning to stain itself with color, and far above her, the spectacular broad-planed rings of the Criosanna, the Woven Belts that circled the planet Tara, emerged from their day's hiding, though even in full sun they could be seen, ghostly, like Earth's moon in daylight. Now they glowed like frostfire as the heavens below them dimmed to a textured deep blue and the newly familiar Keltic stars sprang into sight—the Plumed Dancer, the Spearhead, the Dragon's Eye. The sun that had warmed her all day long was becoming a bonfire beyond the little islands far out in the Bight of Caerdroia; Gavida's Smithy, the volcanic island that Sabia had pointed out on her first day, burned like a pharos in the darker blue of the great bay, many miles out to sea. She had beheld this view, almost identical, on her first day here; it gave her a pleasant sense of familiarity that now she could put names to all these things—as if she possessed them, or they her.

Time she was headed back down the hill, she thought reluctantly, to wash up and change for supper; but, still lazy and agreeably weary, she made no move to do so. At least Turusachan was not more than minutes away, just down a broad processional path called the Way of Souls, that wound up from Highfold between two great spurs of Eryri, the two-horned mountain that towered over Caerdroia. The enormous palace stood below, its many windows cheerful bright squares reflecting the sunset, and she could see people moving purposefully about, though no sound rose up to her ears: cloaked Fian warriors changing the guard outside the main entrance to the fortress, other figures hastening from one tower to another, into the hall of Mi-cuarta, intent on the approaching nightmeal. She could even see her own windows from here, where a small dark form crossed and recrossed the lighted panes: her chamber attendant, turning down the bed and readying things for O'Reilly's return, laying out nightclothes, tidying the mess in which she inevitably left the room.

It was strange to have someone to do such things for her; most definitely not the way she lived at home. Well, it was hardly the way most people lived at home, really; these days, automation and droid servants took care of such things. Sarah had been very uncomfortable her first few days at Turusachan, unaccustomed to personal service: there were people to wake her up and draw her bath or set her shower, people to serve her breakfast in her room, people to attend her in Mi-cuarta if she chose to dine there instead, people to escort her round the city and take her riding or up in one of the ubiquitous little aircars for an overflight of the Great Glen, even up over the dales of the Loom or along the line of the distant Stair. People to dress her; people to arrange entertainment for her; people to tell her whatever she needed or wanted to know; people to do just about anything she could think of.

And then there were the ones she needed to engage with on a serious basis: officers of the Court, scientists, linguists, librarians, historians, combat masters and dancing masters. Above all others, Aeron, and Gwydion, and Morwen, and Rohan, who seemed to pretty much run the entire Keltic empire among them. Well, she said 'empire', though no Kelt ever called it one; but that was really what it was, and might be even more so in time to come. It all depended on where things went from here; and from where she sat, that could quite easily be straight to hell. Yet she could not feel, somehow, that it would.

O'Reilly had been sitting there so long, and sitting there so still, that at first she did not notice the little dark shapes flitting amongst the stones as the light dimmed, on the fringes of her sight. When she did, she held herself unmoving, so as not to startle them.

What are they? Too big for bats or rats or cats...Slaine said there were no dangerous wild animals this side of the Loom, and even if there were she had also said none would come so near to the city...what the hell could they be?

Encouraged by her lack of motion—or perhaps they simply had not seen her—the little figures came closer. They were no more than two feet high at the most; they seemed to be playing, tumbling and leaping over each other, and when they finally became aware of her watching them, they stopped dead. But she slowly reached out a hand, charmed and unafraid, and after a moment one or two of the braver ones came creeping over. Up close, she could see that they were teensy wee fairytale-looking things: leprechauns, or maybe hobbits, from the old books she loved. Her grandmother had told her stories of brownies or small-elves that were said to have served the O'Reilly family, she recalled, and of course there was that banshee, and those great legends she'd read as a little girl about that wizard kid with the scar, and his house-elf, and his magic friends—all her childhood fantasies seemed to be coming true around her.

"Hi there. My name's Sarah," she said softly, keeping her hand out. "Who are you?"

The boldest one reached out to touch her hand, and then the rest hurried to do the same; delighted, she offered them whatever she had not eaten of her lunch, which was a ton of food. That seemed to be a hit with them, a more than satisfactory peace overture: they accepted the leftover sandwiches, the fruit, especially the cookies and small cakes and the chocolate squares, greedily but daintily—a great success. *Oh Lord Almighty, whatever they are, I just made them all crazy high on sugar; what do I do now?*

She seemed to have made them her best friends forever as well: they bounced close in around her, no more than a dozen or so, one or two of the smallest and most daring even climbing into her lap, talking to her in their tiny voices. She tried not to laugh, but they were adorable, and amazingly affectionate. True, she had bribed them lavishly with food and chocolate, but she thought they would have responded the same even had she not. And once she had mentioned Gwydion's name, and Aeron's, their excitement knew no bounds; clearly the Queen and her consort were held in high esteem even among such strange little things as these.

They were all having a fine time chatting together when suddenly she felt the air shift and the atmosphere subtly alter, as if a cloudshadow had passed overhead. Almost at the same instant, with a chorus of squeaks and sudden silence, all of the creatures silently backed away. Not from fear of her; not from fear at all, apparently—respect, then? Whatever it was, the diminutive bouncing creatures were suddenly vanished, or at least hidden among the stones, and in their place, where the owl feather had fallen, now stood two tall cloaked figures, unmoving against the dusk, in the shadows of Ni-maen.

Sarah took a deep breath. *Well, okay then, big courtesy question, where's a protocol bard when you really need one? Who says hello first? They're the natives, I'm the visitor, it's their planet, not mine – good arguments on both sides. But perhaps it should be me – worked well enough with the hobbits...*

She cleared her throat, and her lap of crumbs, and stood up, making a graceful bow, as she had been taught by her bardic etiquette instructor. The two newcomers bowed back, though not as deeply or as long as she had, which told her...something. They were clearly Kelts, a man and a woman; and equally clearly strangers, in that she had never seen them before, and yet they seemed not so. Their faces were faces she somehow knew, and despite her surprise and unease, she smiled at them.

They returned her smile. They were stunningly good to look on, she thought, *unnaturally* good to look on; also they had that air of pure silvery otherness that O'Reilly had sometimes seen upon Aeron, in her more queenly or sorcerous moments. Though she had not seen him do so, the man had somehow picked up the owl feather from the ground, and was turning it over and over between his fingers. Then he looked straight at her, deep into her eyes, and she almost fainted.

Holy Mother of God! I thought Aeron and Gwydion had magic and power in their eyes, but they have nothing *like this...*

"Beannacht," she ventured, using the Gaeloch all-occasion greeting that was used for so many purposes: hello, goodbye, peace, blessing be upon you. And for the first time she did not feel selfconscious using it, but found that it came naturally, if a bit tremulously, to her lips.

"Beannacht ar te," said the woman in return, in a more ancient form than Sarah had been taught, and the man gave a courteous nod.

"Greeting to you, Saoirse."

She was cautiously charmed to hear him address her by the name she had chosen for herself here in Keltia, his deep voice resonant on the name in the Gaeloch, making it sound ever so much more thrilling than plain old "Sarah." But... *Just a minute here, how does he know who I am, not to mention my secret little name?*, forgetting that all of Keltia had known who she was before the Sword had even landed at Mardale port. Though that still did not explain how he knew the secret name with which he was apparently so familiar...

"Greeting, lord. And lady," she added hastily, not wishing to be impolite, and feeling she couldn't go wrong with those titles — even Aeron and Gwydion did not stickle to be addressed so, though they preferred their actual firstnames. "I do not know how you are called, and I'm sorry for my ignorance. Have I met you at some feast? It seems that I've seen you before, maybe? I'm not very good with faces."

She would not have been in any case. The glamour was on her: it seemed that the tall lord stood before her clad in a cloak of gold, the sunset burning upon him and around him; as for the woman, her hair was soft night itself and her eyes were sparking stars. O'Reilly blinked to clear her own eyes, and saw with some relief that the glamour was gone: the two strangers were dressed ordinarily though elegantly, like any well-born Kelt, the man in tunic and trews and boots, the woman in a long gúna and grass-green slippers.

"But you're *not* a man, are you," said Sarah, with sudden certainty and a pounding heart. "Or a woman either. You're—"

They smiled, and again the glamour almost blinded her, so that she sat down hard on the bench. "We are of the Sidhefolk, right enough, and you are of Erith, first of your people to return to us."

"Sidhefolk! How can that be? I have met Sidhefolk, well, one anyway, and you look *nothing* like that one."

The woman laughed, not unkindly. "Let me guess: you were out riding and you saw something on the hill that looked like a moving tangle of silver ribbons, and you stopped to speak to it."

"Yes! Well, no. Well, not exactly. How did you *know* that? We were out riding, yes, and we met a woman and her child, out for a walk, and we stopped to talk to them. And then this bright ribbony thing came gliding down the hillside like a sailing ship, and stopped beside us. The woman said some greeting, and told her little girl to curtsy to the Shining One; the people I was with—Prince Kieran and his wife—sort of nodded to it, and it seemed to nod back at them. It didn't say anything to us, just kind of hovered for a moment or two, and then it was gone. But the woman had said 'Shining One', and I know that's another name for—"

"—for Sidhefolk," said the man, in an amused voice. "That which you saw was an appearance we can put on ourselves at will, for any reason, or no reason."

"Well—yeah? It was very beautiful, really," added Sarah lamely. "I asked Slaine, Aeron's cousin, about it later, but she didn't have a whole lot to say. Nobody seems to, where you people are concerned," she said a little more pointedly, gathering nerve as she spoke. "Why is that, I wonder?"

"I am quite sure we could not say either," said the woman, blandly.

"Couldn't you? Clearly you're not evil, or anything like that...so why are they afraid to talk about you, or to you?"

"Clearly you have no such problem," remarked the man, and now the amusement in his voice was plain to be heard. "Well, then—Saoirse ní Rahillagh—I am Gwyn ap Neith, king under the hill, and this is my queen, Etain."

After that quietly ringing statement, there didn't seem to be too much to say for a moment or two. Then O'Reilly leaped to her feet: suddenly it had dawned on her that it was not exactly respectful to be sitting in the presence of royalty, and she gave the faerie rulers the kind of court obeisance, to the point of subsidence, that Aeron herself detested.

Etain laughed gently. "No need for that, do get up... We ought to chide you, wicked lass, for giving treats to our little friends. Sugar is their favorite thing in all the worlds; even just a square or two of shakla causes them to behave like overactive toddlers. No matter; they will settle down after a while. I can see that they like you."

She raised her beautiful voice, called something to the little hidden giggling hobs in a strange language, not the Gaeloch, and the creatures came creeping back, abashed, though they looked at the queen with adoration.

"There now," she said to them fondly. "Come and sit by your new friend. But be still awhile yet as we speak."

"So," said O'Reilly, trying out her own voice again. "I've been told that no Kelt has seen you for a couple of centuries or more, not publicly or in your proper forms anyway, never mind silvery ribbons; and certainly no people where I come from have ever seen anything like you for about ten times that long. Or maybe ever. Is there something going on that we need to know about? I mean, that Aeron needs to know about."

"As for Aeron," said Etain evenly, "she will find out what she needs to know in the hour she needs to know it— no later, no sooner. As for you, this is the first time we have spoken with one of your ship's company, right enough, but we have kept watch on you since the moment you passed the Curtain Wall."

"Really?" asked O'Reilly, impressed. "Way out in space like that? You can just— go *out* there?"

Gwyn laughed. "Not in these forms we cannot, nay. But true it is that we can send our Sight wherever we like, anywhere within the Bawn, the space within the Wall's bounds. And so we watched you come here, and have seen what you have done since you came."

"That's just a little— unsettling." *Well, downright creepy, if you want to call it what it is...I don't much like the thought of otherworldly creatures stalking us and spying on us...*

"Does it not make sense that the Sidhefolk would wish to meet the new arrivals? And of those, the only one who is distant kin? Truly: your clan on Erith is descended from us long since; the Uí Raghallaigh had many dealings with the Sidhe before ever we came to Keltia, and the connection did not cease once we were here."

"I don't know as I can say about being related," she said warily. "Though Gwydion—*Prince* Gwydion mentioned something about being sidhe—something?"

"Sidheanach. You are of the sidheanachta," said the queen. Her voice was even more thrillingly beautiful than the king's, and Sarah felt herself falling under its spell. "Descended of both our houses, my lord's and mine; and of another that may prove to be most important of all." But what that house might be, Etain did not say.

"It comes to my mind that you have been searching out your ancestry in the bardic records," observed Gwyn, and Sarah nodded.

"I have!" she said, her mind clearing at once. "And I have found that I am also related, albeit very distantly, to Aeron and Morwen both."

The king smiled. "And this pleases you?"

"Are you *kidding*? To be related to the two of *them*? And to you also, as you tell me? To be related to *anyone* here? I'd be happy to find a family connection to the humblest household there is. It's *fabulous*. It gives me—I feel—" She sought for the words. "As I told Aeron, it lets me claim this place. It lets me feel more at home here than I ever felt at home on Earth."

Etain's turn to smile. "What if we were to tell you that you had more of a claim on Keltia even than that?"

Sarah's bright-faced eagerness grew at once quiet and wondering, and she pulled into herself a little defensively, like a tiny snail. "Well, how can that be, then?"

Gwyn laid his hand to her forehead, gently, the way a parent would test a child for fever. "It can be, Saoirse, because you come of not only the Uí Raghallaigh lineage, as kin to us, but of a kindred that gave Keltia its highest bard and one of its bravest spirits—Taliesin ap Gwyddno."

O'Reilly caught back a gasp, and she suddenly became aware that her two companions had been speaking to her, since the first formal Gaeloch exchange, in her native Englic. But she couldn't think about that just yet...

"Taliesin the High Bard? *Arthur's* Taliesin? How is that even possible?" Then her mind supplied its own quick answer from her intensive reading, and she drew in a long shaky breath. "Of course, his mother—his mother was from Earth. Are you saying—what *are* you saying?"

"We are saying that you come of a common cousinage with him: his mother and a long-time-since foremother of yours were sisters. One, called Honora, or Onóragh as we would render it, stayed on Earth, to wed and have children, of which a daughter long-descended through many-times generations came to be you—you even share her name as one of your own. The other, Kathleen—Cathelin—met her beloved, Gwyddno, on your own homeworld, where he had gone on a mission. Given the choice, rather than lose him she chose to come to Keltia with her beloved, where they produced Taliesin."

Sarah's legs had failed her again, and once more she had collapsed abruptly on the low bench, uncaring of the discourtesy, though the royal couple did not seem to mind in the slightest; two of the smallest hobs immediately cuddled up against her knees, and she absently patted their heads.

"But that was—a *really* long time ago. Fifteen hundred years at least!"

"Even so," said Etain, solemnly, and Sarah shivered, realizing that this woman, this queen, this—*being*, was far, far older still. "We knew her—Cathelin. She was our friend; she died under the hill among us, and she sleeps there yet. She was lovely and gifted and brave, and she passed all that on to her son."

O'Reilly was still working on the basic premise. "Wait wait wait wait wait. So—you're saying that Taliesin, *the* Taliesin, is my cousin. My *actual* cousin. My *first* cousin, many, *many* times removed. How is that possible?"

Gwyn looked amused. "Just because it was long ago does not make it any the less true or possible, alanna. Aye, that is what we are saying; is this displeasing to you?"

"No! Oh no, God, no! It's—it's *wonderful*. I'm just—well, 'surprised' wouldn't really cover it, would it..."

"I do not know; would it?" said Etain, teasing gently. "Perhaps it would not. But because of this high kinship, you have a right to be a Kelt. In truth, you already are. If so you choose to be," she added.

"Though now is not the time we would have chosen to disclose this," said Gwyn soberly. "But it is in our minds to do so, because of what will soon be upon Keltia and all who dwell herein."

"War," said Sarah. "You mean war."

"War, and worse to follow. Soon now, and then later as well. We know that you will not stand away from it."

"You think? I would *love* to be able to fight for Keltia. But if there is war, our orders are to return to Earth, all of us."

"And you do not wish to go."

"Are you *insane*? Of course I don't want to go back! I've only just found this place, I'm happy here, I have friends here, I feel at home for the first time ever in my life—" She ran out of steam, and sat looking up at the royal couple with the saddest expression in the world on her face. "Sorry, didn't mean that about you being insane. But...could you— would you—help me stay?" she asked in a very small voice. "If it isn't too much to ask?"

"To ask? Nay," said Gwyn. "To grant? Also nay. But you must be sure this is what you truly wish. What you are asking will set many things in motion, for good and for ill, and will complete many patterns that have stood uncompleted for long and long."

"I'm sure, Your Majesty," said Sarah, with the conviction of a thousand warriors at her back ringing in her voice. "I am *so* sure."

"Very well then," he said, and the air trembled around them all as his power made itself felt. "You must be the one to tell Aeron yourself, and to ask her permission; she will only shout at me if I ask for you, and I have no wish to be on the receiving end of her wrath. But I can speak for her answer aforetimes, and that answer will unquestioningly be aye, for I know she cares for you, and for Haruko also. But there are things that must be done here and now, since you have chosen."

Gwyn glanced aside at his queen, exchanging with her a look of perfect understanding. "All the pieces must be set out on the fidchell board," said Etain quietly to her mate, "and in their proper places, if the game is to be played out aright."

And the king nodded, saying no word, but held out his hand, and Sarah took it, letting him help her to her feet; but he did not release her hand once he had done so.

Etain looked down at Sarah then, and smiled. "You have wished, and we have willed it. Now let us give you something with which it may be helped to happen. There will be need for you to wear this, and to bear this, in the storm that is coming."

O'Reilly stared as Gwyn traced three circles round in the palm of her left hand, with the first two fingers of his right. Irresistibly, she was reminded of a game her beloved grandmother used to play with her when she was a toddler, where Gran would trace circles in her palm and tug her hair and then go up her arm with two chopping motions and tickle her ribcage. *Round ball, round ball, pull Miss Sarah's hair! One slice, two slice, tickle under there!*

She held herself to stillness as her palm began to prickle a little under his touch, only too aware that this had far more serious purpose to it than a little baby game, and by the faint smile on the king's face he seemed to know what she was remembering. And then she gasped to see forming in the center of her palm three glittering linked silver spirals, a perfect match to the ones she saw now in the king's own palm, gleaming softly and sharply in the last of the light. As the spirals, burning-cold now as a ribbon of space-ice, blazed out and then began to sink into her palm, down beneath her skin, she started to panic, and tried to pull her hand from Gwyn's. He only held it harder and closer, in a strong, unbreakable grip, until the spirals had vanished into her palm, his thumb moving reassuringly back and forth across her fingers—again, just as her grandmother's had used to do—and bit by bit the panic left her.

"How did—I don't—what—"

"Peace, child," said the queen. She held out her slim pale hand, palm uppermost, and the triple spirals glittered there as well. "This is the sign of our shared kindred, the Aes Sidhe, and our personal kinship with you also. A mark of protection on you, and the mark of power in you. We do not often bestow it on mortals; though you are the third to have received such favor in recent years."

"Why is that, then?" Now O'Reilly was trembling: her hand shook in Gwyn's as he continued to hold it hearteningly and she to clutch at his arm with her other hand, until she calmed down again.

"It is not any common thing. We have not done so with others like yourself, other sidheanachta," he told her gravely, "even though there have been times in Keltia when such a mark on all eligible to bear it would have benefited everyone and everything, and made life vastly easier all round. But those days are gone, they will not come again. Different days, long ago; in these days, *you* are different, you are newly revealed to be come of a high lineage. Now things are changing, dán is drawing in; and a time will come when you and those others who bear this sign shall need all the power it can call to you, and when it will give you all the strength you shall need. You need not ask who the others are, for I may not tell you; though I would think you might well guess. They do not remember being given it, any more than you will. But when the time has come for remembering, you shall all of you remember; and when you do, we shall be there. And others also."

Sarah tried to smile, but her face felt as frozen as her hand had. "Can you really do that? Make me forget? But I don't *want* to forget, I want to remember! Suppose I stamp my feet and hold my breath until I turn blue and kick and scream and absolutely refuse to forget?" *I won't, I won't, I won't, you can't make me...*

Etain's laugh pealed out, delightfully, delightedly. "You are welcome to try, lass! But it would be all to no avail. Nay—accept the gift and be at peace. Your companions in this have done so; follow their excellent example, and let it be with you in easiness."

Gwyn was smiling as well. "You will remember *us*, at least—that you have met us and spoken with us; but the gift itself, not yet."

O'Reilly could sense them beginning to fade, though they each gave her a ceremonious kiss of blessing before they did so, Etain upon the brow, Gwyn lightly upon her mouth, to take away the memories.

"Oh no no no, please don't go yet, I have so much to ask you, oh *pleeeease*—"

But the faerie king and queen and their strange, merry entourage were vanished, seeming to fade into the stones of Ni-maen as someone approached from the direction of Turusachan below. As he drew near, a distracted Sarah recognized him: Desmond Aoibhell, the Ard-rían's cousin, brother to Slaine. She had noticed him at supper on numerous nights, had danced with him at some of the balls held in Turusachan's festal rooms, even shyly flirted; he was very tall, like all the Aoibhell kin, though he bore little resemblance to Aeron or her own sibs. He was frowning slightly, but not at her, as he came along the path to the bench where she sat.

"Greeting, Sorcha. I hope the day finds you well."

She looked wildly around. "Where are they? Where did they go?" She glanced up, thoroughly rattled, as a white shape soared close above them. "Oh, another owl. There was one before..."

She fell silent before the sudden watchful look on Desmond's face as he glanced up, following the owl's flight, and she was abruptly seized by an ancient terror, as she had not felt before—a fear of the waste places, of the panic places. It all suddenly seemed very strange and alien to her, and he saw her fear and took her arm to steady her.

To cover her shivering, she smiled shakily at him, holding hard onto his arm, and sighed with relief at his courtesy and his presence. "Thank you—I'm a little...confused. I think. And it is still so strange to hear my name in your tongue. I like it a lot, though."

"That is well, then, as I hope we continue to have many chances to say it to you." He looked curiously about him, frowning again a little. "As I came up the Way of Souls, I thought I saw someone here, talking to you."

"You did. That's who I was asking about. They just— went. There were some little small creatures as well, before that," she added. "Hobbits? Goblins? House elves? Anyway, they were funny little things, and we talked of Earth—Erith—and what I have done since coming here.

They said they know the palace people, especially Aeron and Gwydion."

"Oh, those," said Desmond, smiling. "Those were just sidhaun smallfolk, local inhabitants. Little hobs and cobs, small fae ones that live in this valley; they are harmless, and even amusing. But never give them sugar!"

"I'll keep that in mind for next time," she said ruefully.

The prince laughed. "Ah, I see my warning comes too late...well, I could see where you would be surprised. Gwydion is a particular favorite of theirs."

"I thought they were cute," she muttered, and he laughed again.

"They are, or can be. But make no mistake, get on their bad side and you will see how swiftly they can turn. They are fierce and snarling fighters; in Arthur's wars against the Marbh-draoi they helped us very much. Of course, they had been commanded to..." His voice trailed off, and she looked at him curiously.

"Commanded? By whom? Do they have a leader? A king? The two people I was speaking with before you came..."

Before he could answer, a pulse seemed to run through the air itself, as it had before. Another owl, or perhaps the same one, baffed by just above their heads, so close that its pinions brushed their cheeks, and a long, elegant feather fell at Sarah's feet. She stooped to pick it up, distracted, still shaking a little, but rapidly returning to her usual self.

"I should have asked before—what brings you here, my lord? Isn't it almost time for supper in Hall?"

"Close to, and I will escort you down to it; I came up to

pay a visit to my mother's grave, as I like to do whenever I can. She would not in the ordinary way have merited barrowing here, not being of royal blood—though of an old and honorable family, to be sure. Caerdroians of such lesser rank have been barrowed since the time of the Ships in another valley to the east, or wherever else they wish to, even far from the City. But my father, Elharn, being a prince and the son of the Ard-rían Aoife, he will lie here when his time comes, and so she has been set to rest in this place and await him. "

"I am very sorry for your loss of her; was it sudden?"

"Nay, a long illness, like a fading—no pain in it. We can cure most things, even such afflictions as were a death sentence on Erith long since, and for all we know still are, but some yet elude our healers. It was a gentle and easy passing, any road, and now she awaits her next life, or for my father to join her and pass together with her to the Summerlands. Her name was Seren, which means 'star' in the Kymric tongue."

She smiled shyly, though something tugged at her memory and pushed its way through into her present thought. "Lovely name for a princess. And I like that your people think like that. As I said, I was talking to two people earlier, when the little creature thingies were here."

Desmond stared down the little valley in the growing blue dimness, but no one now was visible. "Do you know who they were, these strangers bespeaking you? Had you met them before? Did they give you their names?"

"Did you truly not see them?" She stared at him in turn, disbelievingly, a little alarmed at the sharpness of his voice.

"No, I didn't know them. I hadn't met them before. I don't remember much, but I remember that. They were sidhaun." She brought out the newly learned word proudly. "Well, High Sidhefolk, clearly. The lord said that he was called Gwyn, and the lady's name was Etain. They were both beautiful. They said they were a king and queen. I thought Aeron was the only queen around, and Gwydion to be king when they get married? So who were they? Are they important?"

After that, Desmond could not get her down the hill to Turusachan fast enough, all idea of visiting his mother's grave set aside. He did not seem afraid, she thought, as she practically ran beside him, his hand firmly upon her elbow, just concerned; but he did appear determined to get her back to lights and company as quickly as he could, and most importantly, as he said, to Aeron.

Who welcomed them to her solar, and listened to O'Reilly's story with a most curious expression on her face, a blend of watchfully suspended judgment and a kind of dawning wonder, until she had heard all the tale the Terran girl had to tell. Gwydion sat in his usual window seat perch, one knee raised, boot flat on the stone, to hear her account.

When it was done, and Sarah had faltered into silence, and Desmond had added all that he could, admittedly not overmuch, Aeron straightened in her chair and looked not at either of them but at Gwydion, somberly, as if something they had long expected had finally come to pass.

"And so it begins. Gwyn has returned, and shown himself to one of our own, all unexpected...we would do well, I think, to implement that plan we spoke of, you and I, and bring that object to where, and to whom, we decided."

He nodded, but did not elaborate, or explain to the others what he and the Queen were so cryptically speaking of.

"*Excuse* me?" asked O'Reilly, an edge of irritation to her voice. "Is anyone going to tell me what is going on here? Before my head explodes?" She suddenly realized she had spoken rudely, and to the monarch and consort at that. "Oh—sorry, I mean—but I'm not one of your people, what is all this about, why would it happen for me? Whatever it means?"

Gwydion laughed softly. "Apparently you are more truly one of ours than you or we had any idea, Lady Sorcha, and of a higher kinship. We should have realized, when you went to Seren Beirdd and looked up your ancestry. You are of the sidheanachta, as I told you. And now, as it appears, you are kin to the highest among us: cousin to Taliesin Pen-bardd, and cousin by marriage to Arthur Ard-rígh, at many centuries' remove. More than worthy to merit arms and a title... As to the Sidhefolk, anyone in Keltia may greet or meet them, if the Sidhe are of a mind to allow it; but some there are, some families, some bloodlines, some individuals, who draw such contact to themselves merely by—existing." He paused, and sought Aeron's eyes.

The Queen let her gaze rest on O'Reilly, who was growing increasingly unsettled. "Be easy, m'chara," she said gently. "This is no bad thing. He whom you saw, whom you spoke to, who told you of your descent from Taliesin—he is mighty in our midst. He is Gwyn ap Neith, as he told you, and he is king of all sidhaun, as he also said, and is liegelord too of all sidheanachta. And another distant kinsman of yours, and ours as well."

Sarah's jaw threatened to connect with her knees, then she closed it, not wishing to look like an idiot in front of these three. *Probably too late for that*... "So the woman with him—"

"The Lady Etain, his queen, who was queen to St. Brendan the Astrogator before him."

"I see." *Yeah, no, I don't, I really don't*... "Do you—do you know him? Them?"

Aeron's slight smile widened. "Let us say it is more that they know us. What did you think of them?"

"Oh, well..." Sarah floundered for a bit, then felt the strong, warm pressure of Desmond's hand around hers. "It's all true, then? What they told me? Yeah, I kind of had a feeling that it was...even while they were telling me, I didn't doubt what they were saying. But I thought they were—sad, somehow. And yet also tremendously strong." She struggled for the complete memory, but Gwyn's magic was powerful and had defeated many far greater, and she was not the least match for it. "There was something else," she said at last, defeated. "Something they said to me, or gave me, maybe both? But I cannot remember."

To her surprise, Aeron laughed aloud. "Now that does not surprise me! But Gwyn and his queen are known for that. No matter: if they gave you aught, a word or a gift, it will show itself in its own right time."

Unconsciously she closed her left hand into a gentle fist, as if she wished to keep secret something that her fingers hid. Her palm had seemed to spark with stinging cold, as if it had been burned with sudden frostbite, and across the room Gwydion seemed to feel the same, running his thumb over his folded fingers, while Sarah O'Reilly—or perhaps Saoirse ní Rahillagh—laid her open palm over her heart, as if for warmth or reassurance. Though none of the three remembered what gift it was that lay in their hands.

A sudden wind blew around the tower, rattling the mullioned window in its frame; it laid equally sudden silence upon them all, and Desmond glanced curiously from face to face. Then Aeron shook herself, and seemed to come back from wherever she had been, and looked at Gwydion.

"Well, whatever it might mean, it is more than we know. Though not perhaps more than we shall come to know. But that is a bitter cold wind for autumn. Pull the window to, my heart. A cold wind indeed."